> ## "I don't ...
> ## I heard your name."

"Kate Sinclair," she said. To Morgan's surprise, her voice was gentle.

"Will you state your business?"

She nodded. "I certainly will. I thought about writing and I thought about telephoning, but I was sure you would think I was some kind of oddball. But now..." She stared at him, her bottom lip caught between her teeth, and to his horror, her eyes filled with tears.

She pulled a clean white handkerchief out of the straw handbag she carried and pressed it to each eyelid in turn. He would have been touched by the gesture if he had not been so wary.

"Ms. Sinclair, I wish you'd get to the point," Morgan said.

"I'm sure you're very busy. I had to see you, and I didn't want the people who work for you to know why. This baby," she said, folding her hands protectively over her abdomen, "this baby is yours."

Dear Reader,

Excitement is in the air at Harlequin! We're about to bring you some rousing new stories. Next month you'll not only notice a different look to your American Romance novels, you'll notice something new between the covers, too.

If you've ever dreamed of sailing the high seas with a swashbuckling modern-day pirate . . . riding off into the sunset with a dark and dangerous man on the back of a motorcycle . . . lassoing a cowboy Casanova and branding him your own . . . then the new American Romance is for you.

Fall in love with our bold American heroes, the sexiest men in the world. They'll take you on adventures that make their dreams—and yours—come true.

Your favorite American Romance authors will be on hand, as well as some fresh exciting voices.

So join us next month for the adventure of a lifetime!

Debra Matteucci
Senior Editor & Editorial Coordinator
Harlequin Books
300 E. 42nd St., 6th floor
New York, NY 10017

PAMELA BROWNING

MORGAN'S CHILD

Harlequin Books

TORONTO • NEW YORK • LONDON
AMSTERDAM • PARIS • SYDNEY • HAMBURG
STOCKHOLM • ATHENS • TOKYO • MILAN
MADRID • WARSAW • BUDAPEST • AUCKLAND

Published August 1992

ISBN 0-373-16451-3

MORGAN'S CHILD

Chapter One

If only I didn't have to go to this ridiculous tea party, Kate Sinclair thought as she set off lickety-split down the ramp from the Yaupon Island ferry and zigged across the oyster-shell path past Ye Olde Pribble Gift Shoppe and the Merry Lulu Tavern.

She dodged a kid trying to maneuver a skateboard down the sticky asphalt street and spared a worried glance at the sky hunkering too low on the horizon. The storm would probably hit before the party was over, which is what Willadeen Pribble and the Ashepoo County Historical Society deserved for throwing a tea party this time of year. Everybody knew that late June was a time for fierce afternoon thunderboomers.

At the end of the street loomed Plumm House, home of the historical society and the largest structure in Preacher's Inlet, South Carolina. It was a huge Victorian mansion embellished with lots of unnecessary gingerbread, and once Kate had privately tagged it "plum ugly," much to her father's amusement.

"Why, it's Kate Sinclair," exclaimed Willadeen Pribble, as if Kate's knock was a complete surprise. Her hair looked like a chocolate kiss, piled atop her head with a swirl, and it bobbed when her head did.

"Do come in. Our own little lighthouse lady," said Willadeen, her lips arranged into a forced smile.

Kate, who at five foot ten was anything but little and by Willadeen's standards not even much of a lady, reluctantly stepped inside. She managed to murmur a brief hello before her hostess sailed away to the kitchen, leaving Kate thankful to be on her own.

The next person Kate saw was Courtney Rhett. She was surrounded by a gaggle of gray-haired ladies who seemed to have turned the various blossoms of a whole flower garden into fabric and plastered it around their posteriors. Courtney, by contrast, looked slim and chic in stark Mondrian blocks of color on a white linen sheath.

"Punch?" murmured one of Willadeen's minions as she pressed a glass cup filled with tepid red liquid into Kate's hand.

The room was crowded, and Kate was relieved that no one was paying her the least bit of attention. She wandered closer to Courtney, mostly because the refreshment table was located to Courtney's right. Kate hadn't eaten a thing since early morning.

She had managed to grab a few morsels of food from the table and was positioning herself to maneuver around the grand piano, whose upraised lid seemed to provide a screen of sorts, when she distinctly saw Courtney Rhett wink. Not at her, certainly.

But when Kate was standing behind the piano lid wolfing down what tasted for all the world like a catfood sandwich, she noticed Courtney easing away from her group and sauntering casually in Kate's direction. Kate stopped eating in mid-bite, suddenly on alert. Why would Courtney Rhett seek her out?

Kate had read the society pages of the Charleston paper often enough in the past to know that she and

Courtney weren't exactly in the same social stratum. Courtney was old-money Charleston aristocracy and a St. Cecilia's Ball debutante, while Kate was of a distinctly scientific bent and longed for nothing so much as to resume her research on the lowly oyster.

"I remember meeting you at something or other around here," Courtney said. "I'm Courtney Rhett."

"Kate Sinclair," Kate said. "We met last year at the board meeting of the hysterical society when they were discussing renovations necessary to turn the lighthouse into a museum."

"Hys*ter*ical society?" Courtney asked.

"I mean his*tor*ical society," Kate said, hastily correcting her gaffe.

Courtney laughed, a long, full-bodied peal that caused several of their fellow guests to turn and stare.

Courtney ignored them. "So," she said as she tapped a cigarette out of a gold case and lit it. "How'd these old bags get you to come to this shindig?"

"I beg your pardon?" Kate said.

"I knew the minute I saw you that you don't belong here any more than I do," said Courtney. "My grandmother donated a fistful of money to preserve Yaupon Light, and now that the society is finally going to turn it into a museum, I'm delegated to represent her."

Kate remembered Courtney's grandmother, with whom her late father had developed an unlikely friendship. "I'm sorry your grandmother couldn't make it," Kate said.

"Grandma Robillard is in a nursing home and no longer attends teas. Lucky Grandma. How do you manage to swallow those awful little sardine things? I'd rather eat road kill myself."

Kate smothered a smile. "I'm hungry. This was meant to be lunch. And since you mentioned it, I rank historical-society affairs right up there with trips to the dentist for a root canal. I'm only here because Willadeen felt obligated to invite me and I felt obligated to attend."

Kate left a lot unsaid. In the past month she'd had to realize that she was totally unable to untangle the legalities of her grandfather's will, which had bequeathed the deactivated Yaupon Light to the historical society after her father's death, and that had made the gulf between Willadeen and herself grow even wider.

"Oh, so you're the Katie everyone is saying has been stonewalling the society and keeping them from converting Yaupon Light into their museum," Courtney said, favoring Kate with a long appraising look.

"According to the terms of my grandfather's will, I don't have to leave the keeper's quarters until next September. My father only died a month ago," Kate said.

"I heard Willadeen clucking about how you refuse to leave one minute earlier than the will specifies," Courtney said.

"She and some of the others are pushing me to get out of the keeper's quarters as soon as possible, but I don't have anywhere else to go, so for the next fifteen months, I'm staying put," Kate replied. "It *is* my right, you know." She didn't add that the reason she didn't have any place to go was her dispute with the Northeast Marine Institute and the resulting congressional investigation. It was clear that Courtney Rhett would have no interest in behind-the-scenes skulduggery in the scientific community.

"Oh, I wasn't on the side of the historical society," Courtney hastened to assure her. "Willadeen's talk about museum display cases and new rest rooms bores me—a cardinal sin as far as I'm concerned. Say, would you like a little more punch in your punch? I brought some white lightning along for emergencies." Courtney bent over and produced a flask from under her skirt.

Kate stared openmouthed at the little silver bottle. "Thanks, but no," she said firmly, but Courtney sipped quickly and delicately from the flask, licked her lips and with remarkable sleight of hand returned the flask to its place of origin.

"Frankly, Katie, I didn't expect you to be as dull as the rest of these women," Courtney said, focusing a pair of wide violet eyes on Kate's face.

"I don't drink and I don't smoke, and I don't apologize," Kate said, her gaze beginning to wander the room in search of an escape route.

"Well, don't get all het up about it," Courtney said. "I wish I could say the same thing. If I didn't drink and I didn't smoke, I'd go ahead and have those frozen embryos implanted and *zap!* in nine months I'd be a mommy. But as it is, I don't want to give up my bad habits. I played a pregnant woman on the stage during my brief career in the theater, and I must say that I didn't like it one bit."

Kate's attention homed in on what Courtney was saying; she made little sense out of this new direction in the conversation.

"*What?*" she said.

"The *embryos,*" Courtney said as if explaining to an idiot. "The story about my court battle with my ex-husband has been in all the papers."

"Yaupon Island is not on the paperboy's route," Kate reminded her.

"Oh. Well, my ex-husband and I went to court to fight for the embryos we produced in our marriage. What I mean to say is, I had the eggs and he had the sperm, but when we—well, let's just say that we tried to have a baby and we couldn't, so we let the doctors mix the eggs and sperms together in a petri dish, and the sperms fertilized the eggs and became embryos—you know, little bitty babies.''

"You're talking about in-vitro fertilization," Kate said in amazement.

"Sure, and I was going to have the embryos implanted in my uterus, but then Morgan and I divorced. So the embryos became part of the divorce settlement, and I won custody."

"Custody—as if these embryos were actual, born children?" Kate asked, becoming interested.

"Yup. And I was going to have a baby after the divorce, I honestly intended to do it. Against my ex's wishes, of course, but by that time I didn't care what Morgan thought."

"And now you've changed your mind?"

"I got scared is more like it. I mean, here I have these embryos and all, and I've been having these migraine headaches so bad, and I'm afraid to go ahead with a pregnancy. I have to take all this aspirin, which isn't good for a baby, and what am I supposed to do—go around with this awful headache and my stomach out to *here?*''

"Good point," Kate agreed. She saw Willadeen Pribble heading her way, but so did Courtney. Courtney pulled Kate into a curtained alcove behind the piano and sank down on the window seat, patting the space beside her.

Kate sat, too, gazing hungrily at the table through the chink between the curtains and wondering if anyone was going to bring out more sandwiches. Ham would taste good, or maybe chicken salad.

Courtney went on talking as if her tongue was wound up and had to run until it stopped.

"If I could only find *someone* to bear the baby for me! I'd be a good mother, I know I would. I'd love dressing a baby up in frilly white hats and taking it for walks along the Battery in its pram, and there's a trust fund set up by my grandmother so I have no financial problems, and Disney World would be so much more fun with a kid along."

"Yes," Kate said thoughtfully. "I suppose you're right."

"But where would I find any woman in her right mind who would carry a child for me?" Courtney asked.

Kate stopped thinking about how hungry she was and started considering, really considering, what Courtney was saying.

"I mean, that's nine months of someone's life down the drain! Who'd willingly do that for another person?" Courtney took another drag on her cigarette.

Kate cleared her throat. "I might," she said. She was glad that Willadeen Pribble wasn't anywhere around to hear her say it.

Courtney exhaled a cloud of smoke and stared at Kate as if seeing her for the first time. "Really?" she asked.

"I *might,*" Kate repeated. She'd always wanted to be caught up in other people's pregnancies. She was fascinated with the way their stomachs rose up out of their clothes day by day and month by month, astonished at the way the mother's skin could shape itself to embrace the baby, and she was curious about the mysteries of giving birth.

Besides, Kate was thirty years old, and she never wanted to be in love again, which made marriage highly unlikely.

"Why would you do it? For money?" Courtney asked.

"Because—because pregnancy intrigues me," Kate said. "Because I've never had an opportunity to be pregnant, and my future is so unstable that I can't bring up a child properly, so single motherhood is out of the question. And because I was responsible for nursing my father until he died, and during that time I had no choice but to think about death. I want to stop thinking about it and think about life for a change. Also, I—I've always longed for the experience of giving birth."

"Are you for real?" Courtney asked incredulously. "You mean you'd consider it?"

"Oh, I'd consider it, all right," Kate said.

"Either you're a crazy woman, or—but I don't think you're the least bit crazy. I like you," Courtney said.

"Do you really want a baby?" Kate asked.

"I'd love to be a mother. I just don't want to be pregnant," Courtney said.

"Then—"

"Will you? Honestly?"

"I'd like to. I would," Kate said impulsively. She envisioned herself stepping cranelike through intertidal mud flats as she moved from one oyster bed to another. She would be the picture of beauty and grace, and she would give birth effortlessly, steeped in joy and sensitivity toward the new life she was bringing into the world.

Courtney smiled, a gleeful smile that nevertheless lit up her beautiful features, and that made Kate feel even better. She didn't know anything about Courtney's ex-husband's looks, but if the baby would look like Courtney, with her reddish-gold hair and violet eyes, it would be a beautiful baby indeed.

"You're exactly the kind of woman I'd want to bear my baby," Courtney said. "You're decent, intelligent, educated—don't you have some advanced degrees?"

"I have a Ph.D. in marine biology," Kate said.

"So you're actually *Dr.* Sinclair?"

"I don't use the title socially," Kate said.

"No matter. Of course, if you decided to do this, you'd have to go to the fertility clinic. There'd be tests and you'd need to take hormones to make the embryos attach to the lining of your uterus and so on," Courtney warned.

"I don't mind," Kate said. Such talk made her feel very comfortable; oyster larvae had to attach to a suitable surface in order to become adult oysters. Human embryos had to "set" to become babies, too. What could be more natural?

"I'd pay your medical expenses, of course. What's your fee?"

"I—well, whatever's fair. I don't know how such things are done." Kate still couldn't quite believe that this conversation was taking place.

"I'll have my lawyer draw up some papers," Courtney said, and she named a sum of money that seemed exorbitant to Kate.

"I can't accept that much," Kate said. "Maybe just my living expenses."

"Good enough," said Courtney. "Shall we shake on it?"

Kate extended her hand, and Courtney's fingers gripped hers.

"Done," Courtney said. She stood up. "I'd better get back to the group, or Grandma might find out I'm shirking my duties. My lawyer will be in touch. We'll need a contract—he'll attend to it."

"I see that they're putting out some more sandwiches," Kate said.

"Enjoy," Courtney said, and with a little wave she disappeared among the weaving clumps of pink and blue cabbage roses.

"Kate, dear, I do hope you're having a good time," said Willadeen, whose ample bosom materialized at Kate's elbow just as Courtney took her leave.

"Lovely," Kate said as she scooped several sandwiches onto her plate, spared a nod for Willadeen and walked away as a jolt of thunder rattled the windowpanes.

Several of the ladies oohed and ahhed and shot nervous glances out the windows. A few of them broke off from their tightly clotted groups and left, and, still munching, Kate took advantage of the commotion surrounding their departures to slip out a side door and head for the dock.

After a hurried side trip into the Merry Lulu Tavern, where Gump, the ferry captain, was engaged in emphatic conversation with an assortment of cronies, she persuaded him to head back toward the island.

Gump's white beard and mustache bristled in irritation as he cast the ferry off from the dock. He spared a dubious look at the clouds overhead. "Get struck by lightning, don't blame me," he grumbled as he coaxed the ferry's engine to life from the wheelhouse.

"We're way ahead of the storm," Kate called up to him as she clung to the lurching railing.

"Says you," was the shouted comment.

"Oh, Gump, don't fuss," Kate said.

"You get fool ideas," was all he said, and Kate wondered what Gump, her friend and protector since childhood, would say about her latest.

After she disembarked at the landing on Yaupon Island, Kate ran through the first spattering of raindrops to the lighthouse. It was a place that had seen much history, having been built before the War Between the States. In 1898, when Yaupon Light had been superseded by larger lighthouses, the federal government, which owned the bluff where it stood, had ceded the lighthouse and keeper's quarters to Kate's great-grandfather, and it had been in her family ever since.

Kate had always loved the island, but she especially loved the weathered brick lighthouse, in whose quarters she had lived from the time that she was a small child. It was going to be a terrible wrench to leave, but leave she must. In the meantime she intended to enjoy every minute on the island, even if it meant butting heads with Willadeen from time to time.

Once inside the keeper's quarters, she caught a glimpse of herself in the cloudy full-length mirror on the old wardrobe in the hall. She spread her long fingers across her abdomen, feeling the sharp jutting of her hipbones on each side of the soft round place where the baby would grow.

Oysters almost always attached themselves where other oysters were already established; they congregated because togetherness increased their chances for reproduction. Kate had not congregated, and she'd thought she had no chance to experience what must be a woman's most exalted condition.

Now, as the result of a casual conversation, she might bear a baby. From an empty life, a life which lately had seemed to have no purpose, she could progress to nine months filled with hope and the satisfaction of doing something special for someone else.

After the strain of the past couple of years, after losing her father and everything else that was important to her, she longed to be needed by something or someone again. The time of her pregnancy would be a time of gathering the world to herself once more, of reclaiming some of what she had lost. It was a way of making a statement: *I'm my own person, and I choose life.*

CHOOSING LIFE meant that Kate paid several visits to the fertility center in the fall.

However, what Kate had thought would seem like an entirely natural procedure turned out to be unnatural in the extreme. Fortunately it was not a protracted process. In October Kate stoically endured the indignities of implantation and went home to the lighthouse to wait happily for the first confirmation of pregnancy.

The island was the perfect place to wait. Kate went for long solitary walks, absorbing the serenity of sea, sky and marsh. She knew she was pregnant, knew that in the warm recesses of her body a new life was taking hold, settling in. She was determined that the first sounds that this baby would hear would be the murmur of the waves upon the shore—it seemed so basic, so elemental.

She felt protective of the baby. For the time that they would be together, she was bound not only to shield this child from all harm but to nurture it as any mother would do.

She knew scientifically that the tiny creature inside her was Courtney's baby, not hers. But until she turned it over to Courtney, it was her child, no child of her body but a child of the heart, for sentimentally she knew that surely it grew there as strongly as it did in that more practical organ, her uterus.

When she received confirmation of her pregnancy, she whirled around the kitchen of the keeper's quarters a few times and wished there were someone with whom she could share such welcome tidings. But who would understand? Pegeen, her friend in Maine, who had not heard from Kate in over a year? Certainly not Willadeen or any of the women she knew from the mainland. Surrogate motherhood, Kate suspected, was still not considered a polite topic among the gentry of Ashepoo County.

Of course, she had to tell Gump, who could not be expected to react favorably to the news. She put the task off as long as possible and finally told him one day at the Merry Lulu Tavern after she'd been to a rummage sale on the mainland.

"Thought you were *taking* stuff to the rummage sale, not *buying* it," Gump said when she appeared with two paper bags full of her purchases.

"I unloaded a lot of things that I'm cleaning out of the quarters closets," Kate told him, hiking herself up on the bar stool beside his.

"Then what's in the bag?"

Kate hesitated. "I bought some clothes," she said at last. "Maternity clothes." She waited for his wrath to fall.

Gump stared at her openmouthed. "Now who might they be for?" he asked finally.

"For me," she said meekly. Gump was the only person who could still make her feel like a shy, knock-kneed little girl.

He was speechless. At last he raised the beer mug to his lips and drained it.

"There's somebody in your life I don't know about. How did you manage it?" he said.

"The somebody is the baby, Gump, and I managed it through in-vitro fertilization." Quickly she filled him in on the embryo implantation process, and when she was through, he was shaking his head in disbelief.

"This is the most damn-fool thing I ever heard of," he muttered.

"I wanted to do it," Kate insisted, following him out of the bar as he stumped along. Gump had a limp as the result of an old war injury; she often suspected that he overemphasized it when he was upset.

"Gump? Is that all you're going to say about it?" she asked him after she followed him into the wheelhouse.

He didn't reply, and he didn't speak to her all the way back to the island.

Finally, one day when she went down to the ferry dock on the island to pick up her mail, Gump came off the ferry, leaned against a piling and worked his jaw a few times. After a minute he said, "Well, Kate, I can't say I approve. But you can count on me. Heck, you can come stay with me if you want. You have no business living on this island in your condition."

"I like it here. I won't leave before next September," she said. To that his only reply was an outraged "Harrumph!"

Soon winter arrived in full force, and by January no tourists nosed around the island, knocking on Kate's door or lining up outside to take pictures of the lighthouse, which was a local landmark. Kate had the place to herself. The baby was now a little fish inside her, or maybe an oyster, and Kate was the protective shell.

Sometimes at night Kate took off all her clothes and studied her body in the mirror with the dispassionate eye of a scientist. She found it was hard to be objective when she was so fascinated with the changes she was experiencing.

When she pressed her fingers tentatively into the small lump in her lower abdomen, it was hard, not soft as she had expected. Her breasts, which had always been ordinary, took on a new look, rounding into lush globes, pink-tipped and exquisitely sensitive.

Because her breasts felt hot and fevered and uncomfortable, Kate blithely took to going braless for the first time in her adult life, enjoying the sensation of her full breasts swinging free beneath loose clothes. Sometimes during cold snaps when harsh winds swept off the sea, her chilly hands stole under her sweatshirt to cup her breasts, cooling the gently rounded contours and making her cheeks flush with pleasure that she quickly identified as sexual.

But there was no man in Kate's life, and she dismissed the vivid dreams she began having as some strange fluke of hormones. She often dreamed of a man beside her, inside her, of tumbling together between fluffy warm blankets—dreams she did not welcome, and she never saw the man's face. She did see the face of the baby she began to dream about—a sweet round face atop a blanket-wrapped body that was shaped like her burgeoning belly.

The baby's growing bulk pressed uncomfortably against the zipper of her jeans and stretched them to the limit. It pushed upward against her diaphragm until she found it increasingly difficult to breathe when she climbed the circular lighthouse staircase to the platform outside, where she liked to stand to dry her hair in the sun.

The baby seemed like a miracle, a miracle so special that Kate wanted to hug it to herself and did, when she was lying alone in bed at night with the wind whipping around the lighthouse.

She liked to curl her body protectively around the child within her, listening to her blood pulsing in her ears and knowing that it was her blood that nourished the baby, her heart that comforted it, her voice that it heard when it was awake. And she began to talk to it, too, crooning the words that mothers have always spoken to their babies, telling it how happy it would be when at last it was held in the arms of its biological mother, Courtney Rhett.

And then Courtney came to visit, and nothing afterward was the same.

THE KEEPER'S QUARTERS at Yaupon Light had no telephone, which was the way Kate liked it. She and Courtney communicated only by mail, left by Gump in a metal box on the ferry dock if Kate didn't meet him to pick it up.

Courtney's letters were actually from her attorney and included twice-monthly checks and, once, a contract that Kate barely read before scrawling her signature at the bottom. Kate's letters to Courtney usually consisted of a hasty "Everything is okay, thanks for the money."

For one whole month, Kate's fifth month of pregnancy, no letters arrived, which also meant no checks. Kate asked almost daily, "Anything from Courtney today?" and Gump would shake his head, pursing his lips in silent disapproval.

Then, one morning in April Courtney arrived in a white motor launch that idled at the dock. She was accompanied by a man whom Kate had never seen before. Kate peered curiously through the kitchen window, taking in the determined way that Courtney was planting one foot in front of the other as she made her way up the path to the lighthouse.

Kate, setting aside the dish she had been drying, untied the apron from around her bulging waist and met them at the door. When she saw Courtney in her white blazer with the spiffy navy-and-white polka-dot handkerchief draped artistically from the chest pocket, she became even more aware of her own decidedly unfashionable outfit, which consisted today of a limp rummage-sale maternity blouse and a chopped-off pair of gray sweatpants with a drawstring waist that accommodated her swollen stomach.

Kate smiled and opened the door. "Hi, Courtney," she said. "It's good to see you. Come in."

Courtney swept past, followed by her male companion, whose shirt was flung open almost to his waist, revealing a gold horn on a chain winking out from a curly patch of chest hair.

"Won't you sit down?" Kate said, sweeping a pile of scientific journals from one of the kitchen chairs and tossing them indifferently onto a heap beside the stove.

"It's not a social visit," Courtney said with a hint of discomfort. She didn't sit.

"Oh?" Kate said, beginning to feel a chill despite the warm wind blowing in from the sea.

"It's about the baby, Katie. We've—Damien and I—we've just gotten married," Courtney said.

"And?" Kate prompted, beginning to get the idea that she wasn't going to like what she was about to hear.

"And Damien doesn't want the baby," Courtney said.

Kate's eyes darted from Courtney's face to Damien's and back again. "Doesn't want," she repeated, her breath stopping short of her lungs.

"That's right," Damien said. "It's no kid of mine. Courtney and me—we've got places we want to go, things we want to do. We don't need a kid."

"I see," Kate said, although she didn't see at all.

"I'm sorry, Katie. I'll still pay your medical expenses, of course," Courtney said glibly.

"Of course," Kate breathed. She caught hold of the table and lowered herself heavily onto the chair. She felt the baby lurch uncomfortably against her bladder.

"My lawyer will stay in touch," Courtney said, turning to go.

"But—" Kate said, and stopped. She couldn't believe this.

Courtney turned, and for a moment Kate thought she saw a flicker of doubt in her expression. But no, she must have been mistaken, because Courtney's eyes had turned as hard as stone.

"Courtney's lawyer can help you place the baby for adoption," Damien said. "It's in the contract you signed, in the small print. Come along, Courtney."

He took Courtney's arm and pushed her toward the door. Behind them the sea, blue and shimmering, gently rocked their waiting motor launch; sea gulls swooped and spiraled overhead.

Courtney and Damien were already halfway down the path when Kate appeared in the doorway.

"You have to take this baby," Kate screamed like a banshee in full voice. *"You have to!"*

Courtney refused to look back, although Kate knew she must have heard.

"And I *hate* to be called Katie!" Kate shouted after them, but her words were carried away on the wind along with the insignificant cries of the gulls.

Chapter Two

Morgan Rhett leaned over his desk in his elegant office at Morgan Rhett & Company in the historic district of Charleston, South Carolina, and studied his ex-wife's picture on the society page of the local paper.

Looking at the grainy newspaper photo brought back all the misery of their marriage. He'd never marry again after that experience, he was sure of it, even though his decision precluded any hope of a normal family life. At the moment he couldn't imagine why he'd ever married Courtney. She was so smug, so overbearing and so full of herself.

So Courtney tied the knot again, he mused, reading the account of the wedding. She had married that creep Damien Cobb, the plumbing contractor who had taken advantage of all those folks who were rebuilding after Hurricane Hugo by installing inferior fixtures he'd bought at some bargain-basement plumbing sale.

People said that Damien Cobb was flush, but then, so were his customers. Morgan had heard that sewage from some of the houses had flushed everywhere but into the sewers and septic tanks, leaving the homeowners wallowing in filth. Which, come to think of it, was exactly what Courtney was doing by marrying the guy.

He walked with measured steps to the dart board on the wall and taped his ex-wife's picture to it. He was taking aim when the door of his office opened.

Quickly he adopted a neutral expression and slid the dart into his pants pocket, hoping that his head would hide the telltale picture.

"Mr. Rhett, I hate to bother you, but there seems to be some kind of emergency in the waiting room," his secretary, Phyllis, said, her usually dulcet tones overlaid with a patina of concern.

"Emergency? What kind of emergency?"

"A woman. She's determined to see you, but she doesn't have an appointment."

"What's her business?" he asked sharply.

"She won't say. And frankly, Mr. Rhett, I'm not sure you *should* see her. She's obviously distraught. And— and she's *expecting*," Phyllis said.

"Expecting what?"

"A *baby*, Mr. Rhett. She looks—unwell."

Morgan lifted his eyebrows. "You don't mean she's going to deliver the baby in my waiting room, do you?" Long ago he'd realized that his secretary was one of those people who could not say that someone had died; he had passed away. No one was ever pregnant; she was expecting. Queen of euphemisms, that was Phyllis. She was, however, a fine secretary. She protected him from people like this woman.

"I'd tell her to go, but she's deposited herself on the love seat and says she's not leaving until she sees you. She could be mentally unbalanced," Phyllis said.

"Does she look dangerous?" Morgan asked in alarm.

Phyllis considered. "Not dangerous. Determined," she said finally.

Morgan sighed. So many people came to see him to try to convince him to invest in dubious real-estate schemes that he sometimes thought he needed a bouncer, not a secretary.

"I'll come to the waiting room and see what this is all about," he said. He wanted Phyllis to leave so he could remove Courtney's picture from the dart board. He didn't want to give her and the other women in his office fodder for gossip.

"Oh, I don't know if you should meet her," Phyllis said.

Morgan's impatience finally got the best of him. "If you can't get rid of her, what are we going to do? Let her *pregnate* until she gives birth? I'll be there in a minute," he said, dismissing Phyllis with a wave of his hand.

Phyllis looked embarrassed. Morgan had no idea if there was such a word as *pregnate,* but it was worth inventing it just to see the shocked look on Phyllis's face.

"Very well, Mr. Rhett," Phyllis replied. She cloaked herself in self-righteousness, mistakenly thinking it was dignity, but Morgan Rhett was not fooled. He knew dignity when he saw it, which wasn't often. There was so little dignity left in the world today.

He reached for the piece of newspaper with Courtney's picture on it and crumpled it before tossing it in the wastebasket. He thought that with any luck the pregnant woman would be gone, but when he walked through the door into the waiting room, there she was, spread out across the love seat and taking up enough space for two people. Which she was, strictly speaking.

"I'm Morgan Rhett," he said smoothly. "How can I help you?"

She glared up at him. "You can talk to me. *Privately,*" she said.

Morgan was acutely aware of Phyllis and the two other women who worked in the office, the bookkeeper and the receptionist, who were hovering nervously in the doorway.

"Maybe if you can give me some idea about your business," he said, for once his self-confidence starting to waver. This woman looked angry. She looked worried. And she looked very, very serious.

"It's personal," she said, and then she unmistakably lowered her eyes to her huge belly and lifted them back to his. He stared at her, dumbfounded. She was implying—she must mean—

He wheeled and shot Phyllis and the other two women a meaningful look so that they beat a hasty retreat.

After he forced himself to put on a courteous expression, he turned back to the woman, who had stood up. Now that she was on his eye level, he saw the panic behind her eyes. He still wasn't sure if she was dangerous or not.

"My office is this way," he said, wondering what the hell was going on here. He'd never seen this woman before, and he had an idea that she was going to be trouble, big trouble.

He ushered her into his office with its deep-piled Persian carpet, its mammoth desk and its blue-on-blue view of the harbor with Fort Sumter in the distance.

"Please sit down," he said.

She sat. Here in the natural brightness of his office, removed from the subdued lighting in the waiting room, the woman looked prettier. Softer.

Her blond hair hung past her shoulders in sunbleached stripes, and she was appraising him with eyes as clear and gray as the summer sea at dusk. The smooth planes of her face were agreeable to the eye, but she was clearly a person of no sophistication, and as for those clothes, they were outlandish—a huge brownish-green dress with a ridiculous flirty ruffle around the hemline and low-cut armholes that exposed more than was strictly decent.

He caught a glimpse of one rounded breast through an armhole and quickly turned his eyes away. She wore a flowing tie-dyed scarf around her neck, marvelous colors, but she must have thrown it on as an afterthought because the colors had nothing to do with those of the dress, which looked like a camouflage tent for an army tank.

"I don't believe I heard your name," he said.

"Kate Sinclair," she said. To his surprise, her voice was gentle.

"Will you state your business?" he said.

She nodded. "I certainly will. I thought about writing you a letter, but I couldn't think of any way to phrase it, and I thought about telephoning, but I was sure you'd think I was some kind of oddball. But now..." and her words dwindled away. She stared at him, her bottom lip caught between her teeth, and to his horror, her eyes filled with tears.

She pulled a clean white handkerchief out of the straw handbag she carried and pressed it to each eyelid in turn. He would have been touched by the gesture if he had not been so wary.

"Ms. Sinclair, I wish you'd get to the point," Morgan said.

"I'm sure you're very busy, and I'm sorry for the way I acted in the waiting room. I had to see you, and I didn't want the people who work for you to know why. This baby—" she said, folding her hands protectively over her abdomen "—this baby is yours."

Morgan leaned back in his chair and regarded her with distaste. Then, without meaning to, he winced. He'd forgotten where he'd hidden the dart.

"I've never seen you before in my life," he said, changing positions and unobtrusively sticking his hand in his pocket. The point of the dart had maneuvered itself into a most inconvenient place and was pricking into a very tender part of his anatomy.

"Courtney is an acquaintance of mine. It was the embryos, you see. She wanted to have a baby without actually bearing it, so I volunteered."

Morgan wasn't having any luck with the dart. He couldn't reach it without twisting his torso into an awkward and obvious position.

"Now I think it was the stupidest thing I've ever done," Kate continued, oblivious to his discomfort, "but at the time—at the time—" and she buried her face in the handkerchief. Her shoulders shook uncontrollably.

Now she wouldn't see, so Morgan writhed uncomfortably and plucked the dart out of his pocket.

She didn't notice, he thought thankfully when she lifted her head. He slipped the dart into a desk drawer and accorded her his full attention. Her eyes were red rimmed, and her skin was blotchy. Altogether she looked most unattractive.

"Am I to understand that my ex-wife asked you to serve as a surrogate mother?" he asked, ending his sentence on exactly the right note of disbelief and thinking that he was handling this well.

"Yes," she whispered, looking as though she wished she were anywhere else.

"And you claim that this child of yours is actually the result of those fertilized embryos that were given by the court into the custody of my ex-wife?"

Kate nodded miserably.

"Would you mind telling me what in God's name this has to do with me? *She* insisted on custody, and *she* was awarded it. I have nothing more to do with the matter." His eyes blazed with fury.

"Courtney doesn't want the baby now," Kate said. "Her new husband says there's no room for a baby in their lives."

"Oh, yes, Damien the plumbing contractor. You'd think he'd have more interest in plumbing, wouldn't you? Well, all I can say is that it's no concern of mine. You'll have to work all this out with Courtney. And Damien, of course. Now, if you'll excuse me, I have work to do." Morgan stared at her until her gaze faltered.

"It *is* your child, Mr. Rhett," she said softly. "It's part of you."

If he had let them, the words would have caught at his heart. He'd wanted a child. He came from a big family. But Courtney hadn't been able to conceive normally, and the in-vitro fertilization idea had been their one hope.

He slammed his hands down on the desk, hard. He had to do it in order to keep them from trembling. If only she would stop looking at him with her pleading gray eyes, if only she weren't sitting there looking so pathetic in that awful dress!

"*That child his nothing to do with me. Nothing at all,*" he said firmly, but to his horror, his voice broke on the final word, and she blinked at him.

It was the last straw. "If you don't leave right this minute," he said, "I will have you escorted out. I mean it."

She gasped, a pained intake of breath. It startled him; she couldn't be going into labor, could she? But no, she was pushing herself to her feet, her legs splayed wide to bear the weight of the child. She looked more miserable than any human being he had encountered in quite some time, but she was moving—albeit slowly—toward the door.

She paused with her hand on the knob. "I won't trouble you again," she said clearly and distinctly, and for a split second he felt that it was he who was the interloper and she who was in the right.

And then, thank goodness, she was gone, and he heard Phyllis and the other two women murmuring in the hall. But he didn't want to know what they were saying. Let them gossip, let them whisper; Kate Sinclair and her baby had nothing to do with him.

It wasn't until about half an hour later when he was trying without success to concentrate on the new condominium deal that it occurred to him that it was Kate Sinclair who possessed in abundance the quality that he so admired. She had dignity.

KATE WANDERED blindly along hot streets crowded with students on spring break from Charles Towne University. She pressed through queues of tourists lined up for carriage tours of the historic district. Eventually she found herself walking on the East Battery, where the brisk breeze from the harbor dried the tears on her cheeks. The tears in her heart, however, were another matter. Now she thought she knew the true meaning of despair.

She leaned against the railing for a moment. Behind her rose an impressive line of great mansions painted in pastel colors, but she was blind to their picturesque beauty. She had to figure out what to do.

It was much too late to have an abortion, even if Kate were so inclined, and she wasn't. She could follow the terms of the contract, which stated that in case of default of the natural mother, the baby should be put up for adoption. But Kate felt that this baby shouldn't go to strangers. It had two parents who were capable of taking care of it, and she had no doubt that the baby would be as pretty as Courtney and as intelligent as Morgan Rhett. It would be a wonderful baby, a baby that anybody would want. Anybody but its parents, that is.

It was all her fault. This baby would not exist if she had not decided to follow such a foolhardy course in the first place. Now it all seemed ridiculous in the extreme, her volunteering to bear a baby for someone else so that she could have the experience. This was an experience, all right. Some experience.

Carriages full of tourists passed by on the street behind her, and she envied them. They were so carefree, so happy. Out in the harbor, people rode in boats to visit historic Fort Sumter, the fortress first fired upon by the Confederates in the War Between the States, and Kate now felt as much under bombardment as any fortress. Courtney didn't want her baby, and neither did its father.

What are we going to do? she whispered to the baby. *What in the world are we going to do?*

She couldn't summon the effort to move. It had been a hard day, starting when she rode the early ferry from Yaupon Island to the mainland, rented a car, drove north to Charleston, fought for a parking space in the downtown parking garage and then endured her disastrous meeting with Morgan Rhett. Now she felt exhausted and numb, but not numb enough to ignore the blisters on her feet, which had been caused by wearing old shoes too small for her feet now that she was pregnant.

A man broke away from a sedate group strolling along the Battery a hundred feet away or so, and she looked around in alarm. His tie was flying out behind him in the breeze, and he began to run toward her. She realized only when he was a few feet away that it was Morgan Rhett.

"Thank goodness I've found you!" he said, grabbing her arm. She stood there, too stunned to speak, too tired to move.

"I was afraid—" he said, and then he stopped talking and looked deep into her eyes. She stared back, spooked by his change in manner. "Are you all right?" he asked sharply.

She shook her head back and forth in an effort to clear it. "No," she said. "No, I'm definitely not all right." She was slowly realizing that what she had seen in his eyes only a moment ago was the glimmering of a conscience.

"You'd better sit down," he said, appropriating her arm, and she said nothing when he steered her down the steps to street level, across busy East Battery Street and into the park on the other side. He found an empty bench and gave her a little push in its direction. She sat down and tried to breathe deeply. She felt faint, and walking had stirred up the baby.

"Ms. Sinclair," he said.

"Kate," she reminded him. "You might as well call me by my first name, considering we have such an, um, intimate relationship."

"Intimate," he said. "Well, I hadn't thought of it that way."

"Your child is, right at this moment, aiming dropkicks at my kidneys," she said. "Cells created by you occupy a large part of my body. That's pretty intimate if you ask me."

"I didn't," he said, tugging at his tie to loosen it.

"Why did you look for me? Why didn't you let me go?"

He looked even more uncomfortable. "I thought about it. If it's my child—"

"It's yours," she said unhappily.

"I don't know that. You can't prove it. I don't know what kind of life you lead," he pointed out.

She focused wide eyes on him. "Oh, that takes some nerve. You want to know how many men I've slept with, right?"

"And you don't want to tell me, right?"

"It so happens that there haven't been any men, none whatsoever. For almost three years I've been living on Yaupon Island in the keeper's quarters of the lighthouse, where I nursed my sick father until he died. This baby came straight out of a laboratory, and I'll thank you never to mention it again," Kate said.

He seemed chastened. "I'll have to contact the fertility clinic, of course, and ask them to verify that you received the embryos," he said.

"Why don't you just ask Courtney? It'd be a whole lot easier," Kate said.

"We don't speak. It wasn't an amicable divorce."

"No wonder. You're not easy to talk to," she snapped.

"Some people think—"

"I'm not interested in anyone else at the moment. Are you going to take responsibility for this baby or aren't you?" she demanded.

"*If* what you say is true, and *if* I can prove it, and *if* you're what you appear to be—"

"Which is what?" Kate said hotly.

"A woman who is down on her luck and has a bizarre story to tell," he shot back.

She slumped suddenly. "Well, you've got that right, I guess," she said. All the fight seemed to have gone out of her. He noticed that her skin, though tanned honey gold by the sun, had pasty undertones.

He spoke on a sudden impulse. "Look, have you had anything to eat lately?"

She passed a limp hand over her eyes. "No," she said.

He took quick stock of her; she looked exhausted. "Let's go get some food," he said. "We can talk in the restaurant."

"I don't think I want to do that," she said in a small, quiet voice.

"What you mean is that you don't want to walk there," he said.

She lifted her head, surprised.

"I'm observant," he said. "I was holding on to you as we crossed the street, remember? You felt as though you were about to collapse. Let's not take any chances. My car is parked down the street, and I'll drive over here. You'll hop in—"

"My hopping days are over," Kate said morosely, easing one shoe off her foot and inspecting the blister from afar. She watched with a sense of helplessness as a run in her panty hose inched up her leg.

"You'll get in the car, and we'll drive somewhere quiet. All right?"

"All right," she agreed.

"I ought to have my head examined," he muttered under his breath.

She pinned him with her eyes, eyes remarkable for their intelligence. "I may be tired, but there's nothing wrong with my hearing. Please stop insulting me."

Morgan swallowed. Again he felt as though she had the upper hand. Well, in this case maybe he had been out of line.

"I'll be right back," he said, and the whole time he was hurrying to his car, he was wondering what gave Kate Sinclair the right to act like some kind of duchess.

KATE WAITED for Morgan, her expression bleak. She supposed he couldn't help being skeptical, but it was hard to see his point of view when she was so desperate for him to take the baby, or at least find a good home for it.

It hadn't been easy for her to beard Morgan Rhett in his own den. He was well-known in Charleston circles, and although Kate had never met him, she knew who he was. He owned real estate up and down the South Carolina coast; he had been one of the developers of Teoway Island, a prime beach, golf and tennis resort fifteen miles south of Charleston.

It was just that she hadn't expected him to be so handsome, with those broad shoulders, square-jawed face, patrician nose and deep-set ultrablue eyes that missed nothing. She suspected that the expensive, perfect suit hid a muscular, perfect build, product of frequent workouts at a local gym.

He was such a well-put-together package that she'd pegged him as a natural ladies' man, a real smooth-talking, fast-acting bachelor. Kate could, in her mind, picture him with Courtney, but the idea made her shudder. How could Courtney have married a creep like Damien Cobb after having been the wife of the oh-so-perfect Morgan Rhett?

A car squealed to a stop at the curb in front of her and the door on the passenger side flew open. The car was a metallic-beige Mercedes sedan, one of the big models.

Kate heaved herself up off the park bench and wedged herself into the front seat with a bit of difficulty. Once she was there, she sank into the cushioned leather upholstery with relief. She didn't look directly at Morgan Rhett.

He stopped the car at a crosswalk to wait for pedestrians to pass. "We'll go someplace small and quiet," he said, easing into the lane that would take them to less-crowded Mount Pleasant across the bridge, and Kate nodded. She didn't care where they went as long as it had a rest room.

He drove his car as though he were part of the machine. No, he was master of it, Kate decided, sending him a sidelong glance from beneath her eyelashes. She had an idea that if Morgan Rhett decided on a course of action, nothing could sway him from it.

That was good for her purposes; now her job was to figure out how to persuade him to provide for this baby. Unfortunately she'd never been good at talking her way around men. In fact, most of the time she'd rather not bother. It was usually easier to walk away.

But this time she couldn't walk. Waddle, perhaps, but not walk.

"You're smiling," he said. "What's so funny?"

Kate forced a straight face. She hadn't been aware that her facial expression showed any emotion whatsoever, and she hadn't realized that he was looking at her.

"Nothing about this situation is remotely funny," she said as sternly as she could. Maybe he would respond to authority in her voice.

"Oh no? It amuses me that just when I thought she was gone for good, Courtney has managed to insert herself into my life again in a different form," he said wryly as they crossed the Cooper River bridge.

She stared at him. "You have a strange sense of humor," she said.

"That's what my ex-wife thought. Well, here we are," he told her, pulling up beside a building fronting on a nondescript dock on Shem Creek.

He came around and opened the car door for her, and although she gave herself several unsuccessful pushes, she could not unbend from the car seat. She looked at him helplessly as he offered his hand. She took it, noticing this time how square and strong it was, how immaculate his fingernails.

She was acutely and embarrassingly aware that the two of them made an odd couple as she preceded him into the small seafood restaurant that looked dingy and weathered on the outside but was all tinkling silver, coral-colored tablecloths, and wide-windowed view of the docks on the inside.

When they were seated at the best table in the corner of the small loggia, Kate said, "Order something for me, I don't care what it is. I'm going to the ladies' room," and she hurried away in the direction of the sign she'd seen on the way in.

She was horrified at the way her hair looked when she glanced at her reflection in the ladies' room mirror; it looked as though she'd combed it with an eggbeater. She tried to rearrange it, but it wouldn't hang properly, it only clumped. Finally she wound the tie-dyed scarf around her head and gave up. She wasn't trying to impress this man with her looks.

On her way back to the table, she saw two women who were lingering over dessert cast longing glances in Morgan's direction, although he didn't seem to notice. As Kate approached, he was staring out the window at a fishing boat as it eased up to the dock. He looked up and saw her, and, proper gentleman that he was, he stood until she was seated.

He sat down and said abruptly, "What exactly do you want from me? You might as well spell it out."

She regarded him coolly, her heart beating a mile a minute. "I want you to adopt this baby," she said.

"Adopt my own child? That's ironic," he answered.

"The contract that Courtney and I signed provides that the baby will be placed for adoption if Courtney for any reason changes her mind. It shouldn't be reared by strangers when it has a perfectly capable parent—"

"Me?" His eyes were steely.

"Yes."

"Why should I want to do this?" he asked. His tone was abrupt.

"You have the means to care for the child and bring it up properly. I don't like the idea of putting the baby up for adoption, the way the contract requires in case of Courtney's default, and I can't take care of it," Kate said.

"What do you do for a living?" he asked.

"I study oysters," she said.

"Oysters?" he repeated, sounding surprised.

"As in the world is your," she said, and then she was afraid that she had been too sarcastic. Her father had always said that you could catch more flies with honey than with vinegar, and she sensed that it would be well to observe that maxim now.

"I see," Morgan said. "And so your idea is that you'll give birth to this baby, I'll pay your expenses—"

"Courtney is doing that," Kate said stiffly. "It was part of the original agreement, and her lawyer tells me that she intends to live up to it. She just doesn't want the baby."

"What makes you think I do?"

She shifted uncomfortably in her chair. "Nothing, except that you're the father," she said miserably.

"I don't feel one bit paternal about that—that lump under your dress," he retorted. "However, if it *is* my biological child, I don't want anyone else rearing it. Rhetts live up to their responsibilities."

"It's not—not just a lump," she said. "It's a baby, a real, live person, a child who will need attention and regular visits to a pediatrician and new shoes periodically and—and a lot of love."

"I can't give it love," he said. "I told you, I feel nothing."

Remarks such as that one made her emotions surface, much to her embarrassment. She looked down at the tablecloth and fought back the tears that came much too easily these days. Kate had never been a weeper, not until now, that is.

"Kate, I need to make inquiries, surely you understand that. That will take time," he said.

"But if you could prove that the baby is yours, *then* would you take it?" Kate said on a note of desperation.

"I am no longer married, Ms. Sinclair. A baby doesn't fit into my life-style. But I don't want my kid to grow up with somebody else's last name. How Courtney could have abandoned this child after arranging for you to bear it is beyond my comprehension. If it's mine, I'll provide for it." His blue eyes were as cold as ice.

Kate blinked away her tears. This was a concession of sorts.

"Now, here's our food. You look famished, and the steamed oysters here are the best in the world," he said.

Kate focused her blurry eyes on the waiter, who was wheeling a huge container of oysters to their table. With a flourish of his gloved hands he began to crack the shells, exposing the exquisite little oyster bodies, dead and smelling of the sea.

"I think I'm going to be sick," Kate murmured, and, clapping a hand to her mouth, she bolted for the ladies' room.

Chapter Three

"Why didn't you tell me that you don't eat oysters?" Morgan Rhett demanded.

"I didn't think of it," Kate said before sinking her teeth into a chicken leg. She chewed, swallowed and blotted her lips on a paper napkin. "It's just that I hate to see dead oysters when my life has been dedicated to keeping them alive. Maybe that's silly, since the reason we're trying to save them is that we're trying to increase the world's food supply." She shrugged and managed a short laugh.

"What is it that you do with oysters?" Morgan asked.

"At the moment, I have a part-time job collecting water samples from the creeks around Yaupon Island. I send them to the mainland to be tested for bacteria, which is how officials know when to close the oyster beds due to pollution. Before, I worked full-time for a marine lab, breeding disease-resistant oysters, oysters that aren't susceptible to a protozoan parasite called MSX. I have a Ph.D. in marine biology," she said.

"MSX—it sounds like a motorcycle, not a parasite," he said.

She grinned. "It's the Black Death as far as oysters are concerned," she said. She drew a deep breath before continuing. "Anyway," she went on, "I can't breed oysters on Yaupon Island because I need a research facility and money and—well, I was participating in a program and had to leave. By the way, thanks for not giving up on me after my run to the ladies' room. The chicken is delicious."

"Here, have some potato salad," Morgan said, shoving the small container across the picnic table.

The wind ruffling his hair created a small imperfection in his looks, and it made him seem more real to her, less like the fierce stranger whom she'd confronted in his office earlier. After they'd driven to the park near the beach, he'd shucked his jacket and rolled up his shirtsleeves. Kate didn't feel nearly as intimidated by him in this setting as she had before, although he still exuded confidence and energy.

A crisp bit of batter had fallen on his paisley tie, and Kate wondered whether to tell him about it. He saw her looking, glanced down, and brushed the crumb away, but it left a greasy mark. He didn't seem to care. If Kate's judgment was correct, the tie was silk, but then Morgan Rhett probably owned a lot of silk ties.

"Have you been sick a lot?" he ventured.

"I usually feel terrific, but the first three months or so were awful. Morning sickness," she said with a grimace.

"You're seeing a doctor regularly?" he asked.

"Of course."

Morgan had relaxed as he sorted out her story; she hoped she had managed to make herself real to him. Certainly he seemed to have stepped off the pedestal that she had inadvertently placed him on due to his power, influence and reputation. Not that he seemed any less powerful, but she hadn't realized before that he was—well, so sexy. *Virile* was the word that came to mind, perhaps suggested by the rock-hard muscles outlined by the taut fit of his trousers. At some other time, some other place, Kate would have tried to impress him.

But there was no point in that now. All she wanted was for him to like her. If he liked her as a person, maybe he'd help her out of this jam, and he couldn't like her unless he knew her better.

"I tried to buy the Yaupon Light property for development a few years back," Morgan said. "The man who lived there sent me packing."

"That was Dad," Kate said. "According to the terms of my grandfather's will, you couldn't have bought the property—it was already destined for the hysterical society's museum."

"Hysterical society?"

Kate colored. "I mean the hist*or*ical society," she corrected herself.

He laughed. She hadn't heard him laugh before, and she liked the way it lit up his whole face. Perhaps he wasn't as straitlaced as he seemed.

She pushed the picnic fare away from her. "I really must be getting back to Preacher's Inlet. I parked the rental car in the parking garage near your office, and the parking fee will be enormous. If I wait any longer, I'll miss the last ferry," she said.

He was staring at her. She rubbed at the skin around her mouth because she thought she must have dribbled mayonnaise there, but the napkin came away clean. If she hadn't known better, she might have thought he was giving her the twice-over, the way men usually did when they were attracted to a woman.

She felt a flicker of excitement and quickly extinguished it. Morgan Rhett, lusted after by attractive young women in restaurants and other places, would have no interest in her. Nor did she want him to. No, all she wanted was for him to accept this baby as his own.

Morgan glanced at his watch. "What time is the last boat?" he asked. He had a deep, resonant voice; it was a pleasure to listen to it.

"Seven o'clock," Kate said. "That is, if Gump hasn't been enjoying himself too much at the Merry Lulu Tavern."

"It's already six-thirty. You won't make it," he said.

She looked at her watch in dismay. "My watch has stopped," she said. She should have checked the time, but it had crept up on her. *Like my panty hose,* she thought. She'd be glad to get back to the island and her stretched-out sweats.

Except that getting back to the island tonight was impossible.

"I have no place to stay in Charleston, and I can't afford to pay two days' rental fee on the car," she said, sounding more woeful than she'd intended.

Morgan tossed the paper containers and plastic forks into a nearby garbage can. "What will you do?" he asked.

"I don't know," Kate said, disconcerted by his watchful blue eyes. She felt extremely anxious, and anxiety wasn't a normal emotion for her. To her dismay she felt her lower lip begin to tremble, so she bit down on it, hard.

"Well, don't fall apart," Morgan said with an unexpected degree of kindness. "You can drive back to Preacher's Inlet tomorrow."

"But—but—" Kate said. She could not cry again. She believed in holding back the big guns for the important battles, and with this man she was fighting to see that he took care of the baby. She should save her tears for when they would do her the most good, but her tears refused to cooperate. They stung high behind her nose and threatened to spill out the corners of her eyes.

"Kate, look at me," Morgan commanded. She opened her eyes, expecting the Great Flood to gush forth. *We could build an ark,* she thought glumly. *Two by two we could climb aboard. But getting stuck with a woman who is ready to go forth and multiply certainly wouldn't be much of a bargain for Morgan Rhett.* The fact that she was still able to think in a comical vein only proved that her emotional state was haywire.

Morgan helped her to her feet.

"I know a place where you can spend the night," he said quietly. "We'll turn the rental car in, and I'll see that you get back to Preacher's Inlet tomorrow morning."

"I'll be a bother— I didn't intend—" His very sincerity put her on guard, and a thought occurred to her. "What do you have in mind?" she asked in a more suspicious tone of voice.

He opened the door of the Mercedes and waited for her to traverse the short space between picnic bench and car. He took his time answering.

"I can assure you that if I had dishonorable intentions, I wouldn't choose a—how pregnant did you say you are?" She thought she detected the shadow of a grin.

"Six months," Kate replied, telescoping herself awkwardly into the front seat. She was beginning to get the hang of fitting her large self into this car. It certainly beat the compact rental car for comfort and size, although she still thought the Mercedes was ostentatious. She wiped her damp cheeks with the back of one hand.

Morgan walked around and opened the door on the driver's side, slinging his jacket onto the back seat. He got in and slanted an enigmatic look at her. "If I wanted to seduce someone, it wouldn't be you," he said.

She eyed him warily, sure that he meant to comfort her but not feeling the least bit consoled. No woman liked to feel that she was totally undesirable.

"What do you mean, you know a place where I can stay?" she asked.

"I have a sister," Morgan said. "Well, actually, I have two sisters and a brother, but Joanna is my only sibling who still lives in Charleston. She lives in a big house on Tradd Street only a stone's throw from my place. She has a guest room and will ask no questions. Oh, she also has three small children. Would that be a problem?"

Kate felt overwhelmed. "Everything is a problem right now," she said. "I don't know what to say. I can't *cope*, and I can't *cope* with not being able to cope!"

She fought panic; everything had seemed so easy and natural in the beginning of this pregnancy, and now her life seemed to be one big snarl.

"You'll be fine with Joanna," Morgan said soothingly, which was what Kate wanted to hear, but she didn't know these people. She'd only just met Morgan Rhett, and now he was going to deposit her on his sister's doorstep like some kind of stray, which she supposed she was but didn't like admitting, and his sister Joanna was probably exactly like Courtney, and spending more than one hour with Courtney would have driven Kate out of her mind.

Kate lay back and watched the ships gliding past below as the Mercedes headed back across the bridge. The hot gleam of sun on the tight-knit traffic on busy Meeting Street made her close her eyes against the beginnings of a headache.

She didn't open them again until Morgan stopped the car in front of a white-painted, pierced-brick wall covered with wisteria vine. They were in the historic district; indeed, Tradd Street was considered one of the most desirable Charleston addresses in which to live.

"I'll go in first and explain to Joanna," Morgan said.

"Explain?" she said in alarm. The air seemed heavy, turgid, and she couldn't draw enough of it into her lungs.

"Well, I can't just show up with a pregnant lady," he said. "Don't worry, I won't tell her about you and Courtney and me and the baby," he assured her, and before Kate could reply he was out of the car and through the door to the house, which opened directly on the sidewalk.

Kate heard joyful shouts, children's voices raised in greeting. In a minute or so, a blond cherub of a boy who looked about six or seven appeared and climbed on the iron gate in the middle of the wall, staring solemnly at Kate.

Morgan's baby could look like that, Kate thought, enchanted by the wide blue eyes and the soft tendrils of hair fluttering over his forehead as he swung to and fro amid the drooping wisteria blossoms. Who wouldn't love such a child? Who wouldn't want it?

Morgan reappeared in less than five minutes. She detected a spring in his step; he looked like he enjoyed solving this problem.

"Come on in, Joanna says she's happy to have you," he said enthusiastically, and this time he automatically reached down to pull her up beside him, his hand warm against hers. She stood uncertainly for a moment, tugging at her too-short dress and yanking the scarf from her hair before stuffing it deep into her purse.

"Well, come *on*," Morgan said, urging her along with a firm but gentle hand at the small of her back, and she thought that she had already put this man through enough today. She'd better follow along and do exactly what he said.

Halfway to the door she stumbled, and Morgan caught her elbow just in time to keep her from sprawling. She leaned against him, heart beating fast, embarrassed by her loss of balance, and then she pulled forcefully away.

"You're okay?" he asked anxiously. She realized that his upbringing had probably been that of a proper Southern gentleman: he stood when ladies approached his table, and she was sure he carried a clean handkerchief at all times. His kindness to her was no more than good breeding.

"I'm fine," she mumbled, although she wasn't sure that was true.

"Come along then," he said, and Kate wondered somewhat irrelevantly exactly what Morgan had told this sister of his and how she viewed his bringing a strange woman—a strange and *pregnant* woman—to her house on the spur of the moment.

Beside a tall magnolia tree in the garden, a striking brunette disengaged herself from the clutching hands of yet another blond child, this one female, and hurried up the stairs of the piazza where Kate and Morgan stood waiting.

"Joanna, this is Kate. Kate, Joanna," Morgan said hurriedly. "Now, Kate, if you'll give me the keys to your rental car, I'll take care of returning it."

"But—"

"No arguments. The car's in the parking garage near my office? What level?"

Kate fished the keys and the parking stub out of her purse. "Second level," she mumbled.

"Done," Morgan said, pocketing the keys. "What time shall I pick you up in the morning?"

"The first ferry for the island leaves the inlet at seven," she said.

"Too early. We'll catch the nine o'clock. There *is* a nine o'clock?"

"Nine-fifteen," Kate said weakly.

"I'll pick you up at eight so we won't have to rush. Thanks, Jo. Kate, be ready when I get here. I don't like to wait."

With that he was out the door, his sheer energy propelling him along, muscles rippling beneath the expensively tailored shirt. From her position on the piazza, Kate saw him tousle the small gate swinger's hair on the way.

Joanna smiled. There was something genuine and good-natured about her, and Kate found it easy to like Joanna immediately. "Don't worry," Joanna said, "Morgan's always like that. In a hurry, I mean."

She picked up the small girl who clung to her hem. "This is Melissa, age three. That's Christopher hanging on the gate. And that," she said dramatically as a wail filled the air, "is Stoney. He's the baby. Don't look so alarmed, he's named Stonewall Jackson Dumont."

"Stonewall Jackson?" Kate repeated, trying to center her attention on matters at hand.

"Actually, he's Stonewall Jackson Dumont the Fifth. There's always been a Stonewall Jackson in my husband's family since the Civil War. Awful, isn't it? Come along, I expect you'll want to use the bathroom. I never dared to get more than a few feet away from one when I was pregnant." Like Morgan, Joanna spoke with a proper Charlestonian accent full of broad *A*s, as in *The cahf went down the pahth in an hour and a hahf.*

Kate followed her into the house, a cool oasis after the heat and humidity outside. Joanna scooped the baby up from his cradle near the door and continued up the stairs past framed countenances of what Kate assumed were Rhett and Dumont ancestors.

"Charlie, my husband, is out of town on business," Joanna said over one shoulder. The baby hung over the other shoulder. He spotted Kate treading heavily behind his mother and smiled a wobbly smile. He had so few teeth that he looked like a jack o'lantern.

"This is your room," Joanna said, throwing open the door on a pink-and-green floral fantasy at the head of the stairs. "There's an adjoining bath through there," she said, indicating a door. "Morgan said that you've recently eaten," she said, turning questioning eyes on Kate.

"Yes," Kate said. At the sight of the bed, so inviting, she suddenly felt exhausted.

"Well, the kids and I have had an early supper, and it's almost bath time. I'll bathe them downstairs and put them to beddy-bye. I noticed that you didn't bring a suitcase, but I have maternity clothes you can have. I'll bring them up later."

"Oh, I couldn't—" Kate began, but Joanna waved away her objections.

"You can keep them. They've seen me through three pregnancies, and Charlie and I won't have any more kids."

"Thank you," Kate said. The words sounded so inadequate, and she felt so tired. Her eyelids drooped with weariness.

"I guess that's about it, so I'm off to fill the tub. 'Bye, Kate," and with that Joanna breezed out the door, shutting it gently behind her.

Kate sank down on the bed. The room was blissfully quiet, and the wide-louvered plantation shutters were closed. She reached out a tentative hand and smoothed the bedspread, which felt soft and cool to the touch.

She got up, went into the bathroom, plaited her hair into one long braid and tied it with a length of thread ripped from her hem. Then, after removing her dress, she climbed between the silky eyelet-edged sheets.

She felt the baby flutter gently against the skin of her abdomen and laid a protective hand there until it settled down.

Oh, baby, Joanna is your aunt. Wouldn't it be nice if—

Yes, it would be nice. It would also be nice if Kate had never found herself in this predicament in the first place.

JOANNA AND THE CHILDREN were already in the kitchen the next morning when Kate limped downstairs, her heels smarting from yesterday's new blisters. She was wearing a blue chambray jumper chosen from the pile of clothes that Joanna had left in her room last night while Kate was sleeping.

"Good morning," Joanna said to Kate as she whisked around the kitchen, opening and closing the refrigerator door, pouring more milk for Christopher, mopping up Melissa's orange juice. The faint sugary smell of Fruit Whoops hung in the air, and the children, sitting at a table in the window bay, were dressed in clean cotton playsuits.

"Bacon? Eggs?" Joanna asked.

"I can fix my own breakfast," Kate said.

"I've already broken eggs into a bowl for scrambled," Joanna said. "It's no trouble to add a couple more. Maybe you could see to Stoney. He's fretful this morning."

The baby was bundled into a swing near the dining-room door. The swing was kicking back and forth on its own, its tinny unmusical melody winding down. Kate used the opportunity to peek into the dining room, where she saw a long sideboard, big gold-framed paintings of horses and highly polished silver things like soup tureens and goblets.

"What should I do for the baby?" Kate asked.

"Oh, hold him for a while. I'll feed him in a few minutes," Joanna said confidently as she emptied the eggs into a frying pan on the stove.

Kate approached Stoney. He stared up at her with suspicion. She wondered how old he was. Three months? Six? She had no idea; she knew nothing about babies.

Gingerly she slid her hands underneath him. He drooped like a beanbag when she lifted him up. His foot caught on the bar of the swing as he came out, and she had to wiggle him to free it. To her surprise, he smiled.

She smiled back. She couldn't remember ever holding a baby before. There had never been any around when she was growing up, and later, when her friends and classmates had started having children, she'd always managed not to have to touch them. And here she was, jiggling this mindless lump of cute. She thought she had never felt as helpless as she did at this moment.

"What's your name?" asked Christopher.

Kate looked around. "Kate," she said.

"Kate. Okay. Are you going to stay here today? Would you like to see my bug collection?"

Ah, a man after her own heart. Kate would rather spend time with a bug collection than she would with this baby, who was drooling down the front of her jumper. "I'd love to see your bug collection," she told Christopher. She felt Stoney's diaper. Did it feel slightly damp?

Stoney began to whimper. Kate jostled him against her shoulder some more, but it didn't help.

"Here, I know what he wants. Can you handle the eggs?" asked Joanna.

"Sure," Kate said, gratefully dumping the baby into Joanna's arms. She appropriated the frying pan and stirred. At least she knew how to scramble eggs.

When she next looked up, she saw Joanna nonchalantly unbuttoning her blouse. The sight riveted her. Yes, she knew that mothers nursed their babies. Yes, she thought it was the proper thing to do. And no, she hadn't ever actually watched anyone do it before.

Joanna settled into a rocking chair in the corner. Kate locked her eyes on the eggs in the frying pan, too embarrassed to look up again. The other children continued to eat, chattering about childish things.

When the eggs were done, when Kate couldn't go on scrambling them anymore, she saw that the baby had latched its mouth onto Joanna's right breast and was sucking away, a blissful expression on his face. Kate heard contented little kitten noises coming from deep in the back of his throat.

"The bacon's on the table," Joanna said. "Go ahead and eat without me. I can warm my eggs up in the microwave later." Absently she caressed Stoney's soft hair, and when she stopped, the baby's little fist reached up and curled around one of her fingers. Kate could hardly pull her eyes away from mother and child.

What did it feel like to nurse a baby? What exactly was the sensation of a tiny mouth tugging insistently at the nipple? How long did they nurse, and how did you know when they'd had their fill? Suppose *she* wanted to nurse—of course she wouldn't, but supposing she did— would her nipples be big enough?

Kate ate her eggs, but she didn't taste them. In a while Joanna matter-of-factly switched the baby to her other breast, closing her eyes and rocking gently as his mouth worked at its task. She looked as contented as her baby.

"When will you have your baby?" Christopher asked Kate.

"In July," Kate said.

Joanna's eyes flew open. "Stop asking Kate questions," she ordered.

"I expect Kate's baby will like bugs. One child in every family should," Christopher said solemnly.

Joanna laughed. "I'm not so sure about that. I've had about all I can take of those fuzzy caterpillars you plucked off the Davidsons' hedge," she said. She bestowed a quick kiss on the top of Stoney's head. "This little critter has had enough this morning," she said as she buttoned her blouse.

The baby opened his eyes, then closed them again, and Kate felt a tug of—what? Yearning? Considering the way her breasts ached, that was too mild a word. She didn't say anything as she stood up and pushed her chair under the table.

At that moment a shadow fell across the floor, and she wheeled to see Morgan Rhett standing in the doorway blocking the sun.

"Good morning," he said, opening the door and leaning inside. He looked Kate over appreciatively as

Christopher whooped and tackled him around the knees. "Are you ready, Kate?"

"I will be in a minute," she said. "I have to get my things."

"Take your time," Morgan said. "I like visiting with my sister."

He pulled a chair away from the table and straddled it. Kate, feeling more ungainly than ever, felt her skirt brush his knees as she passed.

As Kate gathered her things from the guest room, she thought about Morgan and the way he had fit so naturally into the domestic scene downstairs in the kitchen. He seemed very different from the buttoned-down, tight-lipped man she had confronted in his office yesterday. He seemed—well, kind.

It struck her suddenly that perhaps this bit of kindness and caring was all that she would ever get from Morgan Rhett. After today, depending on what he decided about the baby, she might never see him again.

Reality pierced through her like a knife. This baby— Courtney and Morgan's baby—deserved a life in a place such as this peaceful house on Tradd Street. It was clearly an existence of privilege and comfort. Christopher and Melissa and Stoney were her baby's *cousins*. Because of who they were, they would have a happy and secure childhood and lives full of promise.

I want that for you, she said fiercely to the baby. *You deserve it, and I'm going to fight for it the best way I know how.*

She glanced in the mirror and was shocked to see how ferocious she looked. That, she supposed, was only natural. In a dispassionate way she thought about animal mothers in the wild and how they fought to the death to protect their young. This might not be her child; it was Morgan's child. But because of the physiological changes that had taken place in her body, she reacted as if it were her child, and in fact, for practical purposes, she was the only mother it had.

However, she'd have to remember to catch this particular fly with honey. With Morgan Rhett, vinegar would simply not do the job.

When Kate returned to the kitchen, a deliberately sweet smile unfurled across her face, Morgan paused in his conversation with the group gathered around him. He answered Kate's smile with a slow, lazy grin of his own so that her smile immediately became genuine in response. And in that moment something about the way he looked at her made Kate catch her breath.

It was ridiculous to take note of it, since she was always short of breath these days. Still, the dust motes suspended in the air between them might have been unspoken thoughts; the balm of sunshine across Morgan's hair might have been a blessing.

She forced herself to turn away from him and said polite but sincere thank-yous and goodbyes to Joanna.

I must be out of my mind, Kate thought to herself as she preceded Morgan out the door. *I have no business getting romantically interested in Morgan Rhett.*

It wasn't as if he'd return her interest. To him she was just another problem to solve, another person to be reckoned with, perhaps a deal to be made.

When he held the car door for her, she swept past him, head held high. There was no reason to look in his eyes. In fact, there was every reason to keep her emotional distance.

And the main reason was right at this minute turning flips somewhere below her displaced navel, reminding her exactly why she happened to be with Morgan Rhett in the first place.

Chapter Four

Morgan hadn't intended to ride the ferry to Yaupon Island with Kate that morning, but when he saw her feet crossing the wooden ramp to the deck, his feet followed of their own accord.

"I thought you were going back to Charleston," Kate said. She stared up at him from the outside seat where she sat, her hair whipping in the breeze, a package of Joanna's discarded maternity clothes balanced across her knees.

"I changed my mind," he said, sitting down beside her.

She looked away toward the island, her eyes squinting slightly in the sun. A group of tourists trooped aboard and filed along the railing to the bow of the ferry, where they stood snapping pictures of each other.

"Why?" she said.

He wasn't accustomed to explaining himself or his actions to anyone. "Curiosity," he replied.

Her expression reflected mild disbelief. "About the island? Or about me?"

"I've been to the island before. So it must be about you." The truth was that ever since Kate's precipitous run for the rest room yesterday, he had been in the process of realizing how difficult it must be to be pregnant. He couldn't imagine what kind of woman would volunteer to bear a child for someone else, and he wanted to know if the decision had resulted from strength or weakness. He couldn't say why he wanted to know this, only that at the moment it seemed important.

A man who wore a scruffy captain's hat limped up the ramp and said sternly to Kate, "I missed you when you didn't come back last night. Waited for you. Almost missed my supper." His voice was gruff but kind.

"I couldn't get back in time," she said.

"Next time call the tavern and let them know. They'll tell me," he said before stumping away.

"Is he a relative or something?" Morgan asked.

"Gump? Well, you might say that," she said wryly.

He waited for her to explain, but she was watching as the man loosened the ferry from its moorings. Who was this guy to her, anyway? Morgan knew that her father was dead, but was this old fellow an uncle? Third cousin twice removed?

"You know, you don't give much away," Morgan said testily, regretting his tone of voice immediately. After all, he reminded himself, a pregnant woman was not to be handled in the same brusque way as a recalcitrant builder or ineffective apartment manager.

She focused wide eyes on him. "What does that mean?" she asked.

"When I ask a question, it might be a good idea to give me a complete answer, especially since you want something from me," he said.

Kate rolled her eyes upward for a moment, closed them and sighed deeply. "Okay. All right. Gump is the father of the man my mother ran off with when I was nine years old. They never got married, so I can't call him my step-grandfather. What would *you* have said in my position?"

Morgan was taken aback. In his family, things were done properly. People became engaged, announced their engagement at a large party, and they married six months later in historic St. Philip's Church, where all Rhetts married. Rhetts did not have extramarital liaisons. He could not recall any married member of his family "running off" with anyone else within the family's history in this country, which preceded the American Revolution.

He delivered his answer thoughtfully. "I would have told you straight out. Aside from that, what an awful blow it must have been. For your mother to leave you, I mean."

The space between the ferry and the dock was widening now, and the boat's motor settled down to a steady thrum. Two other passengers sat down on the narrow bench seat beside Morgan, and he inched toward Kate.

Kate ignored the length of his thigh pressed against hers. "The day that my mother left was one of the worst days of my life," she said. "Afterward Gump helped us—my father and me. Gump felt awful, you see, because if he'd been a better father, maybe Johnny wouldn't have persuaded my mother to leave Dad and me. Personally I don't think Johnny had that much to do with it. My mother wanted to be free of the island, my father and me. She hated living at the lighthouse."

"And how about you?"

"I love the island. And living there. I wish I never had to leave," Kate said quickly. The wind was now blowing her hair off her face, and he admired her strong profile—the squared-off chin, the straight nose, the fine line of her forehead. It was a face of great character—presuming that you could read character in faces, and he'd always thought he could.

"So it was just you and your father after your mother left?" he asked.

She nodded. "I lived with a family on the mainland when I was in high school, and after that I went to college in Maine. When Dad got sick, I took care of him so he wouldn't have to go to a nursing home. He loved Yaupon Island and wanted to die there. He got his wish. Why are you so interested, anyway?" she asked. She noticed that one of the women sitting on the other side of Morgan was ogling him; her breast was flattened against his biceps.

Morgan decided to take his time about answering Kate's question. The woman next to him leaned closer, so he moved nearer to Kate and slid one arm around the top of her seat.

"I want to know a lot of things about you," he said. "How you live, why you let Courtney manipulate you into this surrogate mother scheme—"

"Courtney did not manipulate me," Kate informed him.

"Nevertheless, my ex-wife has a way of getting what she wants," he said with more than a tinge of irony.

To their left a fishing boat with bright blue nets suspended from its outriggers bobbed gently on the waters of Tookidoo Sound. The sea air smelled of salt, a scent that Morgan hadn't noticed in all too long. In Charleston he was never far from the harbor, but air-conditioning in his home and office dehumidified and filtered the air so that it lacked—well, substance. *Like the women I know,* he thought irrelevantly.

"What are you going to do on the island today?" Kate asked in a subdued tone.

"Follow the other tourists around, I suppose," he said. "I didn't bring a swimsuit, so I can't go swimming. Maybe I'll pick up a few shells on the beach, take them to my nephew Christopher."

Kate had an idea that Morgan wouldn't be lonely for long. The buxom brunette who had pressed up against him looked predatory and not the least bit shy. Kate didn't know how Morgan would feel about the woman's intense scrutiny, but there was no doubt in her mind that he would know how to further the acquaintance.

The dark blur of vegetation on the horizon rapidly took on discernible features; Yaupon Island was a low-lying mass of tidal marsh bordered by maritime forest on one side and sand dunes on the other. The ferry landing came into sight, a weathered wooden dock below the promontory where Yaupon Light stood sentinel.

Suddenly Kate knew she wasn't willing to abandon Morgan Rhett to the pleasures of the woman who was even now leaning halfway across his lap to snap pictures.

"You could come to the house for lunch," Kate said, not looking at him.

"Is that an invitation?" he asked. He wasn't sure he'd heard her correctly.

"If you don't mind eating a sandwich," she said.

He flashed a grin and blocked the brunette with his elbow. "A sandwich sounds great," he said.

"I mean, it'll only be something out of a can," Kate said.

"You don't have to apologize. Not after the oyster fiasco," he told her. The ferry approached the landing, and Gump let down the ramp.

Kate called an offhand goodbye to Gump, under whose challenging gaze Morgan felt less than comfortable, and once off the ferry ramp, Kate led him toward the steepest of the three paths. Over her protest, he relieved her of the package of clothing.

The path she had chosen climbed past a stand of palmettos toward the lighthouse and was so narrow that they could barely walk two abreast. They heard their fellow passengers clamoring close behind them. Kate walked slowly. It was a hot day, and perspiration slicked her forehead. At a twist in the path, she stopped.

"I should let the others go on ahead," she said, pulling him into the green-dappled shade beneath a live oak tree. Something happened when she touched his arm; a tiny jolt of electricity rippled through him. Suddenly Morgan was conscious of the swell of her breasts beneath the demure jumper, aware of them in a new way. At that moment, Kate seemed extraordinarily womanly.

Well, of course, she was a woman. She was *pregnant*, for Pete's sake. Nevertheless, he studied her covertly, taking in the sweet curve of her upper lip, the downy softness of her skin. If he had thought she was gawky or rawboned before, he had been wrong. Despite her unusual height, he saw now that her wrists were delicately fashioned and her limbs were lithe as well as long.

"Do you climb this path often?" he demanded after the people had passed and they resumed their climb. Ahead of him he could see the brunette who had been so aggressive. She had enormous hips.

"I have to go to the landing once a day to pick up my mail," Kate said.

"Couldn't Gump bring it to you?"

"I've never asked," Kate said, and as she spoke, it occurred to Morgan that the path was fraught with peril. Little tree roots clutched at Kate's feet, and widespread branches of dwarf wax myrtle clung to her skirt. He thought about her tripping and falling. He thought about her alone in the lighthouse keeper's quarters with no one to call if she were hurt.

"If you didn't show up, would Gump come looking for you? If you were sick, would he know?" he asked.

"If I had an emergency, I'd hoist an SOS up the flagpole at the lighthouse, and Gump would come to see what was wrong. He doesn't climb this hill very often. He limps," Kate said patiently.

"Kate," Morgan said, "what if something happened to you?"

"Don't be ridiculous," she said, clipping the words off sharply, whether due to annoyance or shortness of breath, he couldn't tell. She continued to plant one foot in front of the other, and he took hold of her elbow to steady her. She tried to wrest her arm from his grasp, nearly toppling over in the process.

"You see? This path wasn't made for expectant mothers. You shouldn't live here," he said firmly.

"Maybe you're right," she said. "Maybe I shouldn't live here. In any case the question is moot. I'll have to move out in September, anyway."

A canopy of moss-hung live-oak branches arched a momentarily dark tunnel over them before they emerged into the sunny clearing, the lighthouse towering above them. A sign proclaimed: Yaupon Light—Established 1859, Deactivated 1898.

Kate led him past two circular beds planted with exuberant yellow marigolds. She pulled a key out of her purse; it hung on a frayed old piece of twine. Then she opened the door, and he followed her inside.

He found himself in the kitchen of the small cottage attached to the lighthouse tower. One window overlooked a magnificent view of the ocean, another framed a view of the ferry dock, and under it sat a small table covered by a red-and-white checked tablecloth. A huge enamel coffeepot and a sugar bowl were on the table. The rest of the kitchen was Spartan, to say the least. Morgan had never seen a stove that old outside of a museum.

"Please sit down. Oh, push those envelopes aside. Here, give me a handful," she said, and when she reached for them their hands touched.

Morgan would have thought nothing of it if she hadn't blushed. She turned away so he couldn't see her face and opened the refrigerator and peered into it, her maternity dress falling forward so that the curvy shape of her hips was clearly outlined. He followed the line down her thighs to her calves and to her ankles, which were trim and shapely.

When she had finished assembling it, Kate slid a tuna sandwich across the table to him and pushed the coffeepot aside. He liked the way her hair was shot with gold sparks from the beam of sunshine angling through the window.

Kate wasn't somebody who had impressed Morgan as beautiful before. But now, with the sun streaming on her hair, with her clear gray eyes scanning his face and waiting for him to say something, with the lush curve of her breasts so evident under that jumper she was wearing— yes, she was more than pretty. He wished he knew what she'd looked like in her nonpregnant state.

"Back to our discussion about your safety," he said.

"You were discussing it. I was not," she said aloofly.

"Are you the only one who lives on Yaupon Island?"

"Yes, except for occasional groups of people who visit the Oates hunting lodge for a week or two at a time," she said. She bit off some bread and chewed it, gazing out the window. He wished she would look at him.

"I'd almost forgotten about that place," he said.

"How did you know about it?" she asked him with upraised eyebrows.

"I came here with a group of guys from college one spring break," he told her.

"Oh, so what happened? The bunch of you got your kicks out of shooting Bambi and Thumper?"

He looked her straight in the eye. "I don't hunt. As I recall, most of the hunting took place on the mainland, and it was strictly boy chasing girl."

"Oh," she said. "Sorry."

"I doubt it," he said.

She blinked at him, and he downed the last bit of sandwich. Suddenly he had had enough—of her, of the confines of this kitchen. She was from a different world than he was; she might as well be wearing a No Trespassing sign around her neck. What she wanted from him only *seemed* personal, and he would do well to remember not to get emotionally involved.

"Are you leaving?" she said as he stood up. She looked surprised.

"I'm going to take a turn around the island, maybe walk around the hunting preserve. No one's there at present, I take it?"

"They hardly ever use it anymore," she said, pushing her chair away from the table.

"Don't get up," he said. "Thanks for the sandwich." And before she could say anything else, he was out the door.

She *was* beautiful, Morgan thought as he headed through the dunes toward the wide beach. But her beauty had nothing to do with the problem. He was wary of being inveigled into a flirtation with a woman who was, for him, clearly beyond the pale.

If Kate hadn't been pregnant, that might have been another story, provided they could possibly find anything in common. But the baby, and especially the fact that it might be *his* baby, made problems.

As he dug his hands into his pockets and walked along the beach, Morgan reflected that he wasn't accustomed to babies bringing problems. He had learned from his mother and sisters that babies brought happiness—arrived with a supply of it, in fact, to be doled out without reservation to adoring relatives and friends. He'd never considered babies as liabilities; his mind-set was turned topsy-turvy by this weird situation.

He bent to pick up a shell, dipped it into a foaming wavelet to wash the sand off and decided it passed muster for Christopher. As he dried it off, he cautioned himself that Kate Sinclair might be one crazy lady—he couldn't overlook that possibility.

He headed northward, steeling himself to meet the brunette from the ferry and her friend, who were walking toward him. The brunette wasn't much. But Kate Sinclair *was* beautiful, even though she was clearly off-limits.

KATE WATCHED Morgan Rhett from the kitchen window as he turned toward the dunes. He was wearing a short-sleeved sport shirt with light blue-and-white stripes and a pair of blue pants with Dock-Sides shoes and no socks. It had surprised her on the ferry when she'd glimpsed his bare ankles, because he didn't seem like the type to dress so casually.

That brunette on the ferry. The way she had crushed her breasts against Morgan's arm. No doubt she would be delighted to see him roaming the island alone.

The baby shifted, and she rested the palm of her hand lightly on her abdomen. *At least he's interested,* she told it. *At least he's going to check us out.* Little fingers or toes rippled beneath her hand, and she slowly rubbed her stomach. *Can you feel that? Does it feel good?* she asked it. Remembering Joanna's baby, she dropped her hand. She wasn't good with kids, that much was for sure.

She cleaned up the kitchen, occasionally stopping to massage the small of her back. Would Morgan return this afternoon, or would he take the ferry back to the mainland without saying anything more to her?

She hoped he would go. She didn't want him on her territory; what she wanted from him wasn't a personal relationship. After he got to know her, after he agreed to accept the baby, the two of them wouldn't have to have anything at all to do with each other. Their only association would be brief and for business purposes, like the way she and Courtney had been. Clean. Distant. All matters preferably handled through Morgan's attorney.

As for what would happen with Morgan, there was no point in conjecture. He would contact the fertility clinic, and then his answer would be either yes, he would take the baby, or no, he wouldn't. There was nothing more she could do to influence his decision, so she might as well get on with the things she normally did.

She changed out of Joanna's maternity clothes and pulled on the gray sweatpants and an old loose T-shirt from the Hard Rock Café, Boston, that she used to wear on the Northeast Marine Institute's research vessel.

Time to take water samples, she told the baby. She stuffed her hair into a battered straw hat and headed for Tyger's Creek. On her way out the door, she scooped up her lab kit, which consisted of a woven sweet-grass basket filled with the things she needed for testing water, as well as ice cubes from the freezer to cool down the samples.

Going down the hill on the creek side of the rise of land where the lighthouse stood was easier than going up, a fact for which Kate was now extremely thankful. She tried not to think about climbing back up the sandy path, which was not the same one that led to the ferry landing. This one was narrower, so that, in a way, walking here was much easier. She could grab hold of branches on her way down so she wouldn't fall if her sneakers slipped on the loose sand.

The creek wound through salty marshland on the side of the island closest to the mainland, and it and the mud flats nearby were the home of a large number of intertidal oysters. Kate clambered into the johnboat and shoved herself awkwardly off from the shore with one of the oars.

The boat floated to the middle of the creek, and she slowly and carefully settled herself on the seat and began to row. After the city, the island seemed so quiet and so peaceful; the air was more humid and bore the scents of both marsh and sea.

Kate let the johnboat glide to a stop near the mud flats. She removed a glass vial from a basket, dipped it into the water, then recorded the time, location and water temperature.

When she had stashed the sample on ice, she turned the boat around, bracing herself against the bottom so that she could get a better hold on the oars. If she hurried, she could send the samples to the lab on the next ferry.

She ran the boat into the reeds near the path and stood up, concentrating on keeping her balance. She was so engrossed in maneuvering around the basket in the bottom of the boat that she didn't even notice the blue heron stalking nearby until, with a whir of its wide wings, it took flight in a rush of air.

The sturdy little johnboat barely rocked. But Kate was so startled that she slipped sideways over the gunwale and fell slowly, almost comically, into the creek. She cried out when her shoulder sent a spray of water into the air, and she got a mouthful of muddy creek water. Her hands instinctively wrapped around her abdomen to cushion the baby, and all she could think was, *I'm glad Morgan isn't around to see this.*

Kate sputtered and kicked until her feet sank into the ooze on the bottom of the creek, and before she knew it she was taking stock. Her head was okay, and her arms still worked, and she was standing up. Her old straw hat hadn't fared as well—it bobbed merrily toward the sea— and the baby inside her was protesting such undignified treatment.

She had barely finished her self-inventory when she heard the shout from the path.

"Kate! Kate! Are you all right?"

Morgan charged down the path, looking for all the world like a crazed bull. A *sunburned* crazed bull. She couldn't help it, she started to giggle. And then she laughed, stood there in the muddy water and laughed until her sides ached, unable to move toward shore because she was laughing so hard at the sight of the staid and sophisticated Morgan Rhett with a red face, a sprig of juniper caught in his hair and one shoe flying into the shrubbery as he ran.

"Kate?" he said, stopping at the edge of the water.

"I—I can't help it," she wheezed, tears running out of the corners of her eyes. "You look so *funny.*"

"I saw you fall. Are you hurt?"

"No, I'm not. I just—oh." And she stopped laughing.

He was looking at her, dead serious. She could tell that he didn't think this was humorous at all. He looked frantic with worry, and he was kicking off his remaining shoe.

"If you think I look funny now, just wait," he said grimly. He started to roll up his pant legs before apparently thinking better of it. And then, to her utter amazement, he waded toward her fully clothed, the water swirling around his ankles, his knees. And then she began to laugh again, only this time it wasn't amused laughter, it was hysterical, a product of her roller-coaster emotions, and she couldn't stop.

She pressed her hands into her face, suddenly quiet. All she could hear was the swish of water as Morgan approached, and as she lowered her hands, he grasped her firmly by the shoulders.

"You scared me," he said, and the way he said it made it seem like a capital offense.

"I'm *fine*," she protested, brushing his hands away. She lifted one foot experimentally out of the mud on the bottom of the creek; the other one followed. A wide wake billowed behind her as she headed toward shore.

Her T-shirt clung to her body, and she pinched at it, trying to make it less revealing. When she looked down, she could see through the thin cotton and even through her bra; she could see the large dark circles of her areolae, and below her breasts, the indentation of her navel. It embarrassed her to have Morgan see her this way, the details of her swollen body so explicitly revealed.

"You have no business going out in a boat," he said sternly. "You should sit around and watch television or something."

"Television," she said scornfully. "I get one station, and even that one doesn't come in sometimes." She bent over to push the boat through the reeds onto the shore, but Morgan said, "I'll do that," and gave it a giant heave.

When he turned, his eyes were on the level of the round protuberance under the wet shirt, and Kate turned away, embarrassed. His hand shot out and grabbed her arm, but she yanked it out of his grasp.

"Sorry," he said. "I thought you were falling again."

She wrapped her arms around herself, which didn't hide anything. Little rivulets of water ran off her clothes into the reeds.

"Don't you have something else to do?" Kate said.

"I've already done it," Morgan said. He had come to this end of the island to evade the two women from the ferry who kept following him around. He hadn't known he would run into Kate.

"Would you mind bringing that basket from the boat?" Kate asked him in a small voice.

He leaned over and picked up the basket. "Come along, I'll see you safely to the house. How you're going to make it up that winding path—"

"I can do it," Kate said through gritted teeth.

He made her walk in front of him, and she was aware of him close behind her as she headed upward. Kate eased her way by pulling herself up with the aid of drooping branches. By no means did she want to give him any reason to touch her again.

I will not, she thought grimly, *let him see me breathing hard.* Nevertheless, she was huffing and puffing when they reached the top.

"Of all the harebrained, idiotic things to do," Morgan muttered. "Pregnant women aren't supposed to go gallivanting around in boats. They should stay home and crochet little sweaters or something."

Kate, as miserable as she was, couldn't let that pass. "Don't swing that basket so hard—you'll break the sample. And I don't crochet."

"Somehow that doesn't surprise me," he said. "What kind of sample is in here, anyway?"

"Water," she snapped. "I told you about my job."

"A sample of water was important enough for you to risk life and limb? Since when are bacteria more important than your life or the child's?" Morgan asked heatedly.

They had reached the lighthouse, and she turned to face him in front of the door to the quarters. She wiped the perspiration from her forehead with a flick of her hand.

"The child is more important, of course. I suppose I'll have to think about giving up my job, but I need the money," she said.

"Courtney provides you with living expenses, you told me that yourself," he pointed out.

"Yes, but after I have the baby, after I leave here, I'll need a nest egg. My father's illness took all we'd managed to save, and—oh, why am I telling you this?"

Kate turned away, sick at heart. She didn't want to do any more explaining; she only wanted him to go. She pushed the door open, and to her dismay, he followed her into the house.

"You should get someone to come and live with you," Morgan said. "To take care of you."

"Who? No one wants to live on a barrier island four miles off the coast. The only people who come here are slobs who throw trash on the beaches and ask endless questions about the lighthouse," she said, aware that her voice was rising.

"And besides," she continued in a more normal tone, "the house is too small. There are only four little rooms."

She walked swiftly into one of the other rooms, and he heard her rummaging. When she returned, she had looped a loose shawl in a soft shade of gray around her shoulders, hiding her body.

"I'll be in touch soon," he said. He gestured in the direction of the basket containing the water sample. "Did you say something about sending that to a lab on the mainland? I can deliver it to the ferry if you'd like."

She massaged her temple for a moment. "I'd almost forgotten. Yes, that would be a big help. Here, I'll label it."

Quickly she slapped a label on the bottle and dropped it into a padded mailing envelope. "Give it to Gump on your way back," she said as she handed the envelope to Morgan. "He knows what to do with it."

"You'll hear from me," he said in a tone of voice that made it difficult to discern if he had uttered a promise or a threat.

She watched as he retreated, his clothes still wet, his feet still bare. She hadn't even thought to offer him a towel.

Chapter Five

Two weeks later Kate opened the kitchen door one afternoon and found a wrathful Gump tapping his foot impatiently on her doorstep. She invited Gump into the sitting room for a visit and listened horror-struck while he poured out a story about being accosted on the dock by a man named Tony Saldone, who pretended to know Kate.

"He bought me a drink or two in the tavern, and I told him more than you'd want him to know," Gump said mournfully.

Kate froze while she digested Gump's words. "And then what?" she asked carefully.

"I realized after a while that I'd made a mistake and told the guy to leave me alone. He rubbed the stubble on his chin and shrugged his shoulders, and then he rambled off along the dock. I wish he'd slipped on a loose board and fallen in the drink," Gump said.

"There's only one thing this can mean. Morgan Rhett has hired a private detective to check up on me. He wants to know if there's any chance that someone else could be the father of this baby," Kate said. She should have known that Morgan would be thorough. Still, she was angry, and certainly not with Gump, whose weaknesses at the Merry Lulu were well-known to her.

"I'm pretty sure I set that fellow straight about that," Gump said, but his face became serious. "What if this Morgan Rhett doesn't take the baby?" he asked.

"Morgan *has* to take the baby," Kate said. "He has to."

Gump was silent for a moment. "Any luck yet in you finding a job?" he asked.

"How can I expect anyone to hire me after the big flap at Northeast Marine Institute? In case you've forgotten, I testified against my superior in front of Congress, and his position was upheld. My reputation is nil."

"I didn't think you cared about your reputation," Gump retorted.

"Scientific reputation is one thing," Kate said. "Personal reputation is another. I couldn't care less what Willadeen Pribble and the rest of those women on the mainland think of me."

"Not that they ever lack for gossip," Gump said, shaking his head unhappily as he prepared to leave. "Goodbye, Kate. If any more detectives come calling, I'll clam up."

"Send them to me, and I'll give them a piece of my mind," Kate said. She folded her arms across her belly as she watched Gump depart, thinking that the person she'd really like to tell off was Morgan Rhett.

AT THAT MOMENT Morgan Rhett was pacing back and forth across the hand-knotted Persian carpet on the floor of his office at Morgan Rhett & Company.

"So the ferry captain told you that Kate never has male visitors?" he asked Tony Saldone.

"That's about it," Tony said.

"And how did you pry that information out of him?" Morgan asked skeptically.

Tony winked. "A couple of cups of grog at the Merry Lulu Tavern," he said succinctly. "But when I asked this guy Gump to explain this Sinclair woman's pregnancy, he shut his mouth and said he didn't want to talk about it. Changed the subject, in fact. He started rambling on about Kate's mother and how she left when Kate was nine years old. Said he felt responsible."

"I know, Kate mentioned that," Morgan said, waving away this extraneous information as if it were a pesky fly in his face.

"Well, you want to hear a good story, this one's pretty good. Eloise, Kate's mother, ran off with some guy on a motorcycle and never came back, even after the guy cracked up the 'cycle and killed himself. After that, Eloise departed for Africa and joined some do-gooder health organization."

"All that is irrelevant. You turned up no dirt on Kate Sinclair?"

"As far as her personal life is concerned, no dirt—in spades," Tony said with a laugh. "Even though the woman is enormously pregnant with no man in sight."

Morgan rubbed his chin. "How about her professional life?" he asked.

"Now that's a possibility," Tony said, leaning forward in his chair. "You told me that Kate nursed her father while he was ill. You said that she'd lived on the island with him for two years.

"But the bartender at the Merry Lulu told me that her father had only been sick for about a year before he croaked. What I think we should look into is, why did Kate come home from her job with that big research outfit in Maine one whole year before her father was diagnosed as terminally ill?'' He looked at Morgan hopefully.

"Good question," Morgan said. He sat down in his chair and stared out at the harbor. Today the water looked almost the exact shade of Kate Sinclair's eyes.

"So what do I do now?" Tony implored.

"See what you can find out," Morgan said.

"Righto. How far do you want me to take this investigation?"

"Till you can't go any further," Morgan replied.

"Okay, that wraps it up. I'll report in from time to time and let you know what's going on."

"Fine, Tony. On your way out of my office, pass Go and collect two hundred dollars," Morgan said.

"Two hund—? My fee's going to be considerably more than that before we're through," Tony told him.

"That's what I figured," Morgan said.

"Glad to help you out," Tony said jauntily, hustling off to present his bill for services rendered to date.

Morgan waited until Tony was well down the hall before he opened the middle drawer of his desk and withdrew a manila folder. Inside was a report from the fertility lab, which he read and read again.

When he had finished, he slid it into his briefcase. It was time to call Eddie Oates, his college fraternity brother. He was sure they could work out a deal of some kind. Morgan considered himself a genius at making deals.

THE THIRD WEEK after she went to see Morgan Rhett, Kate began to have nightmares about running up and down deserted streets with a baby in her arms, knocking on doors and asking people if they'd adopt it. The dreams were a reflection of her concern: what if Morgan Rhett refused his own child?

He won't, Kate thought one day as she pursued her self-appointed chore of picking up litter on the beach. And yet she knew he could. Morgan Rhett, she figured, could do anything he wanted to do.

She let her head fall back so that the wind blew into her nostrils, filling her head with the scent of salt and seaweed and little sea creatures, of places far away. She hated picking up the careless leavings of the island's daytrippers; she only did it because she couldn't bear to see the pristine beauty of the island marred by trash. At the moment she would have given anything to be back on the Northeast Marine Institute laboratory research vessel. Ah, well, those days were gone forever.

When she lifted her head again, she saw a figure walking toward her at the high-tide mark, carefully skirting clumps of dried seaweed.

She stared, determining that it was a man, and not only a man, but a man who was wearing a suit. Her breath caught in her throat when she realized that there was only one person it could be.

"Morgan," she whispered, her heart falling to her knees and swooping upward again. She had thought that when the time came he would contact her through the mail. She'd never dreamed he would come back to Yaupon Island.

He was walking swiftly. She waited. As he drew closer, she realized that he was wearing a gray pin-striped suit and black wing tips, which made her want to burst out laughing. Who else but Morgan Rhett would appear on a beach on Yaupon Island in a getup like that?

She stood uncertainly, the water lapping at her feet, the trash bag hanging at her side. When he stood directly in front of her, he stopped and stared at her, his brow slightly furrowed, his lips drawn into a firm line.

"It's mine," he said without preliminaries. "I'm convinced the baby's mine."

She nodded, her chin lifting slightly as she stared back at him. She tried not to say "I told you so."

"The fertility lab corroborates what you said," he went on.

"And how about that detective you sent over here? Did he confirm that I haven't been entertaining men?" She couldn't keep the bitterness out of her voice.

"Yes. And I'll adopt the baby, Kate. It's my duty and obligation," he said.

"Well," she replied on a long exhalation of breath. She wanted to slump with relief, but she kept her shoulders squared and her chin up.

"I want a healthy child. I want you to take care of yourself. I want—"

"And what Morgan Rhett wants, he gets, right?" Kate said cuttingly.

"Look, Kate, you've got what you asked for—someone to take this baby. Don't give me a hard time," he shot back.

Kate turned away and began to walk back toward the lighthouse, spearing odd pieces of litter with her stick, giving a wide berth to what looked like a new turtle crawl. She didn't want Morgan to see the sudden stinging tears in her eyes.

"I had hoped that you'd love the baby," she said, keeping her head turned away.

"Love? I told you I had no feeling for it," he said, walking beside her.

"It's your child," she said in a low voice.

"My responsibility. I believe in taking care of what's mine. I'll hire a good nanny. Oh, I'll see that it grows up with its little cousins—Joanna can provide a maternal touch now and then. The baby will be a Rhett in every sense of the word. It will have a family," he said earnestly.

Kate remained silent. She had what she wanted from him, but suddenly it wasn't enough. She had grown up without her mother, and it hadn't been easy, but her father's love had made up for her mother's absence. This baby might have a family and all the privileges of growing up a Rhett, but could that make up for a lack of love?

"I've moved into the hunting lodge at the other end of the island," Morgan said.

"You *what?*" Kate said incredulously. This alarming statement crowded all other thoughts from her head.

"Eddie Oates's family still owns the place, although they seldom use it anymore. He said that I'm welcome to camp out there as long as I want."

"Why?" Kate said. "Why are you moving here?"

"To keep an eye on you. You're always tramping around on the trails, leaning over in boats and getting dunked in the creek. Who knows what you might do next? There's no one around to rescue you if you have a problem. I told you, I want a healthy baby," he said.

"What about your business?" she said in a quavering voice.

"I'll check with my office by telephone from the Merry Lulu every day. As for my work load, it's light because I was planning on beginning a month's vacation in England soon, but that can wait until after the baby's born," he said.

She looked at him. He was serious. She couldn't imagine Morgan Rhett living on this island, disturbing her, making problems.

"You can't go on living here alone," he said.

"I'm not alone," she said, her voice almost breaking. "I have your little bundle of joy to keep me company."

"That's exactly the point," Morgan said. He gestured at the litterbag. "Are you sure you should be doing that?"

She twisted the top of the bag into a knot. "I'm going home," she said.

"Fine. I'll see you tomorrow morning," he answered.

"No, you won't," Kate said.

"I will," Morgan told her. His eyebrows were drawn together in concern, and all at once a flood tide of sensation swept over her. His scent, English and leathery, blended with the salty, sun-dried scent of seaweed, spinning her away into another dimension where senses ruled and good sense did not. For a moment she felt wildly attracted to him, and she didn't want to think of him that way. Morgan was the father of the child she carried within her—period.

His eyes fell to her stomach. "How much longer do you have before the baby is born?" he asked her.

"Eleven weeks," she whispered.

"Hopefully, you won't exceed your due date. I've always liked England better in the fall, anyway," he said. After a curt nod, he turned and walked away, his wing tips biting holes in the damp sand. He was clearly a man on whose shoulders the habit of command rested comfortably.

Kate headed back toward the lighthouse, head bowed in thought, litterbag bumping awkwardly against her legs.

How in the world was she going to survive Morgan Rhett's presence on the island for the next eleven weeks?

MORGAN SHOWED UP at the keeper's quarters in the bright hot light of early morning and insisted on accompanying Kate on her trip up the creek to take water samples.

"Why you?" Kate demanded in a tone laced with sarcasm. "Why don't you send that detective friend of yours?"

"Look, Kate, you have no reason to be angry about that," Morgan said, although he felt guilty about Tony Saldone's ongoing investigation.

"How would you like it if I'd put a private detective on your tail?" Kate said, jamming her hat on her head and barging ahead of him down the path to the water.

"I wouldn't," Morgan said, hurrying after her.

"I could have," she said. "After all, I'd like to know what kind of person you are. This baby shouldn't go to just anybody."

"You should have thought of that before you informed me that I was the father," Morgan said.

"Well, I didn't think of it, and I still believe you're the one to raise the baby, but I know nothing about your personal life."

They had reached the boat. Morgan shoved it off the creek bank and Kate removed her shoes and socks, wading through the shallows until she was able to climb in.

"Careful!" Morgan warned, but she ignored him.

"My personal life isn't any of your business," he said calmly. He rowed; Kate busied herself with the water-sample kit.

"Anyway," he continued, when he'd determined that the only response he was going to get from Kate was a long, withering glance, "I'm through with post-divorce craziness. I have to admit that I lived on the wild side for a while, taking out all kinds of women, staying up late, going to loud parties. But it's over. I'm thirty-five and ready to settle down again."

"I'm glad to hear that," Kate said, but the remark sounded more caustic than she meant it to be.

"I won't be entertaining women in the house I share with the baby. I don't think it would provide a good atmosphere, and Joanna would read me the riot act if the environment for this child were anything but wholesome."

Kate's look was skeptical.

"Well, you were the one who brought up the subject of my personal life," he reminded her. "I am, after all, a very eligible bachelor."

Was she mistaken, or did she detect a hint of amusement in his voice? Kate stared out over the marsh, able to bear the glare of sun upon water better than the twinkle in Morgan's eyes.

"This baby may end your eligibility," she said.

"Don't be silly," Morgan said. "It will make me even more desirable. Women will fall over themselves for the chance to come over and coo at it."

"*This* woman couldn't care less about you and other women as long as you're a good father," Kate said.

"A good father," Morgan mused. He rowed the boat up to the shore and helped Kate out. He slid an arm around her nonexistent waist, but Kate pulled away and splashed through the reeds to shore, where she sat down to put on her shoes and socks.

"What is a good father?" Morgan said when he had beached the boat.

Kate thought for a moment. "My father was wonderful," she said. "He's a shining example of what a father should be, in my opinion." She took the hand that Morgan offered her and pulled herself to a standing position.

He was right behind her on the path.

"What was your father like? I only met him once," Morgan said.

"He was the one who set me on the road to my career. It was his dream to become a marine biologist, but it ended when he was seriously injured in the Korean War. He came back to the lighthouse to recuperate and never left."

"How did he make a living?"

"We lived in the lighthouse rent free, of course, and he had a small inheritance. Anyway, it was Dad who joined in my island adventures, who patiently answered my questions about marl washed in from the offshore reefs, and who helped me return an octopus in distress to the sea after it washed up on shore during a storm," she said.

"He sounds wonderful," Morgan said.

Kate stopped to catch her breath in the shade of a palmetto tree. "Dad was an admirer of Jacques Cousteau and of Marc Theroux, the famous marine biologist who did such interesting work in the South Pacific. I admired them, too, of course, but I chose my line of work because of my father's early interest," she said.

"He must have been proud of you."

"He was, I think. I wish—" but here she hesitated.

"Wish what?"

"Wish that he hadn't been disappointed," she said curtly. And then, before he could ask her any other questions, she resumed the climb up the path.

Morgan followed her, wishing she'd be more forthcoming with information about herself. He had an idea that he didn't know nearly enough about her, and he found himself growing more and more curious. Who was this Kate Sinclair, really? What motivated her? What brought her happiness? And what, besides his presence, got under her skin?

"Would you mind taking the samples to Gump so he can get them out in this morning's mail?" she said over her shoulder as they approached the lighthouse.

"No problem. I have to go to the Merry Lulu and call my office, anyway," said Morgan.

Kate held the door of the quarters open for Morgan to follow her inside.

"Are you going to be doing anything this afternoon?" Morgan asked.

"It's no business of yours," Kate said, turning away to print the label. She had noticed a sprig of dark curly hair rising above the placket of his polo shirt, distracting her when she'd rather ignore him. *A man doesn't have the right to be so handsome,* she thought.

"If you had an accident, who would save you?"

Kate sighed. "You would, because you're going to be at my heels every minute, aren't you?"

"Yes," he said soberly. "I am."

"I want this baby to be healthy as much as you do," she pointed out.

"I intend to make sure it is," he said.

"Now I know exactly how an oyster feels when accosted by a starfish," Kate said through tight lips as she pasted the label on the bottle.

He looked blank, so she explained.

"Sea stars prey on oysters by wrapping their arms around the oysters. The arms fasten to the oysters' shells with suckers."

"And then what happens?"

Kate shrugged. "The starfish pulls and pulls until the shell opens. The oyster can't hold out forever."

"Is that the way you feel?" he probed, his eyes bright.

"Yes," she said abruptly, but Morgan only smiled his slow smile, and for a moment Kate felt as if the blue of his eyes were blinding her. She was painfully aware of her body, its ovoid shape, its clumsiness.

For a moment she longed to be thin again as she recalled the dream she'd had the previous night, one of the oddly erotic dreams she'd started having early in her pregnancy. In the dream she had felt strangely buoyant and light, and her breasts had tingled with the touch of someone's hands, and she'd tossed and turned restlessly until she was fully awake. Afterward she'd reasoned that she woke up only because she had to go to the bathroom.

But that wasn't the only reason, and she knew it. The reason was standing patiently in front of her, emitting vast quantities of pheromones.

Morgan held out his hand for the bottle, and Kate couldn't help noticing that it was the same strong, sinewy hand that she had imagined stroking her body last night, softly urgent and knowledgeable.

What was wrong with her? She had to stop thinking about it, thinking about him! She was in no position to be acting like a moonstruck teenager over Morgan Rhett.

"Kate, it may come as news to you, but I'm not your enemy," Morgan said as he went out the door. She raised cool hands to her hot face, embarrassed that Morgan, knowledgeable bachelor that he was, might have sensed more about her feelings for him than she wanted him to know.

THINKING ABOUT KATE, thinking about the way her hands had trembled as she wrote out the label, Morgan decided that he'd have to be a fool not to know what was going on.

She was attracted to him. Not that this was peculiar; women often were. But she was pregnant. He hadn't thought that pregnant women had sexual feelings.

Of course, they were still *women,* he told himself. It's not as though they lacked the proper equipment to do something about normal sexual urges, although previously he'd supposed that such impulses more or less shut down for the duration of pregnancy.

Now that he thought about it, that was ridiculous. Of course, husbands and wives must share erotic moments during the nine months before a baby was born. Married couples would still want to express their love for each other in a physical way.

But Kate was a single woman, and he'd never known a single pregnant woman before. She was new territory, and from the looks of things, she was eager to be explored.

Of course, there was the matter of the detective, which she seemed unwilling to forgive, and she didn't like his following her around the island, which he felt was necessary. Where did that leave them? Morgan wasn't sure, but he knew one thing: he was probably as fascinated by Kate Sinclair as she was by him.

As soon as Morgan arrived at the Merry Lulu, he telephoned his secretary. Phyllis told him that no urgent business had presented itself, and the thought occurred to Morgan that he might like not having to attend power lunches. He might even get a chance to find out what blank spaces looked like in his appointment book.

"Say, Phyllis," he said in afterthought. "How about sending me a book about pregnancy and childbirth?"

"Preg—?" Clearly Phyllis had a hard time bringing herself to say the word. "You'll have it tomorrow," she finished briskly.

Morgan hung up, bemused. He didn't have to wonder what Phyllis would think if she knew that he was going to be a father. Come to think of it, he'd enjoy breaking the news at the office, and as for what they'd think about it, he didn't care. One of the advantages of being a Rhett was that you never had to explain anything.

But fatherhood seemed far in the future today. Back on Yaupon Island, Morgan sauntered along one of the twisting, moss-hung paths to the lodge end of the island. A red-winged blackbird fluttered across his path, and he brushed aside a gossamer cobweb still beaded with dewdrops. *A guy could get accustomed to peace and quiet,* he thought, understanding all at once why Kate dreaded leaving here.

Not that he liked living at the lodge; it was a big barnlike building with a long uncarpeted hallway that echoed every little sound. It had noisy plumbing, hard water, ugly overstuffed furniture and a line of ants perpetually running from the kitchen window to the nether regions of the pantry.

Morgan ignored the company of marchers as he had since his arrival and went to the refrigerator to pour a glass of milk. As he stood drinking it, he could look into the lodge's main room with its mounted boar heads and pheasants. There was a fireplace wide enough to put a bed in—funny that he should think of beds. Or was it?

If he thought about beds, what sprang instantly to mind was pillows and golden blond hair spread out upon them. If he thought about blond hair, he fantasized about running his fingers through Kate's hair and ultimately guiding her head toward his until their lips met and blended in surprise and pleasure. Her skin would be smooth and soft, her neck warm, her eyelids heavy with passion, and she would cling to him, incapable of moving and her heart beating triple time.

Oh, he thought about it. He thought about it a lot, more than he wanted to, more than he thought was proper.

He'd had a lot of experience with women, but nothing in his life had ever prepared him for coming to terms with the fact that he, Morgan Rhett, had the hots for a woman who was humongously pregnant and wasn't even his wife.

Chapter Six

Morgan forced himself to stay at his end of the island until he thought he'd go crazy wondering what Kate was doing.

Was she tipped over in some boat, snorkeling, falling off the ferry dock or tripping over a root and sprawled on one of the treacherous island paths? Telling himself that she'd lived on this island all her life and knew how to deal with its dangers didn't help; reminding himself that she didn't want him anywhere around only made him irritable.

So what should I do? he asked himself. His presence on the island wasn't accomplishing its purpose if he stayed in the lodge like a hermit. He found himself daydreaming about her, imagining her eyes warm with laughter, her lips upturned with pleasure—sights that he longed to see.

Finally, after a couple of days had passed, he knew that he had to see Kate again. Now. Today. Out of pure curiosity he'd confirm what he had sensed earlier when she'd given out definite sexual vibrations, but he wouldn't be influenced.

In fact, this time his visit would have a purpose. He'd look her over, *really* look her over, study the size of her, inspect her legs for spider veins, see how the seams of her clothing bulged.

He'd find fault with everything that he could so that it would be impossible for him to find her attractive. He had to put an end to those crazy, maybe even wicked, visions of their bodies pressed together in an endless variety of positions, visions that refused to go away.

He planned carefully. He would remain aloof when he saw her, refusing to smile or say anything personal. He would wear sunglasses so she couldn't see that he was inspecting every inch of her, looking for flaws and faults. He would watch his body language to make sure he wasn't giving her the wrong idea.

All the way to the lighthouse Morgan rehearsed in his mind what he was going to say to Kate when he saw her, manufacturing an excuse for being on this end of the island and planning how to open the conversation. But when he was almost there, when he thought he had the words down pat, he happened to glance upward at the lighthouse tower, and his heart almost stopped.

Kate was leaning on the railing around the metal platform at the top of the lighthouse, her smock plastered against the smooth rise of her stomach, her bright hair blowing in the wind.

He was so stunned to see her up there that he gawked for a moment. Kate, seven months pregnant, hanging over the railing at the top of the lighthouse! Kate, taking chances! He cupped his hands around his mouth so that his words wouldn't be flung seaward by the wind.

"Kate! Come down from there!" he called, the words startling him with their outrage.

She looked down at him questioningly, as if she couldn't quite place him, which, since he had been thinking about her nonstop for the past few days, infuriated him. Her hair flew around her head, shining like a halo. He could barely make out her features; the tower, according to a plaque set into the bricks nearby, was a hundred and thirty feet tall. He knew there was no elevator. She must have climbed all the way to the top.

"Kate!"

"Go away," she called back.

He ran to the door at the base of the tower, but it didn't yield to his frantic tugging.

He ran back to where he could see her more clearly. "What do you think you're doing?" he yelled.

"Drying my hair," was her answer. He thought she might be laughing at him.

He paced back and forth. What if she became dizzy and lost her balance? What if she couldn't manage the downward descent on the narrow spiral staircase? He had climbed another lighthouse once, and the muscles in his legs, unaccustomed to such steep stairs, had ached for days.

"How did that lady get to the top of the lighthouse?" a boy of about twelve asked. He had a camera slung from a strap on his wrist, and someone that Morgan took to be his mother was examining the inscription on the path to the quarters.

"Climbed," Morgan said in disgust at Kate's antic.

"Can we go up there, too?" asked a small girl who must have been the boy's younger sister.

"Yeah, I wanna go to the top," said the boy.

"Where can we buy tickets?" the mother asked, hurrying over.

"You can't, and people aren't allowed to climb the lighthouse," Morgan said distractedly.

"Is she going to jump?" the woman asked sharply.

"No, of course not," Morgan said.

"Then why—?"

"I have no idea," Morgan said.

The woman gave him a strange look. "Come along, Joey," she said.

"But—"

"You too, Debbie," and despite their wails of protest, the children were dragged toward the beach.

Morgan couldn't take his eyes off Kate. At any moment he expected her to plummet over the railing, hair flying, as she uttered a bewildered scream. What would he do if that happened? How could he protect her?

"Kate! Please come down!" he called again.

She said nothing. He thought wildly of Rapunzel in her tower, letting down her hair so that her prince could climb up. He thought about Kate's total irresponsibility and her beauty and her foolhardiness.

Then, in the blink of an eye, she was gone. Disappeared. He blinked again, the reflection of the sun on the glass at the top of the lighthouse blinding him. She must have gone inside.

How many stairs were there in this lighthouse? Each one of them posed the threat of a misstep. She could stumble. She could lose her fragile hold on the railing; she could have a sudden pain and double over, losing her balance.

He waited, and it seemed like hours. He hurried to the metal door in the lighthouse base and pounded on it. He called her name. He was acting like a madman, and all because of—no, not because of the baby. The baby was incidental. At the moment, it was Kate he cared about.

He was ready to renew his attack on the door when it opened with a creak of rusty hinges.

Kate stood there, a step above him, her hair falling softly around her shoulders, her eyes clear and amused.

In that soft yellow smock, her breasts pressing against the fabric, her stomach gently rounded beneath, she looked for all the world like a fertility goddess.

He swallowed and tried not to look as relieved as he actually was. All the words he had planned to say, all thoughts of finding something unattractive or disgusting about her flew out of his head.

"You shouldn't have gone up there," he said, and he was so choked with emotion that he couldn't go on.

"I always dry my hair in the sun at the top of the lighthouse," she explained serenely. "It's so much better for it than the harsh heat of a hair dryer."

He could smell it, her hair, lemon scented with a tinge of salt, a clean smell. The air inside the tower rushed out, cool and sweet. She stepped outside and swung the door closed behind her.

He touched her hair as he had been wanting to for so long. It fell away from her shoulders, shimmering like sun-shot silk. She swung her head around and stared into his eyes, startled.

His hand dropped. He couldn't believe it, but he had been ready to make a move on her.

"You frightened me," he said.

She continued to stare at him. "I can still manage the stairs. I've been climbing them all my life," she said.

"Don't do it anymore. Please. You can dry your hair out on the beach if you must. But not at the top of the lighthouse."

"I'll think about it," she said. She turned away and headed toward the house.

"Kate," he began. He had never seen anyone who looked so completely female. He had the urge to wrap his arms around her and kiss her thoroughly, to run his tongue around those seductive lips of hers, to bend her to him, twining legs around legs, arms around bodies, to crush her breasts against his chest until they could both barely breathe.

If Kate Sinclair didn't want to be kissed, he was a monkey's uncle. Underscoring his jubilation at this thought was the more sobering knowledge that if he kissed her, he might be getting into more than he'd bargained for.

He'd agreed to take the baby; the baby was his responsibility. But Kate wasn't. And if he started something, she might think she was entitled to more than he wanted to give.

Give? All he wanted, he admitted to himself with chagrin, was to take.

She opened her eyes. She looked scared, and he saw her swallow.

So much for sexual desire in the pregnant woman, he told himself. They felt it, all right. Or at least this one did.

"I'll see you tomorrow," he blurted before turning on his heel and heading for the path to the beach. In the face of this new knowledge, not only about her but about himself, all he wanted to do was put distance between them before he initiated something they would both regret.

After all, it was the baby he cared about, he reminded himself on the way back to the lodge. But try as he might, he couldn't imagine the child. All he could think about was Kate. Even now, with the lighthouse receding into the distance, he could still smell the fragrance of her sun-warmed skin and feel the caress of her sweet-smelling hair on his fingertips.

AS SOON AS MORGAN LEFT, Kate commenced trembling like a leaf.

And it was wild, it was insane, but she had desperately wanted Morgan to kiss her.

Hormones, she told herself, *it's my hormones running rampant.* If other pregnant women thought about sex, Kate had never heard about it. Or if she'd heard about it, she'd dismissed it as cockeyed ramblings. But lately it had been constantly on her mind.

Morgan's lips had been only inches away from hers, and he had touched her hair, and she had shivered and wanted to lean into him, to put her arms around his waist and feel the warmth of his body pressing against hers.

Only he wouldn't want that. She had about as much sex appeal as Babar the elephant. She was immensely, hugely pregnant. She was as unattractive as she'd ever been, and besides, Morgan's taste in women ran to small intense ones like Courtney, his ex-wife.

This was *their* baby she was carrying, she reminded herself. The product of *their* union. And even though fertilization had occurred in a petri dish, the baby was a reminder that Morgan had actually been Courtney's husband and had thus gone to bed with her many times.

The thought punctured her longings, let all the air out of them and left her feeling deflated. Deflated, but still huge, and the baby must be swimming laps inside her because it hadn't been still for over an hour.

To distract herself she looked in the cupboard for a snack. Nothing looked good to her. She wanted something tart, something sour, and all she had was stuff like vanilla pudding and canned cream-of-potato soup. She slammed the cupboard door, hard. Today, she thought, nothing had gone right.

Because she had put the chore off long enough, she leafed through some of the professional journals that had been piling up for the past six months. She lingered over the Help Wanted columns for a long time, circling two or three ads. Then, with darkness falling outside, she sat down at the vintage typewriter in the homey little sitting room with its well-worn furniture and began to compose a job application letter.

She had no trouble until she reached the point where she had to mention her previous employer. She was mulling over the proper wording when she heard Morgan at her door.

"Kate?" he said.

With all of her senses suddenly alert, she went to the door.

"Back again so soon, Morgan? What do you want?" she demanded. Her tone of voice didn't give away the fact that only a short while ago she had been fantasizing about kissing him.

"I'll be taking the first ferry to Preacher's Inlet tomorrow morning so I can call my office. I wondered if you needed anything from town," he said. His face showed little expression.

"I go every two weeks or so to the store. I have plenty to eat," she said.

"How about fresh vegetables? Fruit? Are you eating enough of that?"

"My diet satisfies my doctor," she said.

"Next time you go for a prenatal visit, I'll go with you," Morgan said.

"Morgan. This is ridiculous," Kate said.

"What's ridiculous is that you're standing in there and I'm out here getting bitten by mosquitoes as big as Scud missiles and a good bit more accurate," he said crossly.

Kate had to laugh. He eyed her without humor and started to walk away, his flashlight bouncing a beam of light off the dense trees beyond.

She held the door open wide. "Come in," she said with only a trace of impatience.

He turned with an inquiring look.

"Hurry up," she urged, "before the bugs beat you to it."

She led the way into the sitting room, wondering what to say. There was no reason for this visit, no reason at all. It seemed strange to see him in this familiar room, filling it up, taking up more room than he should, walking in as if he owned the place. Why was he here? What did he want?

If he had any plans, Morgan was not giving them away. His sweeping glance assessed the framed photos on the wall of the sitting room, and he surprised her by stopping in front of the largest one and studying it with interest.

"This is you?" he asked.

Kate moved closer, too, somehow pleased that he was interested in her family pictures; she treasured them herself.

"I was a senior in high school at the time," she told him. She remembered how her father had exclaimed over the proofs of this portrait when she brought them home, how he said she was the prettiest girl in the school and insisted on ordering the largest portrait offered. She'd worn her hair the way she did now, but her face had been rounder.

"It's a terrific picture," Morgan said, but Kate was glad when he moved on. It was embarrassing for Morgan to see her slim teenage self when she was so big and ungainly now.

"That's Yaupon Island after a hurricane passed through several years ago," she told him when they stood in front of the next photo.

That picture showed a tangle of debris in front of the keeper's quarters. Kate's father stood with one foot on a palmetto log, hands on his hips, smiling into the camera lens. Kate had taken the picture herself when she was about ten years old.

"I suppose storms are frequent here," Morgan observed.

"We have a couple of big ones every year, though they don't usually reach hurricane strength," Kate said.

"What do you do when a hurricane comes—go to the mainland?"

"Dad liked to, but I always preferred to batten down the hatches and ride it out on the island."

"Daredevil," he accused, his eyes sparkling. He looked around the room. "There are no pictures of your mother here," he said.

"Dad took it hard when Mom ran away with Johnny."

"You did, too, I suppose," Morgan said.

"What nine-year-old girl wouldn't? Oh, Mom used to send me a birthday card once in a while saying how much she'd love to see me, but every time I tried to set a time and place for us to meet, she wiggled out of it. I haven't heard from her in years."

Kate tried to sound philosophical, but she'd always felt that there was an empty place in her life that no one had ever been able to fill. She'd had a hard time forming attachments to anyone—man or woman—because deep in her heart she'd always been afraid of being abandoned again. And in fact, the one time she'd let down her guard, that was exactly what had happened.

This was not something she wanted to explain to Morgan, however. She had to do something about him, though, because he was standing in the middle of the sitting room and looking as if leaving was the farthest thing from his mind at the moment.

She gestured toward the couch. "Please sit down," she said, halfway glad for his company. As much as she enjoyed her solitude, it did get lonely on Yaupon Island sometimes.

"Maybe you can help with the letter I'm writing," she said as she resumed her seat in front of the typewriter. She pulled the paper out and handed it to him.

His eyes scanned it quickly. "Very succinct and to the point," he said.

"I tried to write a letter with punch, one that will make someone sit up and take notice. I need to go to work as soon as I can after the baby is born, and it won't be easy. It's not a good job market for one thing, and for another—well, let's just say that I'm anticipating a lot of difficulty," Kate told him.

"If you need a reference, perhaps I could help," Morgan said. He looked so self-confident. Kate thought that Morgan Rhett had no idea of the uphill struggle she faced.

"The only kind of references I need are those in my field, and that won't be easy," she said quietly, staring down at her hands.

"Kate, what's wrong? Something is bothering you," he said. He leaned forward, his eyes warm with understanding.

She interlocked her fingers and stretched them so that the knuckles cracked. Morgan winced at the sound.

"I'm not sure I want to tell you," Kate said.

"Come on, you don't have to be so secretive," he said.

"It has to do with things that happened a long time ago," she hedged.

"In that case, the best thing to do is forget them and move on," he said.

"Easy for you to say," she said ruefully. "My whole professional career is nothing more than garbage because of what happened."

He leaned forward impatiently. "Are you going to tell me or aren't you?" he asked. He was on the verge of demanding that she spill all the details, but he had learned that demanding was not a technique that worked with Kate.

"Would you like a beer?" she asked suddenly.

"Sure," he said, but she had surprised him with the offer. She got up and walked into the kitchen, where he heard her opening and closing the refrigerator door. She returned with a can of beer and a glass, both of which she set down beside him.

"Aren't you having one?" he asked.

"I don't drink," she said. "I keep the beer around for guests who do."

He poured and took a sip. "We were talking about your professional career," he reminded her.

She ran a careless hand through her hair, and he suddenly remembered how silky it had felt beneath his fingertips. He longed to touch it again, and it was all he could do to keep his hand curved around his glass.

"It happened at the Northeast Marine Institute," she told him, and with difficulty he forced himself to pay attention. "That's where I worked before I came here. I discovered that a co-worker was faking data—in fact, his whole study was fabricated. A friend of mine who worked there, Pegeen, called my attention to some irregularities, and I investigated and uncovered all kinds of proof. I blew the whistle, and I got fired," she said.

"But you were in the right?" he asked quickly.

"Of course, I was," she said with indignation.

"So why were you fired?"

"The co-worker and the head of the department were collaborating on a research paper incorporating the false data. I lost my research job and, when I couldn't pay the bills, I had to sell my house and my car—almost everything I owned. Then my father got sick and—well, here I am." She shrugged and tried to smile.

"Kate, I can't imagine that you sat back and let these people run right over you," Morgan said.

"I didn't. I testified before Congress, only to be publicly dismissed by my department head as a crackpot who resented my co-worker's superior ability. Oh, and I left out one important thing. My co-worker was my fiancé. Mitch and I were supposed to be married at the end of that year."

"You've never recovered, have you?" he asked, watching her carefully.

"Recovered? I lost my house, my car, my job and the man in my life. In short, everything," she said, her eyes flashing.

"But not your self-respect," he shot back, and she blinked at him, surprised.

"You don't give yourself enough credit," he continued. "You stood up to them, Kate, and you were in the right. Not many people would have had the courage to do that." He was touched by her story, and he wished she'd told him before. It helped him understand a lot of things about her.

"Not many people would have been stupid enough to expose two award-winning scientists who can command millions in research grants," she said in a wry tone. "I decide on the spur of the moment to do things, then I have to live with the decision. It's a bad habit."

He knew she was thinking of her pregnancy, of bearing a child for Courtney.

"I've never met anyone who had agreed to be a surrogate mother before. Why did you do it, Kate?"

"Because I thought it was the only chance I would have to bear a baby. I decided a long time ago that single motherhood wasn't for me," she said.

A long silence followed. "A woman like you could marry someday. If you choose, that is," he said.

"No, I've ruled that out after what happened between Mitch and me. I'm happiest when I'm working. My priorities are first to redeem myself and then to immerse myself in my work with oysters. Someday I want to achieve something that would have made my father proud of me."

"What would he have said about your pregnancy?"

Kate gazed into space for a moment, looking reflective. "I've asked myself that many times, Morgan. When I first became pregnant, I thought he would have cheered me on. After all, this was something new. I felt like I was in the vanguard of scientific development, and I thought I was doing something useful for Courtney," she said.

"And now?" he asked, his gaze locked with hers.

"I realize that we haven't begun to scratch the surface of the social implications of the latest developments in scientific and medical technology," she said. "For the first time in my life, science scares me." Somewhere a clock ticked, and in that moment Morgan felt sympathy for her and, yes, pity.

"Kate," he said. "I want to help. There's not much I can do to help you get work. But as for what Courtney did, well, I can make up for it if you'll let me. If I've caused you any grief, I—"

"I could have done without the detective," she said, and her tone was sharp.

"A mistake on my part," he said, thinking guiltily about Tony Saldone, who was at this minute hard on the case somewhere in Maine.

"I know you're a hardheaded businessman, and I'm sure you think that you had to do what you did. But sending a detective to ask my friends about other men! It was so... so—"

"Humiliating," he said in a low tone. "I know. I'm sorry, and I'll make up for it. Let me take care of you, Kate. If you need anything, tell me. I'll get it for you. Not just for the baby's sake, but because you deserve it."

She sighed, and when she spoke it was slowly and without her usual verve. "Since my father died, there hasn't been anyone who would take care of me. I've had to be independent, which I admit came naturally. It's not easy for me to let someone else take over my life," she explained.

"I don't want to take over your life. I only want to smooth the way for you."

"Are you going to start following me around every minute again?" she asked.

"I'm the eldest of four children, and I looked after all of them when we were kids. It comes naturally to me to watch out for you, even though I know you don't like it."

"Having somebody tagging around after me makes me grumpy," she said.

"Pregnant women—"

"Don't tell me about pregnant women! The fact is, I'm always kind of a grouch. I'm impatient with people who are trite, inept, corrupt or immoral. And men often bring out the worst in my disposition. Don't ask me why," she finished helplessly.

To her utter surprise, he laughed. "At least you're honest," he said. When he stopped laughing, he grew more serious. "Do you accept my apology, Kate? I have to know."

"If you can accept my need to grouch once in a while," she said.

He laughed. "Done," he said.

Suddenly and unexpectedly she stretched her hands out to him, and he took them. Energy flowed between them, energy and more.

"Friends?" she said.

"Friends."

At that moment he couldn't pull his eyes away from hers; they looked so deep, so understanding. Somehow he had expected Kate to hold on to her resentment, to make this even more difficult than it already was. He hadn't expected openness and candor.

"You'd better go, or I'll never get my letter finished," she said. She stood up, and he watched how she had to position her legs far apart to bear her weight.

He followed her to the door, mesmerized by the way she walked. She moved with stately grace, like a great ocean liner upon the sea. Her limbs were long and lissome, distracting him from the bulk of her belly, but his eyes kept returning to it because, Heaven help him, he found that part of her beautiful.

Because it's part of her, he told himself mentally, but, of course, that wasn't true. The baby was not of Kate at all. It was *his* baby. *His* baby filling her up, weighting her down, changing her life, and the knowing of it gave him a feeling so intimate that he could only imagine how it must feel to have impregnated a woman through the act of intercourse. It must be the ultimate power trip, to know that you had not only created a new life but had changed another person's, the mother's, life forever.

"I'll see you—tomorrow," Kate said.

He wondered if she ever felt lonely when she slept in the double bed he'd glimpsed through the door of her bedroom; he wondered if she ever woke in the night and wished to snuggle against a warm body.

"I meant it when I offered to bring you something from town tomorrow," he said when they were standing in front of the door. "Isn't there anything you need?"

"Pickles," she said suddenly. "I know it's trite, but— oh, if I only had something sour to eat. I seem to have a hard time tasting things these days—everything tastes like cardboard or worse."

"Pickles?" he said, smiling at her. *"Pickles."* He laughed.

He looked at her helplessly, and then, before he knew what was happening, her face tilted toward him, his head drifted downward, and he felt the warmth of her breath upon his lips. One of her breasts brushed his arm, and before he could take another breath, before he lost his nerve, his lips met hers.

It was a slow, sweet kiss, their lips softly pliant, and he was afraid to take her in his arms for fear of breaking the spell. Only their lips touched, and when it was over, her eyes were luminous in the light from the lamp. He was overwhelmed with tender feelings for her.

"I think maybe I just made the second biggest mistake of my life," she said, sounding shaken.

He was taken aback. Was that a wisecrack or a heartfelt observation? Morgan didn't know. But whatever she had meant, it certainly took the wind out of his sails.

He gripped her shoulders. "Whatever that was, it was no mistake," he said, his voice rough. For good measure he yanked her close and swept his tongue over her lips. She gasped, a sharp intake of breath, and he pulled her closer, backing her up against the door, exploring the exquisite textures of tongue and lips. She might have broken away first, but he pursued the kiss aggressively until he heard her moan deep in her throat, and then he released her, triumph surging through him.

She stared at him, her eyes wide, the irises looking very black. He could feel her heart pulsing beneath his fingertips and realized that he was gripping her shoulders too tightly.

"Good night, Kate," he said, making himself step back. Her lips were parted and moist from his kisses, and she had never looked so desirable. Nor had his thoughts ever been so carnal.

He left her then, slamming out of the house, rushing along the path toward the dunes in the light of a moon that seemed too white, too full, too bright. In his head were images of Kate, her hair flying in the wind at the top of the lighthouse, her lips swollen from his kisses and her eyes filled with uncertainty.

As Morgan approached the lodge, he realized with surprise that someone was waiting for him on the terrace.

He stopped in alarm and narrowed his eyes, aiming the beam from his flashlight to separate the figure on the terrace from the shadows.

The person who was waiting stepped forward.

"I thought you'd never get here, Morgan. What took you so long?" said Courtney.

Chapter Seven

"What are you doing here?" Morgan demanded, striding forward.

Courtney regarded him with a half smile.

"Invite me in and you'll find out," she said. "The bugs, by the way, are ferocious. How can you stand living here?"

Morgan opened the back door of the lodge and flicked on the overhead light in the big hall. The mounted animal heads cast bizarre shadows around the cypress-paneled walls.

"I like Yaupon Island," Morgan said.

"And you like what's on this island, too, right?" Courtney, with her unerring flair for the dramatic, unwound a scarf from her neck and trailed it as she walked to one of the big cracked-leather couches and sat down.

Morgan was sure she must be referring to Kate, but he decided to ignore the gibe. "How did you get here? The ferry doesn't run this late," he said.

"Willadeen Pribble's son has a boat and was only too happy to do me the favor."

"Your husband isn't with you?"

"Damien? He's in Charleston. I had to come to Preacher's Inlet this evening for a meeting of the historical society."

To stall for time, Morgan mixed drinks for both of them, and after handing Courtney hers, he sat down on the edge of a chair and eyed her warily.

"State your business, Courtney," he said. "I'm in no mood for small talk."

"I could ask you the same thing. State *your* business, Morgan. What are you doing on Yaupon Island?"

"I suppose I have your friend Willadeen Pribble to thank for passing news of my whereabouts along to you," he said, taking a sip of his drink and glowering at his ex-wife.

"How clever of you to figure out the obvious. But this isn't the season for hunting—hunting animals, that is. And you don't like to fish. So I said to myself, 'What could bring Morgan to Yaupon Island?' And I thought about the beauteous Kate Sinclair, and voilà!" She waited to see what he would say.

"It's none of your business what I'm doing here," Morgan said heatedly.

"I think it is, especially when Kate Sinclair is carrying our baby," she said.

Morgan slammed his drink down on the coffee table. "You didn't want the baby. You told her to put it up for adoption."

"I didn't tell her to give it to you!" Courtney said, her voice escalating in pitch. "We fought a court battle over those embryos, Morgan. *I* won custody. They were mine to do with whatever I wished."

"The contract you and Kate signed states that the baby is to be put up for adoption if you renege on the agreement. I'm adopting it, Courtney. Adopting my own child!" There was no mistaking the irony in his tone.

Courtney leaned forward, her infuriating smile exposing a row of shiny white teeth. Perhaps it was only the mounted wolf's head in the background, but never had she looked more predatory.

"Read the contract again," she said. "The baby is to be adopted by a *married* couple. *Married,* Morgan. Unless you can find a woman to marry you, it's no go."

He stared at her, nonplussed at this new development.

"You haven't read the contract between me and Kate, Morgan? You should. I'll tell my lawyer to send you a copy." Courtney stood up.

"Get out," Morgan said, barely able to contain his fury.

"I'm going," she said.

"Not nearly fast enough," Morgan answered, hurrying to the door and flinging it wide.

"I'm sure you can find someone to marry, Morgan. Don't you have women standing in line to go to bed with you? Too bad you never knew what to do with a woman when you finally got her there." After firing that parting shot, Courtney disappeared into the night.

Morgan slammed the door after her and stood with his fists clenched, fighting the impulse to run after her and scream epithets. Courtney, as usual, had hit below the belt. Their sex life had been a disaster; he had never known anyone who was as cold and demeaning as his ex-wife. Making love to her had been like cuddling up to an iceberg.

Through the window he saw a shadow detach itself from a tree and join Courtney at the juncture of the path to the ferry landing. It must be the Pribble boy. When they had disappeared into the darkness, he exhaled slowly, his shoulders slumping.

Morgan sat down to finish his drink, massaging his temples thoughtfully. He was sure that Kate had never read the small print in the contract, and she probably had no idea that it specified that her baby could only be adopted by a married couple.

And just as he and Kate were getting used to each other, he didn't want to ruin their burgeoning relationship with an announcement as unwelcome as this one. All his protective instincts were aroused on her behalf. Kate had suffered enough from Courtney's whims, and he would not allow Courtney to sink her claws into Kate Sinclair again.

Besides the big hall and the long line of bedrooms, the lodge contained innumerable bathrooms, a kitchen and a terrace overlooking the ocean. It was a place, when occupied by only one person, that was lonely but well suited for solitary thoughts. He opened a bag of potato chips and lay back on the couch, listening to the rush of waves to shore and exploring the situation in all its complexities as he munched.

Was Courtney telling the truth? Did the contract really say that the baby resulting from those embryos could only be adopted by a married couple? He didn't like his ex-wife, and she didn't like him. But he was pretty sure that even Courtney wouldn't make up something like this.

And Kate—why hadn't she known what was in the contract? Was she so oblivious to legalities that she had plunged into surrogate motherhood without knowing all the ramifications of the contract she'd signed?

Finally, worn out with thinking, Morgan reached for the book on pregnancy and childbirth that Phyllis had sent. There might be no ready answers for the questions he'd been asking himself about the bizarre situation in which he found himself, but the book was most informative and answered some other questions that had come to mind in the past few days.

It did, for instance, have a complete section on sex during pregnancy, a section that Morgan read twice.

TONY SALDONE was jubilant when Morgan reached him at his hotel in Maine early the next morning.

"Good thing you phoned, Morgan. I've got new information about the Sinclair woman."

"Yeah, well look, Tony, you can call off the investigation," Morgan said from the public phone at the Merry Lulu.

"Call it off!" Tony said, sounding injured. "You gotta be kidding."

"I mean it. Fly home and send me a bill."

"Don't you want to know what I've found out?"

"Not especially," Morgan said.

"Kate Sinclair was fired from Northeast Marine Institute for blowing the whistle on the director and a colleague, at least one of whom was fabricating data. She even testified before Congress in their investigation of federal funds being misspent for false research. I cozied up to one of the secretaries who works in the lab, and—"

"Can it, Tony. Kate told me about that."

"She couldn't have told you all of it because she doesn't know all of it. According to Pegeen, who works in the office at Northeast Marine, Kate was right in her allegations about her co-worker's research, and the independent Federal Health Foundation Office of Scientific Ethics is getting ready to blow the whole thing sky-high in a report.''

''How does this Pegeen know?''

''She's a good, good friend of a guy who works for the FHF. You still want me to quit?''

Morgan thought quickly. On one hand there was Kate's understandable aversion to his putting Tony on her case earlier. On the other hand Kate could possibly benefit from finding out what the Federal Health Foundation Office of Scientific Ethics intended to do.

''Well, Morgan, what do you say?''

Morgan felt as if he was double-dealing; he didn't like the smell of this. But if he could help Kate, he would.

''Stay on the case, Tony. Find out whatever you can.''

''Good decision. I'll let you know if I learn anything. And thanks. There's nothing I like more than entertaining beautiful and compliant women on an expense account.''

Morgan hung up the phone slowly. He felt like a two-faced sneak, poking around things that didn't concern him.

Or did they? They involved Kate, and if they affected her, they also concerned the baby. And whatever concerned the baby also concerned him, committed as he was to its welfare.

Which was why, on the spur of the moment, he drove into Charleston and dropped in unannounced at his attorney's office.

Ted Wickes, his longtime lawyer, was a close personal friend, and after Morgan poured out the story of Courtney and Kate, the embryos, Kate's pregnancy and the baby, Ted shook his shaggy head to and fro in amazement.

"Let me make a brief phone call to Courtney's lawyer," Ted said, and within ten minutes Morgan and Ted were inspecting the contract and its small print.

"Looks like Courtney's right," Ted said.

"What are my options?" Morgan asked, tossing his copy of the contract on Ted's desk in disgust.

"You can either get married or take Courtney to court."

Morgan groaned. "Courtney and I have barely finished our last legal battle. I have absolutely no desire to face my ex-wife across a courtroom again. I want to be through with her. I want her out of my life."

"Understandable. So if you still want the baby, get married to somebody else."

"Married. Right."

"Well then, forget the whole thing. Let another couple adopt the kid."

"Allow a Rhett to be reared by someone else? Never! Anyway, I've been thinking it over, and the baby seems like a good idea. Insurance of my immortality and all that. I'd given up on the idea of being a father, because after Courtney and I divorced, it didn't seem to be in the cards, but this baby is mine and I want it, Ted."

"Then you know what to do," Ted said.

"I'm paying you for advice like this? I don't need it," Morgan said.

"You asked for it, my friend." Ted smiled and shrugged into his suit jacket. "Join me for lunch, Morgan? We can try the steaks at the new grill down the street."

Morgan declined the meal. "I have some thinking to do" was his excuse, and think he did.

He was still thinking when he boarded the *Yaupon Island Belle* for passage back to the island. And what he was thinking was that there was only one way for both him and Kate to achieve their objectives.

They would have to get married.

MORGAN HEARD the music when he was still in the shade of the trees sheltering the path from the ferry dock to the keeper's quarters. And he heard a voice, Kate's voice, singing along.

He approached the back door slowly so as not to startle her, and as he drew closer, he saw Kate waltzing gracefully around the kitchen, her head thrown back so that her hair rippled down her back in a shining gold fall, her arms cradling her abdomen.

He was entranced by the sight, and although he meant to move away from the door so she wouldn't see him, she glanced in his direction and stopped in her tracks, her rapturous expression turning rapidly to one of consternation.

Her arms fell to her sides and then flew to her face in an attempt to mask her embarrassment.

"I don't mean to interrupt," he said.

"I was just—well, um..." she said, at a loss for words. She turned down the volume on the radio and came and unhooked the door, holding it open for him. She looked so pretty with her face colored pink with embarrassment, and he wanted to tell her so, but she flitted to the other side of the room, busying herself with something at the sink.

"You dance beautifully," he said, still charmed by her.

"Don't be silly, Morgan. I'm as big as a house," she retorted.

"Do you always dance around the kitchen by yourself?"

She dried her hands on a towel and turned slowly. "I wasn't by myself exactly. I was dancing with the baby," she said.

"Oh. I see," Morgan said. He hadn't realized that the baby was so real to Kate.

"I mean, the baby can hear things, you know? Like the ocean and my voice and—well, I like to play rhythmic music for it, and waltz music seems to settle it down when it's too lively for my comfort. Okay, okay. I see that you're skeptical."

"It's a side of you I haven't seen before," he said.

"You thought I had no imagination?"

"One doesn't usually think of scientists as imaginative," he told her.

She laughed with only a trace of self-consciousness.

"It's a good thing you weren't around the summer when I was a sea gull," she said. "When I was eight, I thought the gulls looked as free and as happy as I wanted to be, so I turned into one. I held my arms out like wings and 'flew' everywhere I went, wheeling and dipping on the air currents. And when my parents talked to me, I refused to answer—I mewed like a gull."

"And they mewed back?" he asked, glad to have something to tease her about.

"Neither of them was inclined to play the game, so it drove them crazy. Finally they became concerned that I might try to fly off the top of the lighthouse or something equally stupid, so my father sent for a chemistry set and I became interested in science. After that I was never a sea gull again." She looked momentarily wistful.

"What a charming child you must have been," Morgan said.

She was quick to disabuse him of that notion. "I was tall and gangly and always had scabby knees," she said. "I wasn't charming. I wasn't like a—"

"Like a what?" he asked, prodding gently.

"I was going to say that I wasn't like a Rhett. Not cute and clean in little cotton playsuits like Joanna's children. Like this baby will be. I'm glad you're going to take the baby, Morgan."

He cleared his throat. "Actually, there's a problem," he said.

She focused wide, unsuspecting eyes on him. "What kind of problem?" she asked.

"With the contract you signed. It specifies that the baby must be adopted by a married couple."

"I don't remember that part," Kate said.

"I've read the contract. It's true," he said, and quickly he related Courtney's nocturnal visit and his call on Ted Wickes this morning.

"I didn't realize," Kate said in consternation. She sank into a kitchen chair, her face ash pale.

He sat down beside her. "Didn't you read the contract before you signed it?" he asked.

"I skimmed over it, but at the time all I could think about was my happiness at being able to bear a baby. I would have become a surrogate mother for Courtney even with no contract, so signing it was only a necessary formality," she said. She stared at him with eyes in which he divined borderline panic.

His only thought was to calm her.

"Don't get upset," he said. "There's a way—"

"A way! What way? I thought this was all taken care of, I'd actually started to feel good about this pregnancy again, and now I find out that because of my own stupidity and shortsightedness, there's a major stumbling block!'' She stood up, and he grabbed her arm.

"Kate! Let's talk about this," he said.

She pulled away. "I don't want to talk. I want to think about it in private," she said.

"A lot of good that will do," he replied heatedly.

"Oh? And you have some other suggestion?'' She glared at him, and he saw the slightest hint of moisture on her lower lids.

"Yes! We could get married!''

Suddenly it was very quiet in the house. The two of them stared at each other over a tremendous void.

Kate was the first to speak.

"You're joking," she said.

"I am not. It's the solution to the problem.''

"You wouldn't marry me," she said.

"Under normal circumstances, perhaps not. These circumstances are anything but normal. I can't let this baby go to anyone but me."

Her laugh was bitter, and he said, "Kate."

"What do you want me to do?'' she asked in a low tone.

"Say you'll think about marrying me.''

She turned away from him so he wouldn't see the anguished expression on her face.

"Can we at least talk about it?''

She let her shoulders rise and fall in a futile gesture. "We'd better, I suppose, but do we have to stay in the house? I could use some fresh air."

"We could walk on the beach if you'd like," he said.

"Okay," she said. He didn't like the look of defeat in her eyes.

When they had reached the deserted beach, he dared to slide an arm around her shoulders.

"Would it be so bad to be Mrs. Morgan Rhett?" he asked, smiling down at her.

"This has to be the all-time irony," she said. "I'm probably the one woman in the world who really doesn't want to be married."

"I never wanted to be married again, either," he said.

She looked at him out of the corners of her eyes. "Why?" she asked.

"I thought once was enough," he said.

"You loved Courtney at the beginning of your marriage, didn't you?"

"I believed I did at the time. I loved what I thought she was, I suppose. Later, when I found out what she was really like, I couldn't stand her. Which is why our marriage—yours and mine—might be successful. With you I know what I'm getting."

"Somebody who is cantankerous, crabby—"

"Cantankerous Kate, Crabby Kate, and also Courageous and Comely Kate," he said.

"Don't lather it on too thick, Morgan, or you'll have a Kate who collapses under the weight of it," she said.

"I mean it. I admire you, you know."

"I didn't know, but thanks. Still, no matter what the circumstances, marriage is a big step. I've never been married before," she said.

"As my wife, you'd be entitled to Rhett family standing in the Charleston community. That means that Joanna would invite you to join the Junior League—"

"I thought it was a kids' baseball league until a few years ago," she informed him.

He laughed. "Well, they'd probably let you play first base if you want. And I'm a patron of the theater, and I'm invited to many dinners and a ball or two every year."

"Let's get this straight. If I married you—and that's a big *if*—you'd want me to live with you? Participate in the upbringing of your child?"

"We could give it our best shot," Morgan said, trying to imagine life with Kate.

Kate rolled her eyes. "I'm not good with babies, and I wouldn't want anything to do with Charleston society. I don't know Rosenthal china from Lenox, and I never even came close to having a debut. I like to dig around mud flats and pole johnboats through marshes. I'd be a terrible wife for you." She managed a brief smile.

"Marrying me would provide you with a place to live," he said. "You told me you have no place to go after you leave the lighthouse."

"True," she admitted.

"I've thought this out carefully, you know, much more than I thought out my decision to marry Courtney. The more I consider it, the better it seems. We could be good for each other. Will you marry me, Kate? There would be real advantages for both of us."

"I don't love you," she said.

"At our ages we know how treacherous love can be and how complicated relationships can become. Perhaps love isn't important in our case," he said.

"I've never thought I could marry someone I didn't love," she said.

"Unusual circumstances call for unusual measures," Morgan replied in a reasoning tone.

Kate shook her head doubtfully. "Against my better judgment, Morgan, I'll think it over. I can't rush into what amounts to a marriage of convenience. Recent experience has shown me the error of taking on responsibilities without investigating all the angles."

He cast a long look at her, saw the curve of her lashes against her cheek, remembered the silken softness of her lips.

"Well, then," he said softly, "consider this one," and he pulled her close and lowered his mouth to hers, capturing her in a kiss in which she participated willingly and which engendered a surge of erotic longing that made him wonder how long she could go on ignoring the tension between them.

Translucent lids drifted closed over her sea-gray eyes as she melted into the sensations, her lips parting, her hands sliding up his chest to grip his shoulders tightly. He longed to mold his hands to the curve of her hips and to bring her body into line with his; he ached with longing for her. When he stopped kissing her, she had opened her eyes and he saw briefly reflected in them proof of a fiery passion that he had until now only suspected.

"If we were married, we could do that often," he said coaxingly, his lips close to her ear. "Come to think of it, we could do it often before we're married."

She pulled away. She wrapped her arms around herself and scowled, which was not the reaction he had expected or hoped for.

"So you meant it last night," he said, resuming their walk. She trudged along beside him, keeping a self-conscious arm's length between them.

"Meant what?"

"That it was the second biggest mistake in your life to kiss me."

She lifted her head. "It's just that—"

"Don't use pregnancy as an excuse," he said flatly. "Last night you wanted it as much as I did. I saw it in your eyes, and only a moment ago you wanted to take it to the limit."

She considered this. "Yes, I suppose I did," she said slowly. "That still doesn't mean that I think it was a good idea."

"You don't want to get involved with me when you're going to have to give up the baby and leave," he guessed.

"Something like that," she said, turning back toward the lighthouse.

"So marry me. Then you don't have to leave."

"If I married you, I wouldn't want to go to balls, banquets or meetings of any group where ladies sit around and drink tea," she said.

He was afraid to ask it, but he had to. "No sex?" he said.

"Morgan, I'm pregnant."

He could only be blunt. "I desire you," he said.

She swallowed, but she kept her eyes straight ahead. "How you can desire a seven-months-pregnant woman is beyond me," she replied.

"You're beautiful," he said.

The sound she made fell halfway between a snort and a chuckle. "Only if you're into whale watching," she replied.

"Cut the smart remarks, Kate. They can't hide the fact that you want to sleep with me as much as I want to sleep with you."

She walked silently, and Morgan considered that this heavy-duty attempt at persuasion might be too much for Kate to absorb at one time. He *was* asking a lot. She had been through so much—the loss of her job, her father's death, the historical society's insistence that she leave the island, her pregnancy and abandonment by Courtney and now the matter of the contract. Her stress level must be sky-high.

As he was trying to figure out if anything he might do could lower it a bit, they reached the path through the dunes. As they grew closer to the lighthouse, they heard an unfamiliar metallic clanking noise that here, on the island, made no sense at all.

They exchanged a mystified glance.

"What's that?" he said.

"Probably Tom and Tessie Tourist rappeling down the side of the lighthouse—or worse," Kate said, stepping up her pace.

When they came into the clearing and rounded the lighthouse, they saw a big yellow bulldozer and beside it a crew of four men studying a blueprint.

Kate stopped dead in her tracks. "What are you doing?" she asked in alarm. "Who said you could bring that—that *thing* onto the island?"

"Willadeen Pribble, ma'am. We're here to put in a new septic tank for the museum. You mean she didn't tell you about it?"

Chapter Eight

Gump was irascible when Kate stormed aboard the ferry, which didn't help much.

"What do you mean, what did I see?" he fumed. "I saw some kind of landing craft run ashore about fifty feet from the ferry dock, and then this bulldozer rolled off it. You don't think I transported a bulldozer over to Yaupon Island on my ferry, do you?"

"Of course not," Kate said irritably, trying to maintain her balance as the ferry bucked and dipped over the choppy channel.

"I bet Willadeen will be sending dune buggies over next. If you've got some kind of complaint, it's her you want to see," Gump said as Kate stormed out of the wheelhouse.

"You could have let me take care of this," Morgan told Kate as she maneuvered her infuriatingly cumbersome body down the steps in order to join him below deck.

"Ha! As if I'd want to. I can't wait to see how Willadeen is going to explain a bulldozer. I'm entitled to another four months on the lighthouse premises, and that doesn't include being serenaded by a bulldozer as it's digging up the marigold beds I so carefully planted."

Morgan reached across the back of the seat and massaged the back of her neck. "You're awfully tense. Does that feel better?"

Kate relaxed against him. It hadn't been necessary for him to accompany her to the mainland to find out what was happening, but he had offered, and, because she'd needed moral support, she had gladly taken him up on it.

They didn't talk until the ferry docked, and as they disembarked, Gump called, "Don't forget this is the last ferry today! You only have about fifteen minutes until I leave for the island."

Kate threw Morgan a despairing glance. "We'd better hoof it," she said, but he put out a hand to restrain her.

"No running," he said firmly.

"I can—"

"Come on. We'll walk extra fast," he said, taking her hand.

They reached Ye Old Pribble Gift Nooke as Willadeen stepped through the pale pink front door and turned to look up.

"Willadeen," Kate said without preamble, "what the hell is that bulldozer doing at the lighthouse?"

Willadeen looked Kate up and down with a faintly disapproving smile. "Didn't they tell you? The septic tank is totally insufficient to serve the rest rooms we need to build for the museum, so they're going to dig up the old one and replace it with a new one."

"I'm still living in the quarters. Do you know what a mess that will make?" Kate said. "They'll be piling dirt all over the place, and the septic tank lies beneath my largest flower bed."

"It will only take a few days for the crew to do their job," Willadeen said. "And we're going to do away with the flower beds when the lighthouse is finally a museum.

We'll plant petunias, pale pink ones, in lovely white planters." Her chocolate-kiss hairdo wobbled, and she looked positively rhapsodic.

"I want the bulldozer gone," Kate said through gritted teeth.

"It will go when the crew has finished," Willadeen said. "Now, if you'll excuse me—"

"Mrs. Pribble," Morgan said.

She looked down her nose at him as though she hadn't noticed him before.

"I don't believe we've met," she said.

"Willadeen, this is Morgan Rhett," Kate said in a faint voice.

"Morgan Rhett! Why you must be Courtney's ex-husband," Willadeen said with a remarkable lack of tact.

"Yes. And I'm sure there's no reason why the bull-dozing couldn't wait until Kate is gone. In another few months, she'll be off the island. Why make her life miserable in the meantime?"

"If Kate's life is unhappy, I'm sure she is the one who has made it so," Willadeen said pleasantly. "Besides, Mr. Cobb tells me that he wants to begin work on the rest rooms right after Labor Day. The new septic tank needs to be in place before that. That's why—"

"*Who* told you?" Morgan said incredulously.

"Mr. Cobb, Courtney's husband."

"*Damien* Cobb?"

"Exactly. The historical society awarded him the plumbing contract for the museum. And, of course, we want the museum to be operational as soon as possible, and we can't open without rest rooms, now, can we?" Willadeen sidled past them. "Goodbye, Kate. And Mr. Rhett." She nodded primly and left Kate and Morgan staring at each other.

The ferry whistle tooted at the landing.

"That's Gump signaling that he's ready to leave," Kate said. She clung to Morgan's hand as they rushed back to the dock.

When they were seated on the outside deck of the *Yaupon Island Belle* with Preacher's Inlet receding behind them, Morgan kicked his legs out in front of him and threw his head back. The sun had sunk into the backdrop of trees on the mainland, and the scent of the sea helped to push the bad taste of their encounter with Willadeen Pribble from his mouth.

"Courtney is behind this. She's the one who put Ye Olde Pribble up to sending the bulldozer," he said.

"I guessed that," Kate said miserably.

"It's not because of you. Courtney thought this up because she hates me. I wonder if she'll ever be out of my hair," he said.

"She was until I came into the picture," Kate said.

"I'm realizing that in the future, I may never be free of her."

"Because of the baby?" Kate ventured a glance at him and was touched by the pain in his expression.

"Exactly," he said. "I've been thinking about how my child will look, how it will act, what kind of adult it will grow up to be. I wonder how I'll deal with a kid who is exactly like Courtney."

"This child is a Rhett," Kate said fiercely. "It will have big blue eyes, dark hair and a patrician nose. It will look exactly like you and Joanna."

He smiled at her, but it was a sad smile. "We don't know that," he said quietly.

Kate sat back in her seat, realizing that Morgan was right. If the child turned out to be like Courtney, how would Morgan deal with it? By disappearing, by staying out of the child's life? How did he feel about nurture versus nature; did he think that behavior traits were acquired or genetic? What, in fact, was the truth? Science hadn't proven either yet.

All in all, this whole experience was proving to Kate that, as the old TV commercial said, it's not nice to fool Mother Nature.

THE NEXT MORNING Morgan woke up early and decided to visit Kate. He wanted to talk her out of staying in the quarters while the workmen were there. He didn't like the idea of the men in the crew looking at her; he was surprised to find that he didn't want anyone to see her but him. She was too radiantly beautiful in her pregnancy, too ripe and far too vulnerable. The worst part was that she didn't even realize it.

When he emerged from the dunes, he saw Kate watering the flowers planted at the base of the lighthouse. He stopped in surprise. He hadn't expected to see her there.

She was wearing something made of thin cotton—organdy, he thought it was called—and it was flapping in the breeze. The bodice was decorated with little tucks, he noticed, before he realized with a jolt that Kate wore nothing under it.

"Morgan! What are you doing here? Why, the first ferry hasn't even arrived yet!" She was so surprised that she sprayed a plume of water into the air, wetting the brick of the lighthouse and raining a few drops down upon herself. They made the fabric of her gown stick to her skin; it shone through, pink and glowing in the pale, morning sunlight.

"I wanted—to talk to the crew when they get here," he said. He felt goggle-eyed over her see-through dress, or maybe it was a nightgown, and he didn't know where to look.

If he looked at her face, he would have to respond to her expression of annoyance, which was directed straight at him. If he looked lower, he'd see the shape of her so blatantly outlined by the white fabric, and he'd see what was underneath—heavy breasts, a belly as round as a melon and below that a hint of darkness between her thighs. Whoever had perpetuated the fiction that pregnant women weren't desirable should be shot, he thought suddenly.

"I certainly didn't expect you to show up when I was enjoying the little privacy I have left," she said in annoyance, stalking to the water spigot and bending to shut off the flow. He was treated to a long glimpse of the back of Kate's thighs; her breasts shifted tantalizingly beneath the fabric.

"Do you always wear thin, diaphanous garments when you water the flowers?" he asked.

She straightened and aimed a long, hard look at him. "It *used* to be private here every morning before the first ferry arrived," she said, and head held high, she strolled with complete unconcern to the door and went inside.

He waited, but Kate didn't come back out, and Morgan was reluctant to knock on the door. He thought she might be hiding behind a curtain at one of the windows, laughing behind her hand at his uncertainty. Although, knowing Kate, she wouldn't laugh behind her hand. No, Kate would laugh out loud so he could hear her, and she would probably enjoy every bit of his confusion.

At that moment he heard men's voices. He turned to see the bulldozer's crew emerging from the sheltering canopy of oaks. Morgan talked to them for a few minutes, which was long enough for him to decide that he didn't want any of them, especially the big burly one, anywhere around Kate.

As the men went to work, Morgan knocked on Kate's door. There was no answer. The bulldozer started up, making so much noise that she wouldn't have heard him knocking anyway.

"Kate!" he called, beginning to worry. "Are you all right?"

No answer.

Really concerned by this time, he went around to the kitchen window and peered in. An empty glass sat on the sink drainboard, but other than that, he saw no sign of Kate.

"Kate!" he yelled, pounding on the door this time.

What if she had fallen? What if she'd gone into labor? What if she couldn't answer him?

He ran around to the window of the bathroom and jumped up on a pile of bricks beneath it so he could peer in.

"You sure you ought to be doing that, buddy?" called the burly crew member.

Morgan ignored the remark and squinted so that he could see inside. He heard water running, and on the other side of the bathtub, located beneath the window, he saw a pair of calves and ankles extended along the floor. They were easily recognizable as Kate's legs.

"Kate!" he exclaimed, and then Kate's face appeared on the other side of the windowsill. Her hair was wet and soapy and she was gazing up at him with an expression of outraged indignation.

"What do you want now?" she asked, scrambling to her feet. There was a blue-striped towel draped around her shoulders.

Morgan stood on his pile of bricks, feeling foolish.

"I knocked and I called, but you didn't answer. I thought you must have had an accident. Or something," he finished lamely.

"I am washing my hair, Morgan Rhett. I have to lean over the edge of the bathtub to do it, which isn't an easy position for me to get in now that I'm so big, and when I get there, I don't want to get up until I'm finished. And since when do members of the well-bred Rhett family get their kicks from peering in bathroom windows?"

She spoke so loudly that Morgan thought the crew member, who was still staring at him, his hands on his hips, hard hat shoved back from his forehead, must surely hear.

Morgan scrambled down the pile of bricks and brushed past the hard hat, who was watching in openmouthed astonishment.

"Just checking on my friend," Morgan said lamely.

"Yeah, sure," the other guy said.

Morgan strode up to the front door of the quarters and walked in. Water was still running in the bathroom, so Kate was presumably finishing her shampoo. He socked his right fist into his left hand a few times and waited, too uneasy to sit down.

When Kate appeared with a towel wrapped around her head, he was apologetic. "Can you blame me?" he asked her.

"Yes," Kate said frostily. "Go away."

"I don't want you here with those men around."

"That's ridiculous."

"Move into the lodge. There's lots of room."

"Those men seem like less of a threat than you do at the moment," she pointed out.

"I walked right in. You didn't even have the door locked."

"You had no business entering uninvited. Honestly, Morgan, I don't know what to think. Yesterday you ask me to marry you—"

"Which I hope you're still thinking about."

"—and today you ask me to move in with you."

"Will you?"

Kate sighed. "First I'm going to dry my hair. Then I'll think about things. Please, Morgan, leave me alone!"

Her tone was so anguished that Morgan thought better of staying.

"No drying your hair at the top of the lighthouse. Don't you have a hair dryer?"

"*Yes*. Now will you please go?"

"I'll go to the mainland and call my office," he said. He didn't hear Kate's exasperated reply.

When he left, the bulldozer was digging up a patch of land and piling dirt indiscriminately around the base of the lighthouse.

"Any luck?" called the big burly fellow.

Morgan ignored the question and kept walking. But he knew that Kate couldn't stay here, no matter what she thought.

AFTER SHE SAW Morgan disappear down the path, Kate dressed quickly and gathered her wet hair into a loose ponytail. Morgan would take the next ferry to town, but he wouldn't be on the return ferry; his phone calls would take too long for that. She wanted to talk to Gump before Morgan came back.

Kate arrived at the ferry landing and boarded the *Yaupon Island Belle* after all the tourists had disembarked.

"You look upset," Gump said, chewing on his pipe.

"Wait till you hear this," Kate said, and she launched into the story about Courtney and the contract and Morgan's proposal.

Gump stared long and hard at one of the channel markers in the middle of the sound after she finished. "Do you love this Morgan Rhett?" he asked abruptly.

"No," Kate whispered, knowing that she could never admit to Gump how she had, with some astonishment at her own passion, returned his kisses.

"You're a woman of integrity. You proved that during the Northeast Marine Institute crisis. As a woman of integrity, you can't marry Morgan Rhett unless you love him," Gump pointed out.

"The baby..." Kate said, not knowing what she wanted to mention about the baby, since it really had no say in this matter, but wanting to make it clear that the welfare of the baby was her first responsibility.

"I know, I know," Gump said, removing his pipe from his mouth. "But you can't solve one problem by creating another."

"I mean, it's not the baby's fault that we're in this predicament," Kate said.

"You think I don't know that? Well, that's what happens when you take nature into your own hands. It ain't natural for babies to be made in dishes in laboratories, and just because we *can* do it doesn't mean we *should* do it."

"Man controls science," Kate said.

"Man doesn't control man, though," Gump said succinctly. "And man sure doesn't control Courtney Rhett Cobb. I don't know how you're going to put this situation right, Kate. It's a mess. I only know that there's no quick fix in marrying Morgan Rhett."

"I guess I needed to hear someone say it," Kate said distractedly.

Gump reached over and patted her hand in a touching gesture of tenderness, a side of his nature that he rarely showed to anyone.

"Is there anything I can do for you? Anything at all?" he offered awkwardly.

Kate smiled a thin smile. "Find Morgan a wife," she said before leaving the ferry to wait for Morgan.

MORGAN WAS SURPRISED when Kate met him at the ferry landing when he returned from the mainland.

"Mind if we chat?" she asked, hoping he wouldn't detect nervousness in her voice.

He shook his head, and she sat down beside him on the hard seat beneath the palmetto-thatched roof that provided shade from the hot summer sun.

The water shimmered tourmaline blue, and the mainland was no more than a smoky green haze in the distance. Kate tried to marshal her thoughts, something that wasn't easy to do with Morgan beside her knowing that something was on her mind and waiting for her to state it.

"I thought this would be a good chance to talk," Kate said. She watched a pelican soaring on a wind current. "I can't do it, Morgan. I can't marry you," she said.

"I see," he said evenly. "What about the baby? I want the baby, Kate."

"Isn't—isn't there someone else you could marry?"

"Of course, there's no one else," Morgan said, dismissing her suggestion outright.

"I just thought that you must have a life. I mean, you told me about all those other women," Kate said.

Morgan made a disparaging gesture with one hand. "Women, yes. One I'd marry, no. In fact," he said in carefully measured tones, "I feel closer to you than to anyone at the moment."

"At the moment," she repeated, unsure what to make of this.

"Because of what we're going through together," he said. "Because I think we have the potential to share something special."

"Because of the way I kissed you?" she asked, her voice almost a whisper.

"We both felt something, Kate."

Kate fidgeted with a loose thread on her dress. "You might have gathered by my behavior that I want intimacy. I don't," she said. She sounded very prim and proper, but all he could think about at the moment was the swaying of her body under that organdy nightgown as she walked into the lighthouse this morning.

"I don't believe you," he said firmly.

Her head shot up and she looked him in the eye. Eyes, rather, eyes warm enough to melt even the hardest heart.

"The first day you met me you said that if you were going to seduce anyone, it wouldn't be me," she faltered.

"I was trying to reassure you," he said defensively.

"Whatever, I got the idea. And I can't imagine that you feel differently about it now. I mean, I'm quite pregnant—*Sports Illustrated* isn't going to ask me to pose for their swimsuit issue anytime soon."

He put out a hand and touched her lips. She flinched, but even as she moved away from him, she felt the heat rise up from her thighs, spread across her abdomen, and linger in her breasts, heat that had nothing to do with the slant of sun through the palmetto thatch overhead.

"You're as beautiful, as sexy and as desirable as any woman I've ever known," he said. His voice was deep and sonorous and had the effect of a verbal caress.

She stood up abruptly. "That's enough, Morgan," she said.

Morgan said nothing, and Kate, her back stiff, her face turned away, despaired. She didn't believe that she was that attractive to him. When she looked in the mirror, she saw a Kate Sinclair who was grossly out of shape, who could possibly get a job as a Goodyear blimp, who could give the Pillsbury doughboy a run for his money. The only difference was that she wasn't as mobile as the blimp, and as for Poppin' Fresh, under these circumstances, she couldn't force herself to be half as cheerful.

MORGAN INSISTED on accompanying her to take water samples later. After she had labeled the vials, he rowed the johnboat around a curve in the creek where they relaxed as the boat rocked gently between creek banks overhung with weeping willows. Kate trailed her hand in the water and felt lazy. To tell the truth, she felt more defeated than lazy, but there was no point in mentioning this to Morgan. She figured he had enough worries of his own.

"You're not angry?" she blurted finally when the silence had dragged on too long.

Morgan shook his head slowly. "No. Confused, maybe, and unsure of my next move, but it's not you that I'm angry with. It's Courtney, for getting you into this."

"I played a part in it. I thought it would be so simple. Just get pregnant, experience it, and walk away afterward. And now—" Her shoulders rose and fell in a shrug of helplessness. "What will you do now?" she asked.

"Sue," he said.

"I thought you said you couldn't stand another court battle."

"Maybe we can reach an agreement out of court," he said. "Maybe we can amend the contract, or tear up the contract or—well, something. Maybe we can make a deal."

"All that sounds pretty lame, Morgan," Kate said.

"If you'll go with me to Charleston to discuss it with the lawyers, I'll set up the appointment," he told her.

"I'll go. I don't know what else to do," she said.

Kate knew that they were both convinced that no one else in the world understood what they were going through and that neither of them had anyone else in whom to confide. They were allies. And yet they stared at each other uneasily, unsure how much to trust each other or if they even should.

Chapter Nine

Trust, Kate thought, was a fragile commodity.

Without trust, love couldn't exist. In the past she'd been betrayed by both her mother and her lover, and Kate was sure she could never wholly trust anyone again; therefore, she'd never love again. It was all very logical.

Not so logical was the difficulty that she and Morgan were in at present, though she kept telling herself it had nothing to do with love. Certainly there was no love lost between the two sets of lawyers, and when she and Morgan conferred with them, Kate felt as if she'd somehow landed in the middle of a free-for-all.

At the meeting the lawyers wrangled, Morgan punctuated his remarks with angry gestures, and Kate sat staring at the shiny finish of the conference table until her head ached, wishing that she were back on the research vessel trying to figure out how to breed disease-resistant oysters. And at the end, after all the bickering, Ted Wickes's advice to Morgan was the same: either get married or take Courtney to court.

"Look at it this way," Ted said to Kate and Morgan over lunch, "you don't want her to get away with this. The woman's a shark, and that husband of hers is—well, there's no name I can call him in polite company."

They weren't pressuring her, but Kate felt under duress, anyway. If she would only marry Morgan, he wouldn't have to initiate a court battle.

But she couldn't marry Morgan. She didn't love him.

After they left Ted Wickes, she and Morgan walked slowly through the waterfront park on the nearby Cooper River. Children splashed in fountains, people basked on park benches, and babies in their prams sucked their thumbs as their mothers visited. Kate and Morgan seemed to be the only couple present without a child, but then the baby stirred and she remembered. They had a child. It just wasn't born yet.

"I could move away," Kate said suddenly. "No one would know where I was. We could arrange for you to adopt the baby in another state before Courtney and Damien found me."

"You're grasping at straws," Morgan said.

"I could go to Maine and hide there. I have a friend—remember I told you about Pegeen?—who would help."

Morgan knew that this was the moment when he should mention casually that Tony Saldone was presently in Maine trying to find out about the plans of the Federal Health Foundation and how the FHF's investigation would affect Kate.

But she had enough to think about. It wasn't the time to sock her with Tony Saldone.

"Look, Kate," he said, "you're not going to Maine or anywhere else. You said you wanted to stay on Yaupon Island, didn't you?"

"Of course," Kate said.

"Then that's what you will do. In fact, I've had enough of the city. Let's get back to the island. Right now."

She looked surprised. He took her hand and smiled at her. "When the going gets tough, the tough go back to the island," he said.

WHEN THEY ARRIVED on Yaupon Island, the crew of the bulldozer was standing around a gushing hole in the ground and shaking their heads.

"Looks like we broke the water line," one of them called to Kate as she and Morgan approached the lighthouse. "Disrupted your water service." He lifted up one foot and stared with disgust at the mud on it.

"Well, you'll have to fix it," Kate said.

"Might take a few days to do that. You can get somebody to haul in fresh water from the mainland to drink, I guess."

Kate stood with her mouth open, looking at the spectacle of her beloved lighthouse standing in the middle of a huge mud puddle, her flowers smashed and scattered. The sharp pungent odor of crushed marigolds filled the air.

Kate lifted her eyes to the heavens. "I wonder what else could possibly happen around here. First the septic tank, now the water. Maine is beginning to sound better all the time." She looked more closely at the excavation; water was running down the slope toward the creek.

"Pack a few things, and you can move into the lodge with me," Morgan said.

"All right, all right, I give up. I'll be right back," she said in exasperation, stalking through the mud into the house.

When Morgan followed her inside, he saw that she had kicked off her mud-spattered shoes and was standing barefoot on the scuffed wooden floor as she threw things into a suitcase.

He wanted nothing more than to gather her into his arms and reassure her that everything—the baby, her job, the final move away from the island—would be all right. Not that he quite believed it himself, but he wanted it to be true for Kate's sake.

Kate saw him staring at her and dropped a hanger. He picked it up for her and handed it over, and when she read the sympathy in his eyes, it was almost her undoing. She curbed the impulse to rest her head on his broad chest, to let him soothe away her worries with caresses.

She drew a deep breath before she spoke. "Morgan, I'm only moving into the lodge because of the water problem," she said. "Not because I want a physical relationship."

Morgan shrugged, but there was a definite flicker of hope behind his eyes. "Sure, Kate. Whatever you say," he said, and she could have sworn he was hiding a grin.

KATE HADN'T BEEN to the lodge in a long time, and it had been permanently off-limits when she was a child. Her father hadn't approved of hunting, and neither did Kate. The lodge itself was huge, and it was surrounded by outbuildings—servants' quarters, a shambles of a stable, a hut where skins had been scraped and tanned. Slowly kudzu vine had encroached and had enveloped all but the main building, which was still in reasonably good repair.

"Pick a room, any room," Morgan said as he led the way to the bedrooms.

Kate chose at random. "This one," she said, and Morgan dumped her suitcase on the bed.

"I don't know about you, but I could use a drink," he said. "Meet you on the terrace in ten minutes?"

"Ten minutes," she agreed, and added, "Something nonalcoholic for me."

"One of my nieces tells me I make the best Shirley Temples in the world," he said, smiling at her as he went out.

Kate explored the rest of the hallway before joining Morgan. His room was two doors from hers. *Still too close for comfort,* she said to herself, but no matter where she went in this house, she would always be aware that Morgan was there, too. She only hoped that while she stayed here with him, she would be spared the sexy, erotic dreams that had been troubling her ever since the beginning of her pregnancy.

Morgan handed her a glass when she came out onto the terrace, and he offered her a chair at the table. They could hear the sea from where they sat, the soft rise and fall of the waves, the shrill crying of the sea birds.

She sipped her drink appreciatively. "Your niece was right," she said, and Morgan smiled, the smile starting in his eyes and working its way down. She'd always, ever since the day she met him, thought he had the nicest smile.

"She usually is," he said.

"You have nieces and nephews besides Joanna's children?" she asked.

"My brother Butler, who lives in Atlanta, has two children, and my sister Pauline in New Orleans has four. They're all older than Joanna's brood."

"Do you see them often?"

"As often as I can. They're some of my favorite people." He paused. "I've been thinking about this fatherhood thing," he said.

"I don't know when you've had time," she answered ruefully.

"Oh, there have been some long nights," he said vaguely. His eyes sought hers. "I'm used to the idea now. I'm even looking forward to it. When I look at your body, big with my child, and think that you're the one to bear the next little Rhett, it overwhelms me."

She watched him, surprised that he had chosen to speak of this. She hadn't suspected that he had any deep feelings about the baby; after all, he'd made it clear that he didn't love it. She waited, sensing that he had something more to say.

He turned his glass in his hands, staring down into the amber liquid. "A lot of my friends have become fathers lately. They took a lot of interest in their wives' pregnancies. They even saw their own babies being born. I'm beginning to think that I'd like that, too." He raised his head and looked squarely into her eyes.

This news was a complete surprise to Kate. "You're putting me on," she said at last.

"No, I mean it. Really," he said.

She fought the urge to snicker and forced herself to give the idea serious consideration. She tried to picture Morgan Rhett wearing delivery-room pajamas and a hospital mask. It was impossible, and she felt her mouth stretching into a grin.

"I *mean* it," he insisted, indignant that she didn't believe him.

"Do you know what it's like in a delivery room?" she asked incredulously.

"Oh—well, I imagine it's bright. Lights, you know, so the doctor can see what he's doing. And antiseptic," he added.

She laughed, and he liked the way she laughed, throwing her head back as though she was really enjoying it.

"You don't know what it's like in a delivery room, either," he pointed out. "How many times have you ever been in one?"

"None," she said, sobering immediately. "I have an idea it's not the easiest place in the world to be, though. Unless you're the main event."

"Oh. Maybe. Anyway, I think I should see my baby born. It would help me—" he searched for the right word; he'd heard Charlie and Joanna use it a time or two. "It would help me *bond* with the child," he said, hoping that the term would make the right impression. When Kate's face relaxed, he knew it had.

"Bonding can set the tone between parent and child for the child's whole life," she said in a soft voice. She studied his face. "You really think you'd like that? To be in the delivery room, I mean?" she asked.

"Definitely," he said.

"I'll ask Dr. Thomas about it next time I go," she said.

"I'm going with you to your next checkup, remember?" he said. "When is your appointment?"

"Tomorrow at two o'clock, and if you still want to go, it's okay with me," she said. She finished her drink and set the glass on the table before standing and walking to the edge of the terrace, her hands pressed to either side of her abdomen in a gesture that Morgan found inexpressibly poignant.

He wanted to go to her, to tell her that he'd always be there for her, but he didn't think she wanted to hear it. And so he finished his drink and made an excuse to go inside, wishing he knew some way to communicate to her all that he felt, and feeling inadequate because the only way he could think of was sexual.

DINNER WAS A CASSEROLE which Morgan produced from
the freezer, compliments of his housekeeper in Charleston, and afterward Kate looked askance at the mounted
boar and deer and wolf heads and suggested that they go
out looking for loggerhead turtles coming ashore to lay
their eggs.

"Anything is better than sitting around this lodge with
those animals staring at me," she said, and Morgan
laughed.

On the path through the dunes he caught her hand to
help her through the shadowy parts, and she clung to his
fingers tightly and did not shake them away when they
were standing on the wide, flat beach.

She slipped off her sandals, and he kicked off his
shoes. Here under the wide sky, with the stars winking
and blinking overhead, she ventured a smile at him, and
he stared back at her, not returning the smile but ac-
knowledging it with his eyes. Behind them waves rose and
fell in majestic splendor, and the sand beneath their feet
shone alabaster in the moonlight.

Kate inhaled deeply of the sea-tinged air. "Wow," she
said. "What a day."

"Yeah."

"I'm not sure we settled much of anything," she said
broodingly.

"Do me a favor. Let's not talk about Courtney or the
lawyers—"

"Or Mrs. Pribble or the bulldozer or getting married—"

He grinned at her, and she smiled back.

"How do we go about finding a turtle?" he asked her.

"We tramp along the beach until we find the telltale
trails. You've seen them, I'm sure—a turtle flattens the

sand into a furrow leading toward the dunes, where she digs a hole and lays her eggs."

"I don't believe I've ever seen the moon so full," he said as they began to walk.

"Of course, you have," she told him. "You're exaggerating."

"Well, it's been a long time since I've looked at it," he amended. A half smile lit her features, and he still held her hand.

"How long since you've gone moon gazing?" she asked.

"Years," he told her. "Usually I'm inside on nights like this. Working," he hastened to add, because he thought he'd given her the wrong impression of himself. Suddenly it seemed important for her to know that he was no longer the man-about-town that he had been shortly after his divorce from Courtney.

But she was intent on a pattern in the sand. "Wait," she said. "This looks like a fresh turtle crawl." She bent over and studied the sand, then straightened and pointed toward the dunes. "The mother turtle is up there, all right. There's no return trail leading back to the ocean."

Kate guided their way into the dunes, little ghost crabs scuttling out of their path, and there, beneath the swaying stems of sea oats, Morgan switched on his flashlight and they found the mother turtle settled into a body pit and laying eggs two and three at a time.

Kate knelt down beside the turtle, which blinked its eyes at them. She must have weighed three hundred pounds, and her shell was crusted with barnacles and moss.

"She's crying," Morgan said when he saw the tears running down the leathery face.

"Tears of exertion," Kate said, watching with a practiced eye as the mother turtle deposited eggs into the nest. They looked like Ping-Pong balls.

"If the nest remains undisturbed by raccoons or other predators, and if she's built it high enough on the beach so that it won't be disrupted by high tide, we can expect little turtles, perhaps maybe a hundred or so, to crack out of the eggs, dig their way out of the sand, and crawl down to the water in about sixty days," Kate said.

The mother turtle, exhausted from her exertions, began to fill in the nest with sand, and after half an hour or so she wearily headed back toward the sea, finally disappearing into the surf.

Morgan switched off his flashlight. "I'd say that human mothers have an infinitely better deal," he said.

Kate laughed. "That's because you've never been one. And as for producing babies, it's oysters who have it easy."

He glanced at her, taking in the curve of her lips, the tiny cleft in her chin. She liked explaining these things to him, he sensed, liked sharing her knowledge.

"Tell me about oysters," he said. He took her hand again, and she laced her fingers companionably through his.

"Well, their sex life is scandalous," she said, warming to the topic. "In warm months, the months without an *R,* their sex organs push the other parts of their bodies out of the way, taking over. And then the female oyster ejects perhaps a hundred million unfertilized eggs in one season, sending them into the surrounding waters in spurts."

"Spurts?" Morgan said.

"Spurts," Kate affirmed. "Then, a neighboring male oyster, hopefully from a good family, spews ten times that many sperm, which encounter the eggs purely by chance. These random encounters result in larvae, who enjoy the only freedom they're likely ever to have by riding water currents for a couple of weeks.''

"When do they settle down?" Morgan wanted to know.

"Oh, when they're about the size of a pinhead, they exude a concretelike substance and attach to something, usually another oyster. And that's it, except that they change sexes."

"I thought that only guests on *Geraldo* and the *Phil Donahue Show* did that," Morgan said.

"Nope. Most oysters change sex at least once during their lives, and the frequency seems to depend on water temperature. In the Mediterranean, they might change sex several times in one season, but in Scandinavia, where the water is colder, they generally stay the same sex all year."

She was so caught up in the discussion that she almost didn't feel the strange twinge in her abdomen. When she realized that it wasn't going away, she stopped suddenly.

"What's wrong, Kate?" Morgan asked, looking alarmed.

"The baby," she said, a peculiar expression crossing her face. "It pushes so hard against my stomach sometimes that it makes me uncomfortable. My, it's active tonight."

"Is that *normal?*" he asked in alarm.

"My doctor says it is. Sometimes the baby gets in a position—ooh, it's doing it again," she said.

While his eyes were riveted on her abdomen, Morgan thought he saw the fabric of her dress move. "I can see it!" he said in excitement. "I can see the baby moving!"

She looked down and laughed in delight. "It's very strong, isn't it?" She looked at him, her eyes bright. "Would you like to feel it? To touch your baby?"

He nodded his head slowly. Just as slowly, still gazing into his eyes, Kate took his hand and pressed it against her belly. At first he felt nothing, but then he noticed a tiny ripple beneath his fingertips.

He wasn't sure that it was real until he felt a good solid thump against Kate's abdominal wall. It was such a strong blow that his hand automatically recoiled, but he pressed more firmly and was quickly rewarded with another thunk. He felt his mouth hanging open and closed it. He swallowed. Suddenly he felt slightly light-headed.

"That's it," she said. "That's your baby."

"My baby," he said in wonder. *"Mine."*

"Yes, Morgan. Your child,' she said softly. Her face was outlined cameolike against the moonlit waves.

He wanted to jump; he wanted to run. He wanted to whoop and holler. But instead he slid his hand around what remained of Kate's waist and brought her close to him. She might have pulled away again, but he didn't give her the chance. He lifted a hand and pressed her head to his shoulder until it rested comfortably, and then he wrapped both his arms around her until he, too, could feel the child moving against his own abdomen.

"Mine," he said again, and then he kissed Kate, a kiss of exquisite yearning, a long deep kiss that hinted at much, much more.

"We shouldn't be doing this," Kate said firmly, pulling away.

"Why?" he said, grabbing her arm.

"Because—because—" she said, and he saw the struggle written on her face.

It was all the encouragement he needed.

"Come back here," he commanded, and he kissed her again.

And even as the kiss made her feel awestruck and giddy and eager to explore all the possibilities of it, Kate froze. Something was happening. Something odd. It felt like a rubber band tightening around her hips and across her abdomen.

"Morgan," she said, twisting her head away. "Morgan!"

He tried to fold her into his arms, but she stepped backward, an alarmed expression on her face.

"What is it?" he said.

"A contraction. I'm having a contraction!" Kate said.

THEY SAT on the old creaking swing on the front porch of the hunting lodge, Kate gazing stubbornly at the distant trees, her legs stuck out in front of her as straight as two hockey sticks, Morgan with one hand resting lightly on her abdomen.

"The book says—" he began.

"Where'd you get a book?" she asked sharply.

"My secretary sent it on the ferry a few days ago," he told her.

"Let's hope it's the only thing that's delivered on the ferry," Kate said darkly.

"Anyway, the book says that these Braxton-Hicks contractions occur at regular intervals and are just practice for the real thing," he said.

"A few days ago you seemed to know nothing about birthing babies. Now you think you're an authority." Kate was not unduly alarmed about the contractions. There had only been three more since the first one, and they hadn't come at regular intervals. Morgan had timed them.

"I'm not an authority," Morgan said. "But I did manage to read the whole book. It covers the complete process, all the way through postpartum depression."

"How about *pre*partum depression? Does it say anything about that?"

He couldn't see the expression in her eyes; they were shaded from the moonlight by heavy vines climbing up the poles supporting the porch's roof.

"Sometimes I wish I'd never come to see you back in April," she said in a low tone. "It only complicated things."

"What else could you have done?" he asked. He reached for her hand; her fingers were clenched. Slowly he massaged her wrist until the fingers uncurled one by one; he caressed each one in turn before lifting her hand to his lips. He kissed the soft tender inside of her wrist, the palm of her hand and the tip of her thumb. She didn't pull away.

He slid his other arm around her shoulders. "I'm glad you sought me out," he said softly in the vicinity of her ear. "I'm glad I know you."

She made a small negative sound and started to put a respectable distance between them, but the motion of the swing and her own awkwardness prevented her from moving.

"Don't," he said.

"I can't, anyway," she said in a muffled tone.

He pressed his cheek against hers and was stunned to feel the dampness there. He leaned away.

"You're crying," he said.

"You noticed," she replied.

"I wish you wouldn't make sarcastic remarks," he said fiercely. "Don't you know I care about you? That it matters to me what happens to you?"

"Sometimes I get so tired of being pregnant," she whispered.

He kissed the damp places on her cheeks. "If it's any consolation to you, nature will take care of that pretty soon," he told her.

"Talk about remarks," she said. She sniffed, and he dug a handkerchief out of his pocket.

"Here," he said.

"Always a clean handkerchief. Always the gentleman," she said, twisting the damp handkerchief between her fingers. She no longer had a lap; her hands rested on top of her stomach.

"Not always the gentleman," he said. "In fact, I have a suggestion that may not seem at all gentlemanly." He was glad for the darkness now. He didn't want her to see how fearful he was, or how uncertain about the wisdom of all this, or how much he wanted her.

"You're going to ask if I'll sleep with you," she said, surprising him again.

"I wish you weren't so perceptive," he said, his hopes plummeting at the tone of her voice.

She was quiet for a long time.

"Well?" he said. "What do you think?"

"I can't imagine it," she said. "I can't imagine that you *want* to. I'm *pregnant*, Morgan."

He couldn't help chuckling under his breath. "It so happens," he said, lazily trailing a string of kisses along the side of her neck, "that I am hopelessly attracted to you, pregnant or not pregnant, and that I want to sleep beside you until I know the contours of your body by heart."

"Why? They change week by week," she pointed out.

"To reach over to your side of the bed and touch some part of your anatomy and to know immediately what part

it is because it's so familiar to me. To make love to you,
Kate. Over and over again.'' He wondered what this
sounded like to her, what her reaction would be.

''I can't believe you're saying these things to me,'' she
said in a small, little-girl voice, which may have been
meant as a defense but made her seem more vulnerable
than she had ever been, and when she was vulnerable, she
was even more desirable to him because her prickly side
wasn't even slightly in evidence.

He rested his hand on the high round mound of her
belly again, caressed the contours and tentatively touched
her breast. A shudder ran through her, and he reminded
himself that he must be gentle, he must take care, because he didn't want to do anything to hurt her or the
baby. Then she was kissing him, hungrily parting his lips
with her tongue, and her mouth blossomed beneath his.

Her lips were soft and yielding, and she lifted trembling hands to cup his face between them, and then she
trailed gentle fingers down his neck to his shoulders and
pulled him close. His own fingers spread wide across her
breast, feeling its warmth and firmness. She pulled his
head down to her breasts and he buried his face in their
warmth, breathing the sweet secret smell of her, her lips
against his hair.

Kate fell back against the cushions of the swing, shiv-
ering it on its chains, and he put out a foot to steady
them. Slowly he unbuttoned the bodice of her dress and
parted the layers of fabric. In the darkness her breasts
shone white as marble, their contours ripe and the nipples swollen and dark.

He curved his hands around her breasts, a picture of
Kate in her white nightgown springing into his mind. Her
breasts **had** swung when she walked. He lifted one to his

mouth and tentatively touched the moist tip of his tongue to her skin.

She inhaled sharply. Beneath his seeking fingers he felt her heartbeat accelerate and she moved restlessly so that the swing shifted again.

"If we're going to do this, we should do it right. We should go inside," Morgan said.

"Is that what the book says?" she asked, but she was teasing.

"The book says that making love is good exercise during pregnancy," he said, his fingers tracing light circles around her nipples.

She laughed uneasily and shrugged away his hands before wrapping her dress around her. "Are you making that up?" she asked.

He stood up and pulled her along with him. She was almost as tall as he was, and he liked being able to look directly into her eyes.

"You can read it yourself," he said seriously, though it seemed ludicrous to talk about reading a book at a time when his skin was alive with the longing to be touched.

"I'd better," she said.

She sounded flippant, but he knew otherwise. He reached out to touch her, but she turned swiftly and walked into the house. When she was gone, the intimacy of her aroma lingered on, bittersweet in his nostrils. He fell back onto the swing, telling himself to slow down, reminding himself that, with Kate, he couldn't move too fast. In fact, perhaps it would be better if he didn't move at all.

But that wasn't what Kate wanted, he was sure of it. And it wasn't what he wanted, either. He wanted everything—to feel, taste and breathe Kate, to rise and fall to the rhythm of her exploding heartbeat, to shudder in her arms and to feel her grow weak in his.

He waited outside, pondering the problem, and he didn't go in until long after the light in her bedroom winked off.

Chapter Ten

The next day they rode the ferry to Preacher's Inlet in uneasy silence, neither of them sure what to say or how to say it. Kate was nervous about how to introduce Morgan to Dr. Thomas and fretted about it as they walked up the street after disembarking from the ferry.

"Just introduce me as a friend if it makes you feel better," Morgan said.

"He'll figure out that you're more than a friend," Kate replied, keeping her eyes on the road.

Morgan looked impatient. "That's okay, too. Why don't we level with him? I'm the baby's father. Your doctor knows that your pregnancy resulted from the implantation of an embryo."

"He thought it was a peculiar idea from the start." Kate sighed. "Now he'll think it's even more so."

"Kate, don't walk so fast," he said as they approached the building on the highway where the doctor's office was located. When they reached the oak tree beside the parking lot, he stopped her.

She tried to shake his hand away, but he held her until she was forced to look at him.

"Maybe we should talk about last night before we go in there," he began.

"I don't want to think about it now," she said, twisting away.

"Nevertheless, it happened. I want to make love to you, Kate. Hell, I think I'm *in* love with you," he said.

"You don't mean that. You're only trying to find a quick fix for this situation," she said, but her eyes never left his.

He exhaled a long sigh of exasperation. "The time we've spent together has been good for me. For once I'm not thinking of myself, I'm thinking of other people— you and the baby. I've changed for the better since I've known you. I've grown. I never wanted this baby, Kate, but now that it's a reality, I can't wait to be a father.

"I'm not sure I know what love is—maybe I've never known. But if it's putting others first, if it's wanting to make a difference in their lives, if it's feeling happy when I think about someone, then I love you," he said. The speech was too long, but it was effective. Kate's eyes widened and she didn't move.

"If—if we don't hurry, we'll be late for my appointment," she said at last in a breathless voice, and he followed her the remaining distance to the doctor's office, satisfied that if he hadn't convinced her, he had at least rattled her composure.

"YOU'VE NEVER LOOKED healthier," Dr. Thomas told Kate as she sat across the desk from him. He eyed her sharply. "How do you feel?"

"Mentally or physically?" Kate asked.

"Both, and if you ask me which is most important, I can't tell you." He got up and paced the floor, making sweeping gestures as was his wont. Kate thought he looked like a caricature of a stork.

"I've seen mothers in perfect physical condition—
perfect, mind you—whose mental attitude goes so
low—" here he dropped his voice to emphasize the word
"—that it drags the physical condition down with it." He
shot her a sharp look. "You're not getting depressed,
now, are you, Kate?"

"Not exactly," she hedged. All in one breath she told
him about the problems with the contract and how Morgan would not be allowed to adopt his own child unless
he married.

He became very grave and resumed his pacing, mut-
tering something to himself and finally wheeling on her.
"No wonder you feel worried. Crazy thing all the way
around, the whole idea. What to do?" He threw his arms
out in exasperation and stopped with his hands on his
hips, his neck outstretched toward Kate in quivering indignation.

Kate looked down at her hands twisted together, stung
by his words. He seemed to think better of them and said,
"Well, you're going to have a fine healthy baby. That
should be a consolation."

"It is," Kate assured him. "And one more thing. The
baby's father wants to marry me."

Dr. Thomas walked to his chair and sat down. "You
expect advice from me?" he asked abruptly, raising
bushy eyebrows. "You get yourself into this bizarre situation and you think I can tell you what to do?"

"You can't tell me whether to marry him or not, but
I—um—I don't know if making love would be good for
the baby," she said.

"Making love? Why not? You think lovemaking is
only physical? You have emotional needs, too, Kate. As
long as you're healthy, as long as there are no physical
reasons to restrict lovemaking, why, I say go ahead! I'm

more worried about your being stuck on that damned island with no way to get to the mainland than I am about
dire consequences befalling you if you decide you want
to make love," he said.

"Gump knows to watch for the SOS flag on the pole
in front of the lighthouse like he did when Dad was sick,"
Kate told him, glad to ease him away from the topic of
lovemaking. "And anyway, the baby's father—Morgan—lives on the island now, too. He's been, well,
thoughtful and—um, helpful."

"Oh. I see. Well, maybe I should talk to him about
getting you away from there the last couple weeks of your
pregnancy."

"He wants to talk to you, but not about that. Besides,
I've convinced him that I want to remain on the island.
You know how important it is for me to stay there as long
as possible."

"I know, I know. You and your father have some kind
of fixation about that island. Nice place, but I'd as soon
live on the moon—it's about as accessible. Well, where
is this Morgan fellow? Did he come with you today?"

"He's in the waiting room," Kate said, and she went
to summon him.

Morgan accompanied Kate into the small office, su-
premely self-assured as always, and sat down in the chair
beside her. Dr. Thomas looked him up and down, seemed
satisfied with what he saw and said bluntly, "Kate tells
me that you're the father."

"Yes," Morgan said. He met the doctor's gaze coolly
and directly, and Dr. Thomas nodded in approval.

"I'm glad you decided to stop in," he said.

"The reason I'm here is that I wanted to discuss being
in the delivery room when the baby's born," Morgan
said.

The doctor's eyebrows lifted in surprise as he considered this. "You are the father," he said finally. "You have the right, I suppose. Although it's my experience that unless there's a bond of some sort between the mother and any nonmedical person in the delivery room, there's no point in it. No point in it at all. Kate tells me—oh, well, it sounds like there's a bond, all right. Why do you want to be in the delivery room—curiosity about the process?"

Morgan cleared his throat. "I care," he said in a low tone. "Not only about the baby, but about Kate as well."

"Hmm. So she told me. How do you feel about having him in the delivery room with you, Kate?"

Kate's eyes sought Morgan's. He was looking at her with tenderness and deep feeling. Her heart turned over; why couldn't she simply agree to marry him? She almost couldn't pull her eyes away; she wanted to go on looking at him, at his dark hair, now tipped with sun streaks, at his eyes, so full of his soul.

"I want him there," she said clearly, watching his face.

"So be it." The doctor shuffled the papers on his desk and plucked a few pamphlets out of the jumble. He presented them to Morgan with a flourish.

"Here, these are about what goes on in a delivery room. Read them and call me if you have questions," he said.

Morgan took the booklets and studied them briefly while the doctor turned back to Kate.

"Kate, your due date isn't until the end of July, so I'll see you again in two weeks. And remember, I'd rather respond to a hundred false alarms than allow you to have this baby all by your lonesome on Yaupon Island."

The doctor stood and offered his hand to Morgan. "I'm glad you came in, Morgan. Kate, you take care of yourself. I mean it."

When they were outside on the sidewalk, Morgan said, "Your Dr. Thomas thinks I'm an interloper."

"He likes you," Kate countered.

"He's a real character."

"He's a fine doctor," Kate said defensively.

"Mmm. Say, do we have to go back to the island right away?"

"Well—"

"Isn't there a nice quiet restaurant where we could eat an early dinner?"

"Preacher's Inlet is the kind of town where McDonald's is considered a trendy place," Kate told him, her lips curving upward in an amused smile.

"I was thinking of someplace where I can snap my fingers and they bring out a tray of desserts," Morgan said.

"I know of a steak house on the highway to Charleston. I've never been in there, but I've heard it's first-rate," she said.

"Want to try it?" Morgan asked, holding his breath. Kate seemed much calmer now; perhaps the doctor had reassured her.

"Sure," she said, smiling at him. "Let's. It's so early that I'm sure we won't need reservations."

When they arrived, they found that the steak house had recently been converted to a hibachi grill called Fuji, like the Japanese volcano.

Kate was dismayed and looked to Morgan for his reaction. She didn't think this was the kind of restaurant he had in mind.

"I love a sushi bar," Morgan said. "How about you?"

"As long as it doesn't include oysters," Kate said with a laugh as the hostess guided them to a room divided from the others by shoji screens and insisted that they take off their shoes. Kate clung to Morgan's arm in order to keep her balance as she slipped off her flats, and it wasn't easy to kneel on the little mat that was provided.

"Now that I'm down here, don't expect me to get up anytime soon," Kate warned him.

"Good, you can't run away," he said.

Outside the room where they sat was a salad bar built into what was supposed to look like a Japanese temple.

"Great," Kate said when she realized what it was. "I'll have to get up again to get my salad."

"I'll go for both of us," Morgan said.

"I hope you say that when it comes time for me to go to the rest room," Kate said gloomily, but Morgan only grinned and came back with two plates of limp salad.

"I'm sorry," Kate said as she finally pushed the plate aside, "but I don't think I can eat any more. The lettuce is brown."

Morgan held up one piece with his chopsticks, which he used effortlessly while Kate struggled to master them. He studied the lettuce critically. "Not bad for lettuce that's been reincarnated," he said before popping it into his mouth. "By the way," he said after he had chewed and swallowed, "I looked around when I went to the salad bar and decided that you're easily the best-looking woman here."

"I wish you wouldn't say things like that, because I don't know how to act when you do," she told him.

He leaned forward and spoke earnestly. "Acting is the last thing I'd expect of you. I like you because you're completely without pretension," he said.

He rested his hand upon hers—a hand so strong that it conveyed instant reassurance. For a moment Kate imagined what being pregnant would be like without Morgan. In a flash she felt the loneliness, the rejection, the anguish she had experienced in the days following Courtney's announcement that she no longer wanted the baby. And then Morgan had come along to share the burden with her, and his involvement had changed everything. She smiled a tremulous smile; it seemed strange to have someone she could depend on—strange, but reassuring.

After dinner, which Kate thought was dismal but Morgan proclaimed passable, they unfolded themselves painfully from the floor mats and, after Morgan paid the check, walked to Morgan's car swinging hands. "Do we have to go back to the island?" he asked impulsively.

"If we don't we'll miss the last ferry," she said. One foot was still asleep; she stopped and shook it, leaning on Morgan's shoulder.

"That wouldn't be all bad," he said as they resumed their walk.

"We aren't going to miss it, Morgan," Kate said with a stern look.

"What did you and your father do when you wanted to go to a movie? Or anyplace at night?"

"We hardly ever did. Sometimes we stayed overnight with Dr. Thomas and his wife, but it wasn't often necessary because there's only one movie theater in Preacher's Inlet, and they run to films like *Kung Fu Race Car Driver* and *Nightmare in Loch Ness.*"

"I used to think that the *B* in B movie stood for *bad,*" Morgan said, unlocking the car door and seeing that Kate was comfortably seated before going around to the driver's side.

"I've seen some passable B movies. Have you ever seen *Vulture Voodoo?*" she asked as they headed toward the dock.

"It couldn't be any better than *Sturgeon General,* where this two-thousand-year-old fish is thawed from a glacier and turns into a man who terrorizes pygmies in an African hospital."

"You're making that up!" Kate said.

"No, I'm not," he said, and Kate snickered.

Morgan parked the car in the lot near the ferry landing and they boarded the waiting *Yaupon Island Belle,* realizing only after they were seated that they were the only passengers going to the island on this, the last trip before the ferry ceased operating for the night.

"Gump's not here," Kate said.

"What do you mean? Isn't he required to be?"

"Yes, but if there are no passengers for the last ferry, he's been known to close up shop early." She stood up. "He's in the Merry Lulu," she said with conviction.

"You sound pretty sure of that," Morgan said.

"That's where he always is," Kate said. "We'll have to go drag him out of the tavern if we want to get back to the island tonight."

"We could enjoy the scenery for a while," Morgan answered, reluctant to break the happy mood that he and Kate shared.

"You don't understand. Gump will retire when the lighthouse becomes a museum. He's got a short-timer's attitude these days, and he's spending more and more time in the tavern. It's not good for him. Come on, let's go."

Kate set off at a fast clip across the ramp and down the dock, Morgan following reluctantly, and when they reached the Merry Lulu, Kate marched right in and brushed aside the curtain of fake fishnet at the door to survey the scene.

A clutch of tourists sat on plastic-and-chrome stools at the bar, which had once been salvaged from a wrecked vessel. Kate and Morgan peered through air thick with the smell of smoke and beer and saw immediately that Gump slumped in a booth, snoring wheezily. He was sound asleep.

Kate poked his ankle none too gently with her toe. "Wake up, Gump," she said.

His eyes flew open and he opened and closed his mouth a few times. "Well," he said finally. "I was wondering when you'd get back."

"You don't look in any shape to take us to the island," Kate observed with a glint in her eye.

"The truth is, I had a few beers."

"Your eyes are as glazed as day-old donuts. You should be home in bed."

"Now wait just a minute," Gump said indignantly. "No reason I can't run you back to Yaupon Island. Kate, my girl, in your condition, you get too impatient." He struggled to a sitting position.

"Come along, Gump, I'll take you home. Morgan, give me a hand." Kate appropriated one of Gump's arms and Morgan supported the other.

"Where does he live?" Morgan asked as they guided Gump past the other curious patrons at the bar.

"Only a few steps away, thank goodness," Kate said.

"Thing is, Kate, I got kind of thirsty," Gump said querulously.

"Thing is, Gump, you get too thirsty too often," Kate retorted.

"Ridiculous," Gump muttered. "Purely ridiculous."

"He's always making much too merry at the Merry Lulu," Kate told Morgan under her breath.

"If it's any consolation, he's going to have a lulu of a hangover tomorrow," Morgan whispered back.

"He keeps a spare key on top of the doorframe," Kate told Morgan as Gump, weaving and mumbling, fumbled in his pocket at the door to the tiny bungalow where he lived.

Morgan found the key and swung the door open. Gump stumbled through a small door to the left of the entrance and landed on his bed, with Kate following and clucking as she removed his shoes.

"Shh," Kate warned Morgan, holding a finger to her lips as she backed out of the room. "Let's not wake him up."

"Wake who up?" Gump demanded, lifting his head and letting it drop back on the pillow. In less than a minute he was snoring again.

Kate turned out the light as they left, and she and Morgan stared at each other beneath the lone streetlight illuminating the deserted street.

"Well, now what?" Morgan said. "We're stranded in Preacher's Inlet until morning unless we want to look up the Pribble boy and ask him to run us over to the island. He did it for Courtney."

Kate could not face Willadeen Pribble again so soon after their last encounter. "I'd rather swim," she said.

"In an hour we could be at my place in Charleston," he said, holding his breath.

"Dr. Thomas lives one block over. He and Gloria—" Kate felt her face flush. She knew what Morgan was thinking, and she was thinking the same thing. Alone, together, anything could happen.

"My place in Charleston," Morgan said more firmly, and all thoughts of staying with the doctor and his wife flew out of Kate's head.

Anything could happen, Kate thought again. And then she said, "Your place in Charleston."

WHEN KATE STEPPED OUT of the car at Morgan's house in historic downtown Charleston she couldn't help gaping. She was prepared for an impressive house, but she hadn't expected it to be so grand.

Through the heavy front door, a wide circular staircase swept upward beneath a shimmering chandelier; Morgan led the way to the second story, guarded at the head of the stairs by a ceramic greyhound. Beyond it the master bedroom was sumptuously decorated in black and white.

Kate stopped momentarily to stare at the huge bathroom with its big shower and black fixtures. "Courtney's idea," Morgan said, turning the corners of his mouth down.

On the other side of the bathroom was another bedroom, this one decorated entirely in white. "You can sleep here," he said, setting her suitcase on the waiting luggage rack.

"It's lovely," Kate said, although privately she thought that the whole house was overdecorated.

"I need to make some phone calls," he said. "Will you be all right on your own for a few minutes?"

Kate nodded, and in a few minutes she heard Morgan talking to his secretary, to Joanna and to a few others. She wandered idly to the window. A spotlight below lit an English-style garden with neat, narrow brick paths dividing low plantings of flowers.

Morgan returned, popping in unexpectedly through the open door.

"I've told Joanna," he said.

"Told her about me and Courtney and the baby and you?" she asked in surprise.

"Only that I'm going to adopt your baby. I didn't want to go into detail on the telephone."

Kate's heart sank. "Morgan, I—"

He touched her cheek. "It'll be okay. After her initial shock, she thought it was wonderful that I'm adopting a child."

Kate turned away and stared out at the garden. Shapes blurred in front of her. She didn't want to look at Morgan at the moment; she didn't want to confront her own feelings about Morgan's taking the baby.

Oh, that was what she had wanted, all right, but what was it her father always used to say? *"Be careful what you want—you might get it."* She'd achieved what she'd wanted, but the thought of relinquishing this tiny scrap of humanity that moved inside her, for whom she was a lifeline—well, the thought was beginning to pain her.

"Kate, look at me," he commanded.

She didn't turn around.

"Is it so hard for you to believe that I love you? That I care about the baby?"

"Since the moment that you told me you'd adopt it, I've never doubted that you cared about the baby," Kate countered. "You've got it backward, though. You should love the baby and care about me."

He swung her around, his expression compassionate. "I couldn't help but fall in love with you, Kate. You're so fiercely independent that I admire you, you're so vulnerable that it breaks my heart, and you're so beautiful that I want to kiss you—"

"Morgan," Kate said in desperation.

"That I want to kiss you all over. Like this," he said, tipping her face toward his and letting his lips meet hers.

Kate felt as if she were falling, spinning into a deep and dark vortex from which she might never emerge. His lips were insistent, pressing, seeking, exploring her mouth with great tenderness and then, when she didn't resist, even greater passion.

If she could have summoned the strength, she would have pushed him away. If she could have run, she would have tried. But there was no escaping Morgan Rhett in his own house, and she had known that before she'd agreed to come.

"Tell me," he insisted, his lips close to hers, "tell me that this doesn't mean something to you. If you dare."

She shook her head to clear it, but it was no use. His lips were upon hers again, his fingers caught in her tumbling hair, and her body was pressed against his so that she could feel his arousal.

"You're not saying much, my Kate," he observed, and she caught a devilish gleam in his eyes. In that moment her surrender was complete. She and his child were one, and it seemed the most natural thing in the world to unite with the child's father in a coupling that her body had been craving almost from the moment she had set eyes on him.

"There are other things I would rather do," she said softly, twining her hands around his neck and kissing him.

He slipped out of his clothes with minimal help from her, standing before her without the least bit of self-consciousness. *If only I can feel as comfortable standing naked in front of him,* Kate thought, but then she had always been matter-of-fact about her body and perhaps Morgan would be, too.

Morgan pushed the dress off her shoulders so that it fell to the ground. When she stood before him without her clothes, he felt as though he could not breathe. He'd had no idea she would be as lovely as this, as purely beautiful, as wholesomely arousing.

The low lamplight in the room bathed them both in its mellow glow. "You're wonderful, Kate," he said, smoothing his hands over her hips with reverence. "There's something elemental about you in this state. You're like—like the mother goddess, the earth mother, the source of all life and love."

"Morgan Rhett, I think you are crazy," she said clearly and distinctly, but he could see the emotion in her eyes, and he knew she was only joking.

"I won't hurt you, you know. I'd never hurt you," he said. He could barely speak; it was as though an ever-abundant life force sprang from her to him through his fingertips, spiraling through him and filling him with wonder.

"I know," she said.

"We're going to be good together, Kate," he said.

"I know that, too," she whispered.

She felt his hands cupping the hot curves of her breasts, and she felt her nipples swelling under his insistent touch. She closed her eyes and floated with the sensation, feeling lost in her fantasy of making love with him, scarcely able to believe it had come true.

He parted her thighs gently, his hand softly seeking her warm center, and with the other hand he held her close, whispering, "Sweet, sweet."

And her frantic hands sought him, sought and held him, wanting him, and somehow they were on the bed lying on their sides and gazing at each other as if they were the only two people on earth.

Slowly he sat and lifted her to him, soothing her, urging her, his thighs solid beneath her.

"Gently," she reminded him, her voice only a murmur.

"Yes," he said, and he was gentle, and she rocked against him, reaching with her hands, their fingers entwining, reaching with her eyes, their eyes holding.

"You can't love me," she whispered, but he only smiled and slid his hand beneath the hair on her neck to pull her closer for a kiss.

Chapter Eleven

Sometime before first light, Kate drifted awake and groped her way to the unfamiliar bathroom. When she returned to the bed and lay down beside Morgan, she didn't fall asleep immediately. Instead she felt the baby stirring in her womb, reminding her of its presence.

Morgan's eyes opened briefly and she saw him smile in recognition before he curved an arm across her stomach. It fit there as if it had always belonged, and she wove her fingers between his. The three of them—she and Morgan and the baby—hovered somewhere between sleeping and waking, all together in one bed. It seemed right.

Morgan was not the kind of lover she had expected. His tight buttoned-down exterior had disappeared completely when they made love. He was uninhibited and yet gentle. And caring. And so considerate of the baby.

The baby. Always the baby. The reason for their meeting, the reason for their mating. Talk about the cart before the horse!

Kate turned onto her side, still within Morgan's grasp, and his arm easily accommodated her change in position. This position, with her knees pulled up, was the most comfortable one in which to sleep these days.

Last night she had acted wanton, delirious with sensation, lost in passion with a passionate man. Still, she had realized that the act was not one that either of them regarded lightly.

Afterward, when they had lain together waiting for their breathing to return to normal, she had wondered, *How can he love me?* She still had no answer to that question. In her mind it simply wasn't possible for a Morgan Rhett to love a Kate Sinclair. They were two distinct types with two distinct backgrounds, and the only thing they had in common was the child. Morgan's child.

She dozed, and when she woke up, Morgan was not beside her. She sat up, hair tousled, and smiled at the wild disarray of the sheets. After wrapping one of them around her, she padded into the bathroom, where Morgan was noisily taking a shower.

He stood in the middle of the huge shower, which was so big that no shower curtain was needed, with three shower jets trained on him.

"Just the person I've been wanting to see," he said, tossing the sheet aside, grabbing her and pulling her into the spray. He smacked her soundly on the lips, and she said, "Suppose I didn't feel like a shower," and he winked lewdly and ran his soapy hands down her sides and said in his best Groucho Marx imitation, "You may not feel like a shower, but you feel pretty good to me!"

He shampooed her hair, frowning as he concentrated on the task, and she soaped his back, making forays into other areas.

"Darling Kate," he said. "I had no idea you'd be so good at this."

"At what?" she said.

"This," he said, backing her up against the shower wall and demonstrating.

"I think" she gasped through clouds of steam, "I think I've had enough."

"Aha! She says she's had enough," he said, stepping out of the spray. He drew a fuzzy terry cloth robe out of a closet and hung it over her shoulders.

"Put this on," he said. "When you're ready for breakfast, I'll see you in the kitchen." He kissed her once in front of her still-wet ear and disappeared into his bedroom.

When she joined Morgan downstairs, he had already set the table in the breakfast room and was standing at the stove, concentrating on the frying pan. "Do you like your eggs sunny-side up or over?" he asked.

"Sunny-side up, and can't I help?"

"No, Kate. Sit down and be decorative."

"I'm about as decorative as a baby blimp," she complained.

He sent a stern look in her direction. "Don't be silly," he said. "I thought I left no doubt in your mind last night how sexy you are."

"Yeah," she said reluctantly. "I guess you settled that question."

"Forever," he said. He set aside the spatula and swept her into his arms, kissing her until her knees went weak.

"I think I ordered eggs," she said when he released her. "Not that."

"Good thing you reminded me," he said, returning his attention to the pan on the stove.

"I had no idea you could be so handy around a house," she told him when they were both sitting at the table and she was digging into the eggs. She hadn't realized before how hungry she was.

"Bachelorhood taught me a lot of things," Morgan said, smiling at her.

"For instance?"

"That having help around the house isn't dependable, and that I would have to learn to do everything myself for the inevitable days when my housekeeper didn't show up. What do you think of the eggs?"

"Scrumptious," she said with her mouth full.

"I fry them in bacon grease. Not so good for your health according to the latest news from the nattering nabobs of nutrition, but delicious on the palate."

"I can always have my arteries reamed out by Roto-Rooter," Kate said. "Or maybe a bulldozer. I know where I can find one. I hope it's gone when I go back to the island. When *are* we going back, anyway?"

"Not for a while, I hope," he said, taking a sip of orange juice. He leaned back in his chair. "Are you so eager?" he asked.

"You know how much I love the island," she said.

"Don't look at me like that," he said, putting his hand over hers. "You make me feel so guilty."

"Guilty?" she repeated.

"If you think I pressured you into making love with me, if you think I was seeking some weird kind of thrill, if you think that I was only curious about making love with an expectant mother, you're wrong."

"I didn't feel pressured," she said firmly. "I wanted it as much as you did."

"Just as I suspected," he said with a gleam in his eyes. "As far as going back to the island, we'll go when we both decide it's time. Fair enough?"

"Fair enough," she replied.

"Friends?"

"I'd say we're more than friends," she said, smiling at him.

He returned her smile. "And now that we've got that out of the way, are you still hungry? Would you like something else to eat?" he asked.

"I'd like more bacon. And I'll get it myself," she said, but he was up before she was.

"Let me," he said. "It's warming in the oven."

She could have stayed where she was, but she trailed him into the kitchen. When he looked up, she was unconsciously standing in the classic pose of pregnant women, one hand pressing at the hollow of her back, legs positioned far apart in order to distribute her weight evenly. She looked so uncomfortable that he went to her immediately.

He gently massaged her back, starting below her neck and eventually gliding supple fingers down the terry cloth seam to the place where her hand had been. She sighed and leaned her forehead on his shoulder.

"That feels...so...good," she breathed. "If only you knew how much I've wanted somebody to do that."

"You should have mentioned it sooner," he said. "I would have obliged."

"I was—afraid of you," she admitted, not looking at him.

He buried his face in her hair and pulled her close until he felt the solid lump of the baby between them.

"You don't have to be afraid of me, ever," he whispered.

"You're Morgan Rhett. I'm nobody," she said. Seeing his house and the way he lived had convinced her of that, more than anything that had gone before.

"You're the mother of my child," he said, which was not strictly true, but neither of them was in the mood to argue.

"You've stopped rubbing my back," she said.

"I'd rather concentrate on other parts," he said, his warm lips finding the hollow of her throat.

The robe fell open, and it was like the previous night all over again, only better. Kate thought her chest could not contain her beating heart, and she thought that she might swoon with pleasure. She had never enjoyed love-making this much before. Was it only because her hormones were stirred up because of pregnancy, or was it Morgan Rhett?

Whatever it was, she wanted it to go on forever, and her hunger wasn't for bacon. In fact, by the time either of them was ready to eat, the bacon was cold.

"I'VE BEEN THINKING," Morgan said that afternoon as they braved the afternoon heat for a comradely walk in the park, which Kate insisted that she needed for the exercise. "I'd like us to take childbirth-preparation classes."

"Why on earth?" Kate asked. He looked especially handsome today, his new tan offset by a white polo shirt and a pair of faded blue jeans.

"It would be good for the baby. It would be good for you. It's not too late for you to do exercises, and besides, you need to learn how to breathe for childbirth."

"Don't you think poling around in a johnboat and picking up litter is plenty of exercise? And I don't need classes to teach me how to breathe, Morgan. I've been doing it all my life. Childbirth is a natural process, and whatever I need to do will happen all by itself."

"Joanna says that childbirth is a travail of tears. Of course, she might have been joking," Morgan said doubtfully.

"That's real encouraging, Morgan. Are you trying to scare me?"

"No, I'm only pointing out that Joanna has had experience."

"You're right. And if it's so bad, why would she have had two more children after she had Christopher?"

"Think of it this way, Kate. If we learn the Lamaze method of childbirth, it will give me something to do in the delivery room besides twiddle my thumbs."

"*I* should lie around on the floor and grunt and groan with a bunch of other women so you will have something to do besides twiddle your thumbs? I have some advice for you—learn to knit."

"I thought you'd go for it," Morgan said unhappily.

"You thought wrong, Morgan Rhett. I'm not going to any childbirth-preparation classes, and that's that."

"Think of the baby, Kate."

"I do. I am. And that's no argument, because the baby will get born, Lamaze method or not."

"Then think of yourself," Morgan said desperately.

"All I can think about is that I need a job," Kate said, and Morgan dropped the subject. He didn't like to remember that Kate would move away after the baby was born. After last night he couldn't imagine being without her.

KATE USED THE TELEPHONE at Morgan's house to make long-distance phone calls in her quest for a job.

She called a friend who worked at the Woods Hole Oceanographic Institution in Massachusetts and he gave her the name of a professor in California who might be interested in her work. The professor said that he had no openings on his staff, but she might try a maritime research center in Nova Scotia that had recently received a large grant from the Canadian government. And so it went, with Kate finally realizing that she was being given a colossal runaround.

"It hurts to be thrown on the trash heap," she said to Morgan that night. "I still have something important to contribute to the study of mollusks."

"I don't doubt that," he said.

"You'd think that in the last three years, I'd have come to terms with being *persona non grata* in my own profession, but I still can't believe it," she said unhappily.

"I read in the paper today that our local Charles Towne University is sponsoring a lecture by Marc Theroux tonight. Would you like to go?"

"Marc Theroux! Of course, I would. It's much too late to get tickets, though," she said.

"It so happens that I already have them," he said, waving them in front of her eyes.

"Oh, Morgan! He's been my idol ever since I was a little girl!"

"Exactly," Morgan said, although he knew little about Marc Theroux. What mattered to him was seeing Kate happy and hearing the lilt return to her voice.

THAT NIGHT Kate listened spellbound in the large university auditorium as Marc Theroux discussed his present work on the reefs off the South Carolina coast. Although Morgan had little interest in the man to begin with, by the end of the lecture he was applauding wildly along with everyone else.

The evening ended with the president of Charles Towne University announcing that Marc Theroux had endowed a fellowship in the marine biology department of the university. The recipient would be known as the Marc Theroux Scholar.

Afterward, as Morgan and Kate were walking home past shuttered houses, their footsteps echoing off high garden walls, Kate said thoughtfully, "You know, I miss my work." She paused for a moment. "Morgan, at one time I probably could have landed that fellowship. I could have been the Marc Theroux Scholar."

"You would have considered working here, in Charleston?" Morgan asked.

"It's a wonderful chance for someone, Morgan," Kate said in a resigned tone of voice. "It's a chance to direct important work in marine biology. Some people would give their eyeteeth for that opportunity."

He slid her hand through his arm. "You could apply now," he said.

"They'd never consider me. No one would take the chance. I'm considered a troublemaker."

"You! A troublemaker!"

"You have to admit I'm unconventional," she said as they approached his house.

He opened the door and she preceded him inside. He caught her under the big chandelier. "I *like* unconventional," he said, pulling her close.

"Which makes you a bit unconventional yourself, wouldn't you say?" she returned, nibbling on his ear. But he didn't say anything, and after a while neither did she.

AFTER THEIR OUTING to see Marc Theroux, Kate thought nothing of it when Morgan suggested that they attend another event at the college later that week.

"Chamber music? It always puts me to sleep," Kate said dismissively when Morgan brought the subject up.

"We can't have that," he said, because the two of them had fallen into the habit of making love until all hours, then sleeping late in the morning. It was idyllic, but they both knew that it couldn't last forever.

"Well, since you were so nice about sitting through two hours of Marc Theroux, I suppose I'm willing to give you equal time," Kate said, smiling at him.

That night it was Morgan's idea to take the car, even though the college was well within easy walking distance. When they got there, however, Kate thought it was strange that so many parking spaces were available at the college if a well-known chamber group was playing that night.

"It's summer," Morgan said as if that explained everything, and he whipped the car into a vacant spot outside one of the university's numerous buildings.

"We go this way," Morgan said, leading her into a structure that looked for all the world like a classroom building, but she wasn't familiar with the university and thought that perhaps there was a small auditorium inside.

Morgan led her down a long hall lined with doors, and Kate was beginning to think he was lost until he said, "Ah, there it is."

A cheerful middle-aged woman held the door open. "Hi," she said, chirping for all the world like a happy sparrow. "Welcome to Lamaze class. I'm Esther."

"I thought—" Kate began with a confused look from Esther to Morgan, but then she saw several other couples sitting in chairs placed in a circle. All the women were clearly pregnant.

Kate wheeled and glared at Morgan, her expression one of outrage.

"Right this way, please," Esther said as Morgan nudged the small of Kate's back so that she had no choice but to move through the door.

Unwillingly Kate sank down on the chair that Esther indicated. There were so many other couples, the women dressed in maternity slacks and tops, the men looking eager. As eager as Morgan, who leaned forward in his chair.

"How dare you!" Kate hissed at him, only to be given a blank look.

For a moment she wanted to get up and walk out. The thing that stopped her was that Morgan might know some of these couples and she didn't want to embarrass him.

On the other hand, why not? *He* had certainly embarrassed *her.* She was plotting her escape when Esther moved to the center of the circle and began to speak. Was it still too late to run for it? Kate glanced at the open door.

"First we'll see a short film, and then I'll answer any questions," Esther said. The lights dimmed and the film started. *Great,* Kate thought, *now I'll stumble over something on the way out.*

As the movie rolled on, Kate began to be interested in spite of herself. It showed sperm and eggs uniting, and babies growing in utero, floating weightless like little astronauts in space.

Morgan tried to take her hand, but she shook it away. She was still angry with him.

"Kate, don't be upset," he whispered after the movie projector was turned off.

"You'd better believe I'm upset. You had no right, I *told* you I didn't want to do this!"

"Now," Esther said as the lights came back on, "I want you all to find a comfortable spot on the floor," and a nervous titter went up from the group.

"As if there is a comfortable place on the floor," Kate muttered, remaining in her chair.

Morgan's eyes pleaded with her. "Please, Kate," he said. "If I'm going to be your childbirth coach, we need to know how to do this."

"I never said you could be my coach," Kate retorted as she reluctantly moved to a spot on the floor. "I said you could be in the delivery room. Big difference."

The class progressed through breathing exercises, which Kate found herself doing in spite of her aversion, and a brief demonstration of physical exercises to do at home. They learned to pant, the woman beside Kate reminding her of nothing so much as an asthmatic beagle she'd lived next door to in Maine.

Kate fairly flew out of the room ahead of Morgan when class was dismissed.

"I'll never forgive you," Kate said, walking as fast as she could. "Never."

"I thought that once you'd started the class, you'd realize how important it was," Morgan said, trying to reason with her.

"I'm going back to the island tomorrow, bulldozer or no bulldozer, water or no water. I can't wait to get back to my own peaceful keeper's quarters."

Morgan opened the car door for her and waited until she got in. He slammed the door after her and hurried around to the driver's side of the car, wondering why Kate was so stubborn. He also wondered if she really meant it about going back to the island tomorrow.

She didn't speak to him all the way home, and when they arrived at his house, she stalked up to her room without a word.

Morgan didn't know what to do. They'd been getting along so well, and he'd ruined it. He had to admit that he'd played this all wrong. He should have understood that when Kate said no to the childbirth-preparation class, he should have taken her at her word.

Now he heard her slamming around in the bathroom, and then silence. It was too early to go to sleep; perhaps she was reading. But there was no light under her door. He could only surmise that she'd gone to bed for the evening—alone.

He read for a while, and he watched TV. He had rented a video of an old cult classic, *Wrath of the Killer Tomatoes,* and he had looked forward to sharing it with Kate, but her absence took all the fun out of it. After giving up on the video, he wandered around his big house, thinking that he'd never noticed how lonely it was with only one person in it. Well, Kate made two people, and baby made three, but they didn't count. At least not tonight.

After he returned to his room, he pounded his pillow into a ball, pushed it flat again and stared into the darkness. He missed Kate lying beside him, her feet tucked between his knees, his arm around her belly. He didn't think he could fall asleep without her beside him, without first experiencing the soothing, satisfying lovemaking to which they had both become accustomed.

He walked through the dark bathroom and pushed at the door that connected to her bedroom. When it opened, he saw that the bed was only a shape in the darkness, and he tiptoed to it. When his eyes adjusted to the gloom, he saw that Kate was staring up at him, wide awake.

"I couldn't sleep," he said, staring at her.

"I can't, either."

His heart turned over. If only she knew how much he cared about her, how he worried about her welfare. If only it meant something to her!

Those feelings were too hard to express, at least with words. He only had one way, and that was by making love to her.

She lifted up the sheet in silent invitation, and he sat down on the edge of the bed.

"You're not too angry?" he said.

"No," she answered.

The sheet fluttered down over them as he pulled his legs underneath it. He was aware of her breathing beside him, and he knew she wasn't going to make the first move. Should he, or would she only take offense?

He waited, afraid to touch her. When he had almost made up his mind not to speak, she said in a small voice, "Morgan?"

He turned to her in sheer relief and she came into his arms.

"I don't like being mad at you," she murmured into his neck.

"I'm sorry. I thought the class was a good thing," he said. "Maybe you were right to be angry."

"I don't like being manipulated," she said.

"I suppose I can't blame you," he admitted.

They lay quietly, listening to each other breathe.

"You breathe very nicely as it is. I can't imagine why I ever thought you needed lessons," he said.

To his surprise she started to laugh. "I'm through with breathing classes, but if you ever find a class on how to get along with the Morgan Rhetts of this world, sign me up," she said.

"We're having the first lesson right now," he said.

"What?"

"Slide your leg over mine—that's it. And move your head slightly to the right—good."

"And now?"

For an answer he kissed her, slowly and deeply, and she sighed with pleasure.

"I sure like this class a lot better than the other one," she said as she rose above him, pale and utterly delectable in the moonlight filtering through the curtained windows.

THE NEXT MORNING they said no more about returning to the island. And yet Kate knew that they must. She wanted to go back, even though it would mean the end of their romantic interlude.

During the next few days, they often slept until noon, and then they ate lunch. Morgan had given the housekeeper the week off.

"She probably thinks I'm in England as planned," Morgan said.

"Do you wish you were?"

"Of course not," he said indignantly, kissing the back of her head. They were lolling in bed after a breakfast of leftover pizza, which Kate adored and which Morgan had thought was disgusting until he'd actually tried it.

"Was eating pizza for breakfast so hard? Did you mind it so much?" Kate asked.

"Pizza cake," Morgan replied with his mouth full, and for that she cuffed him playfully on the side of the head.

"Don't you have to go in to your office sometime?" Kate asked as they gathered up pizza crusts and piled them on the breakfast tray.

"Soon, but not today. I thought we could take a ride over to my place on Teoway Island. I'd like to open it up and air it out."

Kate stretched contentedly. "Mmm. Sounds lovely," she said.

"We could stay there tonight if you'd like."

She smiled at him. "I'll be ready in an hour. Maybe less," she said.

He watched her as she headed for the bathroom. If only he could stop time and make everything stay the same forever! If only she would make the commitment to stay with him after the baby was born. He was resigned to suing Courtney for the right to his own baby; the one thing he still couldn't accept was the impending defection of Kate.

He still hadn't been able to bring himself to tell her about her exoneration by the Federal Health Foundation's Office of Scientific Ethics. He didn't even want to think about her resuming her place in the scientific community.

He carried a picture in his head, a picture of a happy family, and lately it had been surfacing often in his daydreams. The perfect family consisted of a father, a mother and a child. He could not make out the baby's face, but he was the father, and the mother was Kate.

Chapter Twelve

Kate loved the Teoway Island house on sight.

"I built the house when I was developing Teoway as a golf resort. I stayed here a lot in those days," Morgan said as he showed her around.

Kate took in the wide sandy beach on one side, the peaceful green marsh on the other. "It's beautiful here," she said.

"I should come here more often. I suppose I got out of the habit when Courtney and I were married because she never liked it," he said.

"What's so wonderful about this place," Kate said, turning around slowly in the middle of the big living room with its view of both marsh and sea, "is that it's as if no one else lives anywhere near. It's like the island—my island."

He wrapped his arms around her. "There's no lighthouse, but look, that hazy cloud on the horizon is Yaupon Island."

"If Willadeen gets her wish and manages to reactivate the light, you'll be able to see it," Kate said.

Morgan took her hand and drew her into the master bedroom. "We'd have even a better view from here," he said.

She twisted away. She didn't want to talk about the future. By the time the lighthouse was operative, Kate was sure that she'd be long gone.

They lapsed into an easy domesticity in the house, much as they had in Charleston, but here it was Kate who cooked dinner, whipping up a feast from the odd assortment of canned goods she found in the cupboards. The kitchen was marvelously convenient, with its refrigerator that dispensed ice water and its racks of copper-bottomed pans. Even the colors in which the house was decorated—soft peach and gray—suited her.

Late that night they lay in Morgan's king-size bed with the curtains open so they could gaze out the window at the marsh. "This is my idea of Heaven," she said, her head finding a comfortable hollow in Morgan's shoulder.

"Then why not stay here forever?" he said, holding his breath.

She stiffened, then forced herself to relax. "My life isn't heading in this direction, Morgan," she said.

"It could," he pointed out, but Kate didn't reply.

She wished he would understand that she hadn't meant this pregnancy to be anything more than an interlude in her life. Yes, providing life for this baby had given her own life meaning when it didn't seem to have any. And yes, she supposed that she had undertaken this pregnancy to prove in some cockeyed way that there was a certain continuity to life after her father's death. She loved being pregnant—at least most of the time. And her feelings about her pregnancy were all bound up in her feelings for Morgan, so how could she tell whether she truly loved him or only loved her pregnant state?

She did know one thing. She had never meant the pregnancy to be more than a stopgap measure. She had never meant to give up her efforts to reestablish her standing in the scientific community.

"I SUPPOSE I can't postpone the inevitable any longer," Morgan said the next morning after a hurried phone conversation with his secretary, who called before they were even out of bed. "I'd better go to my office for a few hours."

"May I stay here, in this house? It's so beautiful this morning," Kate said. Through the open draperies she could see that the sea seemed cast in warm golden light; overhead a few clouds billowed like freshly laundered sheets against a clear blue sky.

"I'd be happy for you to stay here. *If* you'll promise to behave yourself. No crazy antics," he warned her seriously as he swung his feet over the side of the bed.

"I thought I'd sit on the deck and read a magazine," Kate said meekly.

"See that you do, Kate my darling. I may be gone for the rest of the afternoon."

"Oh?" she said. "Why?"

"I'm going to call Ted Wickes and instruct him to begin court proceedings against Courtney."

She had been afraid of this. She had no idea what to say; she knew how much he must be dreading facing Courtney in court.

"I feel so guilty," she said, her voice a near whisper.

He lifted her hand to his lips and kissed it. "What else can I do? You won't marry me," he said half-playfully, but she saw the apprehension deep in his eyes.

She pulled her hand away and sat up straighter, the sheet barely covering her. Morgan stood and busied himself taking clothes out of drawers while Kate stared contemplatively into space.

How could she let him go back to court when she had the means to spare him that ordeal? He'd done so much for her, after all. She wanted to repay him, and it was true that she felt a deep affection for him.

"Morgan?"

He had sat down on the edge of the bed and was beginning to pull on his socks.

"What, Kate?"

"I have an idea."

"So do I, but we haven't time to do it now," he said playfully.

"No, no, it's nothing like that."

"Too bad. All right then, what is it?" He smiled at her and picked up his other sock.

"We could get married if you wouldn't expect me to remain your wife."

He dropped the sock on the floor and twisted his head around to look at her.

"You're serious," he said after he saw that she was.

"I think so." She wanted desperately to please him, to let him know the depth of her gratitude. She wanted to make things easy for him, but she didn't want to tie him to her forever.

"You'd want a divorce after the baby is born?" The words were sharp.

"Wouldn't it take longer than that? Wouldn't the adoption have to be final before we got the divorce?"

"Yes, I suppose the adoption would have to be final," he said in a subdued tone.

"So then we could be married, but I wouldn't expect a lifetime commitment. It would be with the understanding that we end our marriage as soon as I can find a job or as soon as the adoption is final, whichever comes first." This sounded reasonable, rational. Morgan would have to see the sense in it.

"Is that the way you'd want it?" he asked.

"I'll resume my career as soon as possible. I have my doctorate in marine biology, Morgan. I have a lot to contribute to oyster research, and the work is important."

"More important than being a Rhett?" he said.

"More important than spending my life going to teas and balls," she retorted.

"I see. When would we be married, according to your plan?" he asked.

"Soon. Whenever you want," she said, forcing herself to sound as though the whole matter was of negligible importance to her.

"We could be married in a few days?"

"Certainly."

"I suppose," Morgan said, "that we could be married as soon as I can arrange for a license."

"That would be fine," she said. Her hand of its own volition reached out and tipped the hairs on his arm with one finger, but he didn't respond. Instead he stood and found his shoes on the closet floor, sitting on a low chair to put them on.

"Well," he said. "This is most generous of you, but before we compound all the mistakes that have already been made, I'd better consult my attorney," he said at last, standing up and gazing down at her, his expression unreadable.

"Yes," she said. She hoped he would touch her; she wished he'd kiss her. Their closeness seemed to have evaporated at the very time when she thought he should be happy. She was doing what he wanted, wasn't she? She had agreed to marry him, hadn't she?

Morgan stood in front of the mirror to knot his tie. She watched from the bed as he put on his suit jacket. The wing tips were back, and he looked every bit the upscale executive. He was no longer the loving Morgan who had so tenderly bedded her, or the supportive Morgan who had accompanied her to Preacher's Inlet to confront Willadeen Pribble. He seemed like a Morgan Rhett whom she hardly knew.

"You look ready for business," she told him, forcing a smile.

"Hmm," was all he said. "I wonder where I put my briefcase? Oh, here it is. Well, I'll see you later. I should be back in time for dinner."

"Would you like me to cook something?" she called after him as he hurried down the hall.

She didn't know whether he heard or was merely ignoring her. In a few moments she heard the front door close after him.

MORGAN CLOSETED HIMSELF in his office, away from the inquisitive eyes of Phyllis and the other women who worked for him. His expression serious, he punched out a series of numbers on his phone.

Tony Saldone was not at the hotel in Maine where Morgan knew he was staying, but Morgan left word with the operator for Tony to call him. While he waited for the phone call, Morgan tried not to think about Kate.

It was impossible to keep her out of his mind. Last night he hadn't been able to get enough of her long legs twining around his, her softly caressing fingers, the unrestrained passion of making love with a woman who was so totally sensual. How she had gone for three years without a man was beyond him.

And now she had agreed to marry him.

After Courtney's coldness, Kate's warmth was like a breath of spring arriving on the heels of a long, miserable winter. The thought of lying in bed beside Kate every night for the rest of his life literally made his heart leap with joy.

But she wanted a divorce as soon as possible.

He paced the length of his office, waiting for the phone to ring. Would Kate marry him if it weren't for the baby?

No. She had made it clear that she didn't love him. Although he could have sworn that during the past few nights, all the time that she was making of herself a splendid gift, all the times that he was throbbing to the beat of her heart, he could have sworn that—

The phone rang and he yanked it out of its cradle.

"Morgan Rhett," he said.

"You won't believe what that Pegeen chick told me last night. The Federal Health Foundation Office of Scientific Ethics will issue a report in a couple of weeks that exonerates the Sinclair woman from all wrongdoing. Pegeen says—"

"You mean Kate will be reinstated at the Northeast Marine Institute?" Morgan said, sinking down onto the chair behind his desk.

"Pegeen says it's inevitable. She tells me that the report lambastes the director of the institute and the co-worker of Kate's who falsified data, uh, let's see, his name is Mitchell Robbins. It recommends that the director resign and discredits this Robbins fellow."

"And when will news of this become public?" Morgan said faintly.

"Couple of weeks is all I know. I'll stay on the case."

"No," Morgan said. "You can come home now. I don't need to know anything else."

"You're sure about that? I kinda like Maine in the summer. And Pegeen is quite—cooperative."

"Come home, Tony. You've earned your pay."

"I'll send you a written report in a few days," Tony said.

When Morgan hung up, he picked up the calendar. In a day or so, he and Kate could be married. It would be a mutually beneficial union—he would support her until she found a job, she would stay married to him until the adoption was final. A neat deal for both of them, and Morgan considered himself a genius at making deals.

But would she still marry him if she knew that her exoneration and reinstatement at the institute were imminent?

Maybe yes. Maybe no. It certainly could queer the deal by upsetting the balance.

Which was, in the end, exactly why he decided not to tell her.

KATE HAD DINNER WAITING when he got back to the Teoway Island house. She was wearing a frilly apron that she'd found somewhere. He kissed her, a lukewarm kind of kiss, and when she speared him with a quizzical look, he made some excuse about getting out of his suit and putting on more comfortable clothes, before fleeing to the bedroom.

It was hard to face Kate, knowing what he did about her job situation. It was going to be hard not to tell her. Somewhere in the back of his mind, he nurtured the idea that if she married him, she wouldn't leave him. She would stay on after the baby was born and give up her idea of resuming a career that, as far as she knew, was defunct.

He didn't broach the subject until after dinner when they were relaxing on the deck, her feet pillowed in his lap so he could massage them. Kate leaned back, one arm around the globe of her belly, the other behind her head. She toyed with a strand of fine golden hair, and he felt a lump in his throat just looking at her. She was so lovely, so precious to him.

Didn't she know that he couldn't help being in love with her? Didn't she love him just a little?

He cleared his throat. "I checked into a marriage license today. We can be married on Friday," he said.

"Where?" she asked, turning her face toward him.

"I have a friend who is a judge. He can marry us in his chambers," Morgan replied.

"Good," Kate said, although that kind of wedding sounded so cold. So sterile.

"Are you sure you want to do this?"

"Of course," she said.

He led her to bed then, removing her clothes as she stood quietly, admiring the intricate lacing of blue veins beneath her skin, reverently massaging the sensitive dark tips of her nipples until they rose between his fingers. He slid his hands down to cup her abdomen and felt the stirring of his child; it moved him so much that he couldn't speak. When he finally wrapped Kate in his arms he rocked her silently, unable to express his emotion.

In the dark her eyes were large and glowing, and in bed she was especially inventive, and he thought that if she was this way when she was pregnant, she would be even better when she was not.

And when she was no longer pregnant, they would have how long? How long before Kate got her old job back and left him?

He had married Courtney for all the wrong reasons, and he knew that the reason he was marrying Kate was wrong, too. Oh, it was true that by marrying Kate he could avoid taking Courtney to court, but he was hoping to use the marriage to convince Kate to stay with him. It might not work; in fact, he was sure it wouldn't. But he had to try, because—Heaven help him—he loved her.

ON FRIDAY they were married.

Kate felt a sense of unreality about the whole thing. The judge spoke in resounding tones, lending dignity to the occasion, and Morgan was handsome in his dark blue suit and highly polished shoes, and he looked directly in her eyes as he spoke his wedding vows and said them as if he meant them.

Kate felt graceless and dowdy in her hastily bought white piqué dress with a collar of lace cutwork, a dress she wouldn't have worn under any circumstances in her other life, where she felt most comfortable in madras that had bled from red and blue plaid into solid purple.

She also wore a new pair of white pumps with medium-height heels that pinched her feet unmercifully. They, like the dress, had been Joanna's idea. Joanna had insisted on taking her shopping on Thursday morning, dragging an unwilling Kate into shops with coy banners proclaiming Clothes for the Lady-in-Waiting.

Her bouquet had been supplied by Morgan and was a tasteful and expensive cascade of white orchids. He also gave her an unexpected wedding gift of a lovely diamond-and-pearl pin, which she wore on her collar.

"Is it real?" she had asked when he'd presented it to her, and Morgan had laughed.

"Of course," he said.

"Oh," she had replied, embarrassed. In Morgan's set, it was a given that jewelry was always the real thing, not costume. She'd have to remember that she was a Rhett now—at least, she was a technical member of the Rhett family. She planned to keep her own name. It would make it so much easier when she and Morgan were divorced not to have to change her driver's license, passport and other documents back to her birth name.

At the end of the ceremony, when the judge said gravely to Morgan, "You may kiss the bride," Kate almost looked around to see who the bride was. Then Morgan folded her in his arms, taking his time about it, and kissed her warmly and thoroughly and with just a hint of passion that Kate hoped no one else in the room noticed.

"Congratulations!" Charlie, Joanna's husband, said, clapping Morgan on the back. For Kate he had a quick kiss on the cheek, as did Joanna, and then Joanna put her arm through Kate's and said, "Now for your wedding feast!"

The four of them went back to Joanna and Charlie's house and sat down to a sumptuous repast of Cornish game hens reposing on a bed of wild rice and served on a big heirloom silver platter that looked to Kate to be about the size of the skating rink at Rockefeller Center. In fact, Kate found the big dining room with its long sideboard and pictures of hunt scenes on the walls intimidating, and the conversation was stilted despite Morgan's valiant attempts to make it a festive evening.

Throughout the dinner, Kate, still suspended in an aura of disbelief, kept sneaking glances at the lovely wedding band Morgan had chosen for her. It had been a complete surprise, Morgan producing it this afternoon before the ceremony. Kate's eyes had grown wide when he snapped the little velvet box open to show her.

"I didn't think—I mean, I forgot—" she stammered.

"We can't get married without a ring," Morgan said. "I tried to choose one you'd like."

"It's beautiful," she said, thinking it was exactly what she would have chosen for herself. It was a heavy gold band, extremely wide, and deeply carved in an elaborate leaf-and-circle design that reminded Kate of loops of sargasso seaweed. It was perfect for her finger, and now she clasped her hand around it protectively. She, who never wore jewelry, who in fact owned no valuable pieces, would treasure this.

When at last dinner was over and they were in the car driving back to Morgan's house, Morgan said, "I'm glad that's over, aren't you?"

Kate stared straight ahead. She wished they were going back to Yaupon Island, or even to Morgan's house on Teoway, instead of staying in the city. She stole a look at Morgan, wondering if it was too late to suggest that they drive to Teoway Island tonight. It would take less than forty-five minutes to get there.

"I'm tired. How about you?" Morgan asked her.

"A little," she said, and decided against suggesting Teoway.

"How's the baby?" he asked, resting one hand on her abdomen.

"Practicing punting," Kate said, perhaps too brightly.

"I hope it's not *too* wide awake. Didn't I hear you get up several times last night?"

Kate glanced at Morgan's face as it was momentarily illuminated by the streetlight at the corner when they turned into the driveway of the Tradd Street house. He looked subdued, not quite himself. Maybe all this was more of a strain on him than she realized. Maybe he was having a hard time coming to terms with the fact that he had actually married Kate Sinclair, marine biologist without a job, a person who had never been to a St. Cecilia's Ball in her life and who was so unimpressed with the Rhett name that she refused to use it.

"I didn't keep you awake last night, did I?" she asked anxiously.

"No, no, nothing like that," he said, coming around to her side of the car to help her out. He reached behind the front seat for her bouquet. "You might want to keep this," he said.

The orchids in her bridal cascade were crushed, the edges of their petals brown. Kate didn't want Morgan to see her sentimental streak—she considered it a weakness—but she touched one of the petals gently, as if the tactile sensation on her skin could reassure her.

"It's a lovely bouquet, Morgan," she said softly. "Thank you. And—and I've never had such an expensive pin in my whole life. Thank you for that, too."

His eyes bored into her. "You're welcome, Kate," he said.

"I wish I had something to give you for a wedding present," she said as they started into the house.

"You're giving it to me," he said.

"What? I have nothing." They had reached the bottom of the staircase by this time.

"You've given me a family," he said.

She realized that he was serious, and his earnestness embarrassed her. She started up the stairs.

"I should have carried you over the threshold," he said suddenly.

She paused and looked down at him. "I'm five feet ten inches tall and weigh more than I ever have, Morgan. I'm glad you didn't." She continued up the staircase, but he galloped up the rest of the steps to beat her to the bedroom door. Before she realized what was happening, he had placed one arm around her shoulders and one under her knees and was swinging her into his arms.

"Morgan, stop!"

He looked down at her, an amused expression on his face. "Whatever the future holds, let it be said that we started off right," he said, carrying her through the door of the master bedroom and striding to the big bed.

So close to him, inhaling his scent, thinking how sexy he looked with his hair slightly disheveled, she felt desire curling up from somewhere deep inside her, the same desire that she had come to know so well.

He kissed her, deepening the kiss and letting it become more fervent, and she felt herself tremble in his arms and so did he.

He laid her gently on the bed, never removing his lips from hers, and slid his body close to hers. His tongue traced the line of her jaw, leaving a damp trail, his breath hot on her skin. Even though she was immediately aroused, she nevertheless gasped when he slid his hand up her leg.

"What's that?" he murmured when his fingers encountered a barrier.

"A blue garter borrowed from Joanna," she whispered.

"Doesn't it cut off your circulation?" he asked with interest, his fingers sliding it down over her ankle.

"My circulation has been curtailed for the past eight months," Kate said.

"Where'd you get that dress?" he asked.

"It was a wedding gift from Joanna. She said—"

"I don't care what my esteemed sister said. It makes you look like a huge marshmallow."

Kate pulled away. "Morgan!" she said, not knowing whether to be offended or not.

He pulled the dress up and she sat so he could slip it over her head.

"It so happens," he said, unhooking her bra, "that I love marshmallows," and Kate subsided, wanting only to feel his lips upon her flesh.

He was gentle, and she responded as she never had before. For the first time Kate realized that she was Mrs. Morgan Rhett, a strange circumstance but not without its rewards, one of which was that they would be together at least until after the baby was born.

On this night she wanted nothing so much as to feast her eyes on his long, lean body and on his square-jawed face with its sweet smile, gathering him to her with moans of pure delight. The joy built inside her until she exploded with passion, and then she coaxed him, teased him until he cried out, exultant, again and again and again.

It was a wedding night, Kate thought hazily, to end all wedding nights. Although they might be mismatched socially, they were ideal sex partners. There might be a lot of things wrong with this relationship—or rather, this marriage—but their sexual adjustment was certainly not one of them.

Some people worked a whole lifetime to achieve a union such as this, Kate thought with remarkable lucidity before she finally fell asleep. How lucky that it hadn't taken her and Morgan long at all.

Of course, they didn't have long. They were going to be divorced, weren't they?

Chapter Thirteen

The next day, at Kate's urging, they returned to Yaupon Island.

"Wouldn't you rather go to my place on Teoway?" Morgan had asked her, but Kate turned the offer down flat.

"I want to live on Yaupon Island as long as I can. After the baby is born, Morgan, we'll go anywhere you want, I promise. But right now I can't wait to get back to the island."

"What are we going to tell Gump? And Ye Olde Pribble?" Morgan wanted to know.

"We'll tell Gump we're married. He'll be relieved, and maybe he'll be able to think about something besides me for a change—like sobering up, for instance. As for Willadeen Pribble, I wouldn't tell her if her house was on fire. No, let me change that—I wouldn't tell her if her *hair* was on fire," Kate said.

They told Gump as soon as they boarded the ferry, taking him below deck and sitting him down on one of the row seats in order to break the news. His mustache twitched, and he hemmed and hawed before wishing them good luck, but finally his mustache, always the true indicator of his mood, curved upward to frame a broad smile.

"Only thing is," he said, "you ought to live in Charleston, not on this fool island."

"You said the same thing to Dad when he was sick, but you might as well have held your breath for all the good it did. He wanted to stay on the island as long as possible, and so do I," Kate said.

"Don't mean it makes good sense," Gump said before disappearing up the stairs and into the wheelhouse.

Kate actually felt a thrill of anticipation as they approached Yaupon Island. She had missed the eerie beauty of the twisted live oak trees and the wide gold-and-green stretches of marshland, and it seemed too long since she'd seen the weathered bricks of the lighthouse silhouetted against the sky. She gripped Morgan's arm as the ferry eased up to the landing.

"The island means a lot to you, doesn't it?"

She only smiled and squeezed his arm.

The bulldozer had finished its work, the new septic tank presumably reposing beneath the raw gash in the sandy soil beside the lighthouse, and despite the damage to Kate's flower bed, which somebody had ineffectively tried to repair, the quarters looked much the same. The only negative thing Kate could find to complain about was the oppressive heat, which seemed to hang over the island more heavily today than she remembered. By the time they unlocked the quarters, Kate's forehead glistened with perspiration.

"We've never discussed it, but do you want to stay in the keeper's quarters or at the lodge?" Morgan asked.

"In the quarters, of course," Kate said, looking around the familiar and beloved little sitting room with its family pictures and her old typewriter and her father's bifocals still on the table where he had left them. "This has been my home most of my life. I want nothing so much as to spend my last days on the island in this house." She felt her eyes grow misty at the thought of leaving.

Morgan took her in his arms. "If that's what you want, then here we will stay," he said.

Morgan went to gather his belongings from the hunting lodge, and while he was gone, Kate busied herself with unpacking her suitcase. She was soon interrupted by a knock on the door. When she looked out the window, she saw that Gump was standing there, and Kate hurried—well, *tried* to hurry—to the door as fast as her bulky body would allow.

"What are you doing here?" Kate said. They had just left him on the ferry.

"Your news took me by surprise so that I forgot something important. Here's your mail for the past couple of weeks," Gump said, thrusting it under Kate's nose.

"Mmm, thanks," Kate said as she thumbed through the envelopes, plucking out one with the return address of the Federal Health Foundation and slitting it open with a fingernail.

Gump sat down in a convenient chair. "I had some second thoughts, and I just wanted to tell you, Kate, that if you don't want to be married to this fellow, this Morgan Rhett—"

Kate looked up from the letter. "What?" she said.

"You don't look like a woman in love to me. In *like* maybe, but not in love." Gump glanced at the wide gold ring on Kate's finger and looked away.

"I never said I loved him. It was the best thing to do under the circumstances," Kate said.

"Best thing for who? Him? Courtney? What about you? What about integrity?"

Kate's eyes scanned the letter she held in her hands. She paled but kept reading.

"Well?" Gump said.

"I'm sorry, Gump," Kate said, looking up. "My mind is on something else."

"I said what about integrity? And what's so all-fired important about that letter? What's in it that keeps you from telling me all about this business of getting married to someone you don't even love?"

"Actually, the letter *is* relevant to the topic if we're talking about integrity," Kate said, handing the letter over with a trembling hand.

Gump took the letter and skimmed through it. Kate sat as if lost in thought, her mind seemingly a million miles away.

"What does all this mean?" Gump asked impatiently. "You know I don't understand government bureau-ese."

"It says that according to the FHF's investigation, I'm exonerated of all wrongdoing in the case that caused me to lose my job. The director of the Northeast Marine Institute will be asked to resign, and my co-worker, Mitch, the man I was going to marry, will be fired."

"Kate," Gump said, letting the letter drop to his lap. "This is what you've been waiting for. I'm glad for you."

"But—" and Kate made a frustrated gesture with her hands, which she then allowed to drop to her sides.

"Your reputation will be restored, won't it? You'll be able to get a job now, won't you?"

"I suppose so," Kate said, tears beginning to roll down her face. She didn't know what was the matter with her; tears kept coming, and she was powerless to stop them.

"What's the matter? You should be delighted!"

"I—I—" Kate couldn't finish the sentence. She wasn't even sure what she had been about to say. All she knew was that her pent-up emotions were brimming over, and at the moment she wouldn't have been able to identify her tears as happy or sad, even if her life depended on it.

"There, there," soothed Gump as he patted Kate awkwardly on the shoulder. "You're just easily upset right now."

Morgan, carrying his bag from the lodge, appeared in the doorway. "What's going on in here?" Morgan asked with a frown at Gump and a look of concern for his sobbing wife.

"Oh, Kate here is going through what every pregnant woman goes through," Gump said so cheerfully that Kate briefly thought of throttling him.

"This letter came," Kate managed to say between sobs.

Morgan glanced at the letter and arranged his expression so that when he looked up he looked pleasantly surprised.

"It's good news, Kate. Why are you so upset? Is something else wrong?"

"I don't know. I'm happy. Now that this has happened, I feel vindicated. But all those long months of being reviled by everyone in my profession, and not being able to get a job, and—oh, I don't know. I'm happy."

"Well, since you're so happy and a storm's brewing outside, I guess I'll get back to the ferry. I'll check on you tomorrow and see if you're feeling any happier. Though I don't think any of us could stand it if you was," Gump said, disappearing out the door.

Kate wiped her eyes. Now that Morgan was here, she felt better.

Morgan sat down and regarded her solemnly. "What will you do now?"

"Continue my job search. Try to set up employment interviews. Things like that," Kate said. Her nose was stopped up and she fumbled in her pocket for a tissue, but there wasn't one. Morgan handed her his clean pocket handkerchief.

"You won't start interviewing until after you have the baby, I suppose," he said in as businesslike a voice as he could muster. In truth, his heart was pounding in his chest.

"I suppose so. It will probably take me that long to set something up," Kate said, twisting the handkerchief in her hands.

"So you could possibly leave right after the baby is born?"

"I'll need a couple of weeks to recover, of course," Kate said.

"Of course," Morgan repeated after her.

"If I prepare some letters, will you take them down to the ferry landing so Gump can get them in the mail right away?"

As unwilling as Morgan was to aid and abet her in getting this job, he uneasily agreed. Kate sat down to type at the ramshackle typewriter, and he sat at the kitchen table ostensibly poring over some papers from the office. What he was really doing was studying the letter she had received from the FHF.

It made no mention of the fact that Kate was going to be offered her old job back. Of course, the Federal Health Foundation would have no way of knowing that; it wasn't any of their business. The only reason that Tony Saldone had been privy to the information was because of his relationship with the talkative Pegeen.

Now was the time to inform Kate. If she knew she was going to be rehired at the marine lab, she wouldn't need to be writing letters of application to other research facilities.

And yet if he told Kate what he had learned from Tony, she would immediately know that he hadn't called Tony off her case. Kate would realize that Tony had been checking up on her in Maine and that she had in fact been the subject of Tony's ongoing investigation.

Morgan felt slightly sick to his stomach. *Maybe this is what morning sickness feels like,* he thought. *Maybe this is how Kate felt all those months.* But he knew that this was no sickness of the body—it was a sickness of the heart.

He looked up when Kate came in from the sitting room, waving the letters she had just typed.

"Will you read these, Morgan, and tell me what you think?" she asked.

His heart went out to her. Her brow was furrowed in concentration, and her lips, devoid of lipstick, were so red that he knew she had been biting them as she so often did when she was thinking. Her hair, long and loose and flowing, billowed out behind her, and he was suddenly struck with the vision of how it had looked the night before, strands of gold adorning his pillow. She was so beautiful, and she was his wife.

He took the letters from her, automatically reaching his other arm out and encircling her hips, his hand massaging the curve of her abdomen.

Deftly she slid out of his grasp. He looked up. "Anything wrong?" he asked.

She shook her head. "No," she said.

"Then come back here," he said.

She heaved a sigh. "I'm afraid we're getting too comfortable with all—all this," she said.

"All what?"

"This—this marriage stuff," she said.

"We *are* married, Kate."

"I know, but we've agreed that it's not going to last," she said.

"It so happens that I like to touch you," he said patiently.

"Well, I like it, too. I don't want to get too accustomed to it, that's all." Kate turned around and began to stow some of the packages of food they had brought from the Charleston house in the cupboard.

Morgan tried to concentrate on the letters Kate had written, but he found himself bombarded by confused thoughts. This was his wife, but she wasn't going to be his wife for long. She carried his child, which was really his child, only she wasn't really its mother. They had been married only the day before, but it wasn't really a marriage.

"I'm not sure this is even really a life," Morgan said, clearly and distinctly, throwing the letters down on the kitchen table.

"What?" Kate said, whirling in alarm.

"I think I'll go for a walk," he said. He tried not to see the bewilderment in Kate's eyes as he slammed out the door.

IF KATE HAD FELT like running after him and encouraging him to talk about it, she would have. But she felt heavy, ponderous. The baby seemed to have slipped lower, and even the thought of trying to navigate the path through the dunes to the beach, which was where Morgan had probably gone, was depressing.

When she walked, her feet splayed sideways. Her center of gravity seemed to be somewhere around her knees. She had heartburn. And the weather was hot, unbearably hot.

To pass the time until Morgan came back, Kate looked for something to do. Most of her possessions, as well as her father's, were neatly boxed and ready for storage in Gump's house in preparation for Kate's final departure from Yaupon Island. On the spur of the moment she decided to clean out the refrigerator. A lot of the food was moldy, and she tossed it in the garbage with a grimace and concentrated on scrubbing the interior. Why she bothered, she didn't really know. Willadeen and the historical society would inherit this refrigerator, and she didn't particularly care whether it was spotless for them or not.

Funny how she had become accustomed to Morgan's presence; it seemed lonely here in the quarters by herself. She switched on the one-station TV for company, trying to figure out who was winning the baseball game being broadcast, and during one of the breaks she heard a short weather broadcast.

"...tropical depression," the announcer said, and "...storm reaches the mainland."

Oh, great, she thought, piling boxes of butter and containers of outdated tofu on the kitchen table. *That must be the storm that Gump mentioned.* And Yaupon Island was always harder hit than the mainland when these things headed toward shore.

She cocked an eye out the window and saw a few ominous clouds piling up out to sea. She might as well give up any idea of getting those application letters to Gump. He would almost certainly decide to ride this storm out, as he had so many others, at the Merry Lulu. She glanced at her watch, wishing that Morgan would come back.

Kate had no idea what time the first raindrops fell, but it was shortly after she had finished with the refrigerator and had turned her attention to cleaning the ancient stove, scouring and polishing as if driven to the task. Maybe it was because she didn't want the ladies of the historical society to think she was a bad housekeeper when they finally took possession of the lighthouse, or perhaps she felt especially housewifely now that she and Morgan were going to live here, or—

Or maybe she was about to go into labor.

Kate sank onto one of the kitchen chairs, trying to remember something a friend of hers had said once, something about how she'd had the peculiar urge to clean out every closet in her house when she was in labor.

That was when Kate felt the beginnings of pressure in her lower back.

I must have strained something when I was bending over to clean the refrigerator, she told herself, but when the pressure tightened and became a cramp, she sat up straight and put a hand to the source of the pain. She was sitting like that when Morgan burst through the door, his hair damp with rain.

"Kate, I've been thinking—" Morgan began until he saw the odd expression on Kate's face.

"Kate?"

"Something's happening," she said.

"The baby?"

"I don't know," she said.

"I'll get the childbirth book," he said, running for his bag, which he had left in the bedroom. He rushed back into the room, leafing through pages until he found one that pertained to the first stage of early labor.

"What does it feel like?"

"Like a vise on my backbone," she muttered.

"It's too early for you to have the baby," he said.

"Three weeks before my due date," she said through tight lips.

"Then you can't be in labor," Morgan said hopefully.

"Maybe not," Kate said, relaxing again.

Morgan waved a hand at the food on the table. "What's all this?"

"I decided to clean out the fridge and ran out of space in the garbage can," she said.

Morgan scooped all of the things into a large plastic bag to get them out of the way. "The wind is picking up," he said.

"It's a tropical depression," Kate said, getting up and pouring a glass of cold water from the bottle in the refrigerator. "Did you read my application letters?"

"I read them," he said. "They're good."

"There's no use trying to mail them today. Gump won't be coming back until tomorrow."

"What about tourists stranded here during the storm?"

"Maybe you'd better go check at the landing and see if any stragglers show up. They can stay with us," Kate told him.

"I don't want to leave you," he said.

"Don't worry, it won't take you more than ten minutes to go to the ferry landing," she said.

"Maybe I'll see Gump, and if so, I'll caution him to stand by just in case you decide to have the baby today," Morgan said, dashing out the door. While he was gone, Kate felt another jab of pain, which lasted part of a minute and then was gone. The back of her legs ached something fierce. *Well, baby, is this it?* she asked it. *If so, maybe we'd better lie down for a while.*

Morgan came stomping into the house before she made it to the bedroom. "Tookidoo Sound is getting choppier by the minute, the ferry isn't around, and no tourists are in sight," he reported.

"They must have seen the storm brewing and caught the last ferry," Kate said.

"Any more pains?"

"One. I'm going to lie down."

"You might as well. Want company?"

"No, thanks," Kate said, waddling into the bedroom. But Morgan followed her anyway, looking jittery. Kate lay down on top of the bedcovers and stared out at the silvery gray slice of sky framed by the window until her eyes drifted shut.

The next contraction ripped through her, clamping her like the jaws of a giant animal, which Kate, who was dreaming, thought it was. When she opened her eyes, it was to see Morgan's alarmed face hovering over her.

"You cried out," he said. "Is anything wrong?"

"Another pain," Kate managed to say, trying to push herself into a sitting position. "Morgan, I think I'm really in labor."

She heard Morgan's sharp intake of breath. "You can't be," he said jokingly. "Not until the ferry resumes."

Kate groped for a pillow to stuff beneath the small of her back, and Morgan wedged it in the proper place.

"Don't worry," Kate said. "I'm not planning to have this baby on Yaupon Island. I intend to give birth in a nice clean hospital with Dr. Thomas in attendance."

"I can't tell you how happy I am to hear that," Morgan said, thumbing through the childbirth book.

He sat on a much-painted straight chair beside the bed. "The book says we should time the contractions," he said, glancing at his watch.

"Start timing right now," Kate said breathlessly. The next contraction started at her back and came around to her front. After that, they arrived regularly.

Morgan pulled the curtains wide and stared out at the falling rain. "I wish this storm would let up. I wish Gump would get the ferry running. I should put up the SOS flag anyway, don't you think?"

"Not yet," Kate said. "Would you please get me something to drink? Iced tea would be nice."

She heard Morgan clattering around in the kitchen as another contraction came and went. The tea sloshed over the side of the glass when Morgan set it down on the table beside the bed, and he ran to get a rag.

"The book says you might feel nervous, energetic or excited," he said as he mopped.

"All I feel is calm. You're the one who's acting nervous, energetic and excited," Kate pointed out.

"Me? Well, perhaps. I never expected you to go into labor this early."

"Maybe my labor will stop," Kate said.

"Maybe," Morgan said, but she knew he didn't believe it, either.

"It's happening again," Kate said.

"You should breathe," Morgan told her.

"What do you think I'm—oh, oh," she said, focusing on the pain. She tried to think of the baby, how it would look, how pleased Morgan would be, but it was hard to think about the baby when the pain was building up to a majestic crescendo. At least she tried to think of it that way, but in reality the pain was more like a hard brick wall.

Outside the wind was picking up. It howled around the walls of the quarters, flinging rain against the windows.

"Sounds like a hurricane," Morgan said.

"Hurricanes are much worse than this," Kate said when she had caught her breath again.

"I'm going outside to run the flag up the pole. Maybe if Gump sees it, he'll come to get you."

"Gump won't be seeing anything unless it's the bottom of a beer mug," Kate said. "Could you get me some ice to hold on my tongue? My mouth feels so dry."

As Morgan chipped the ice in the kitchen, lightning split the sky over the ocean and, seconds later, thunder rattled the quarters.

"You'd better not go out in the lightning," Kate cautioned.

"I'm going to raise the SOS flag, no matter what you say," Morgan told Kate.

"I'd rather you get a cold cloth for my forehead," Kate said fitfully. "Anyway, if you get zapped to a crisp by lightning, who's going to help me?"

"Don't bring up things like that, or I might get even more nervous, energetic or excited," Morgan warned before racing into the bathroom and back with a cold cloth.

Kate closed her eyes, sucking on the ice, and Morgan went to the door and stood there for a moment watching litter and leaves and even a soda-pop can blow past in the wind. He found a waterproof poncho beside the door and tugged it over his head, grabbing the flag before rushing outside.

Below the bluff, angry breakers churned and crashed on the shore, and the wind was so powerful that Morgan had to struggle to remain in a standing position. The flagpole was perhaps twenty feet from the door of the

quarters, and he hugged the flag close and ran for it. Rain
streamed into his eyes so that he could barely see well
enough to find the clips that would secure the flag to the
rope, and as he struggled with them he heard a sudden
loud *cr-ack* above.

Lightning! was his first thought as he dropped to the
ground. When he opened his eyes, he realized that it
hadn't been lightning at all. It had been the flagpole, old
and probably rotten, that had snapped off about halfway up and been flung toward the woods.

Slowly Morgan picked himself up and ran back into
the quarters. Kate stood at the entrance to the sitting
room, gripping the wall, staring at him with eyes as dark
as two coals in her pale face.

"What—"

"The flagpole snapped. You'd better get back to bed,"
he said. Without divesting himself of the dripping poncho, he helped her back into the bedroom, where she
climbed back on the bed, and he pulled the poncho off
and threw it in a corner.

"I could be in labor for hours yet," Kate said, trying
to smile.

"How long will this storm last?" Morgan asked.

"No telling. It depends on whether or not it's stalled
off the coast. Uh-oh, here it comes again," Kate said,
grimacing at the onset of the contraction.

"Pant, Kate, like we learned in class," Morgan said,
and, with visions of the neighbor's beagle in her head,
Kate panted. She wanted to ride the pain, to stay above
it, to remember that she was experiencing what women
had experienced since time immemorial. She tried to take
heart in the fact that she was becoming part of an exalted sisterhood united by this one all-encompassing, all-
important experience.

"And to think this is only the first stage of labor," Kate said after the contraction was over. None of her lofty thoughts had helped at all. Actually, she felt as if her mind were out of her body during contractions, looking on, an interested spectator not involved in any way. Her body seemed to have taken over her whole being with a will of its own, that will being the intense need to expel the baby. If this was childbirth, it was not as she had expected, to say the least.

Morgan was consulting the book again. "The average time for the first stage is eight or nine hours with the first baby," he told her.

"This seems to be moving a lot faster than that," Kate said.

Morgan held her hand through the next contraction and the next and the next, talking her through them in a strong, sure voice.

Kate began to lose track of time. She dozed between contractions even though she tried not to, and she had no idea how long it had been since the first one when Morgan said close to her ear, "You're in first-stage transition. I think."

"Is it time to boil the water yet?" she asked, trying to be funny. But her humor fell flat.

"I thought you said you were going to hold off until we could get you to the hospital," Morgan said in a frustrated voice, and in that moment she realized how hard this was for him.

"Believe me, Morgan," she said, "if I could be like an oyster and change sex, this would be the time to do it." But he didn't even smile.

Poor Morgan, he's accustomed to having everything his way. He didn't bargain for this, she thought before a

wave of nausea rippled through her. And then she
stopped thinking about poor Morgan because she could
only think about poor Kate.

Chapter Fourteen

Kate had never considered Courtney a wise woman, but now, in the middle of labor, she thought maybe Courtney had been on to something after all. One thing was for sure—she was not giving birth effortlessly, steeped in joy and sensitivity. She was hot and sweaty and grunting like a pig.

It seemed as if one contraction was no sooner over than the next one stabbed through her, cutting like a chisel, splitting her in two, and always there was Morgan's voice in her ear, fading and growing stronger like the wind itself. "Push, Kate, that's right."

Kate struggled to breathe exactly as Morgan instructed, and the breathing helped, and she felt grateful to him for making her attend the childbirth class where she'd been given rudimentary instruction in how to do it. But she couldn't thank him because she was too busy getting this baby born.

She was surfacing from one of the fiercest contractions yet when Morgan suddenly wasn't there anymore.

"Morgan!" she cried, thinking she was yelling at the top of her voice but hearing no more than a weak squeal, something like a squalling piglet.

And then she heard his voice in the kitchen saying, "Hold on, Kate, I'm getting scissors and things," which was when she realized that there was no changing this, that she was going to have this baby, and Morgan was going to deliver it.

Another contraction—after which Morgan reappeared, his anxious face wreathed in light like an angel's.

"You can bear down now, Kate, hard," Morgan said, and Kate trusted him and blindly did what he said, pushed until she was worn out with it, until she couldn't push anymore.

"Fine, darling Kate, keep it up," Morgan said, and Kate became aware of Morgan lifting her up and cradling her in his arms, arms tender and strong, and his voice in her ear whispering, and her hands gripping his, and another push.

Time blurred, grew faster, fell away. She managed to raise her head and saw Morgan's waiting outstretched hands, so capable, and she heard his voice saying, "I see the head, Kate. Push as hard as you can."

"I *am*," Kate said, putting every bit of energy she possessed into the next push.

"Almost," Morgan said. "You're doing fine."

Kate pushed, unable to hear Morgan's words, only the gentle tone of his voice.

A cry. Not her cry, but a baby's! No stronger than the call of a sea gull at first, and then a great lusty wail of outrage.

Morgan said exultantly, "It's a girl, Kate. A fine, healthy girl!"

A cool cloth blotting her face, and Morgan's wide smile, and Kate thought, *Joanna was right. Childbirth is a travail of tears.* Then her own tears began, but they were no longer tears of pain but elated, happy tears.

Morgan laid the baby against her breast, a fine fat pumpkin of a baby with ears whorled like little pink shells and hair like gossamer threads of sunshine.

"She's gorgeous, Kate, a perfect little doll," Morgan said, and Kate smiled a rapturous smile as she reached for Morgan's hand.

It was then that the exhaustion, complete and utter, struck, and Morgan murmured something soothing and spirited the baby away, and she heard Morgan moving about in the kitchen. Kate dozed, waking up in the night to see the baby in a box at the foot of the bed and Morgan beside her, propped up on pillows and his eyes closed.

"Morgan?" she said faintly.

His eyes flew open.

"Do you need anything?" he asked.

"No," she said. "Only—" How could she tell him what she felt in her heart? How could she tell him that she felt connected to him as she had never felt connected to another person in her whole life, that the experience of giving birth with him by her side had affected her so deeply that she would never be the same?

"Dearest Kate," he said. "You did yourself proud. It wasn't so bad, was it?"

She eyed him balefully. "It hurt like hell," she said, reaching for his hand and bringing it to her lips before falling into a deep and dreamless sleep.

THE NEXT MORNING the baby began to stir when Kate did, and Morgan roused himself to lift the baby out of her cardboard-carton bed.

"Are you hungry?" he said to the baby, sitting on the edge of the bed so Kate could see her. The baby was a tiny scrap, a red-faced mite, but Morgan's big hands were gentle with her. *He'll be a wonderful father,* Kate thought suddenly, and the thought gave her great joy.

"Give her to me, I'll feed her," Kate said, holding out her arms.

"You weren't planning to nurse," Morgan pointed out. "I've rigged up a makeshift bottle, and there's plenty of canned milk in the cupboard."

"But—" Kate said, touching the baby's cheek. The baby seemed so fragile, so delicate.

"Here, you hold her and I'll see about a bottle," Morgan said.

"No, I want to nurse her, Morgan. When—when I hear her cry, my milk begins to flow."

"Oh," Morgan said, looking taken aback.

"It's the most practical thing for me to feed her, isn't it?" Kate asked anxiously.

"Yes. Yes, I suppose it is," Morgan said, backing out of the room and leaving Kate alone with the baby.

Kate gazed at the baby, at the petal-soft eyelids and the sweetly rounded cheeks. The baby didn't look like Courtney, and she didn't look like Morgan. Her looks were all her own, and she was the most beautiful thing Kate had ever seen in her life.

The small rosebud mouth rooted against Kate's breast, and Kate parted her nightgown so that the baby could take her nipple in her mouth. The baby's mouth closed over the nipple, and as the gentle tugging commenced, Kate settled back on the pillows, lulled into contentment.

"WHAT WILL YOU name her, Morgan?" Kate asked, almost a week after a smiling Dr. Thomas had pronounced both mother and baby in the best of health.

"Pearl," he said.

They were sitting at the kitchen table in the quarters eating dinner, the baby sound asleep in her new bassinet beside the stove.

"Why?"

"Pearls grow from little grains of sand that somehow find their way into an oyster's shell. The embryo was implanted in you and grew and—well, it's a jewel of a name for a jewel of a baby," Morgan said. "And I want to name her Pearl. Whatever I want, I get. You told me so yourself."

"Me and my big mouth," she said.

Morgan leaned over and kissed her. "Quite a lovely mouth," he said, and they smiled at each other until Kate got up to lift the waking Pearl from her basket and went to change her diaper.

AS AUGUST WANED, Kate, Morgan and baby Pearl moved to Teoway Island.

Not that Kate found it easy to leave Yaupon Island; she knew she might never return.

"I wish I could climb to the top of the lighthouse one more time," Kate said wistfully. "From there I could see everything—the boardwalk across the marsh, the lodge, all of it," but Morgan only warned her with a look.

Instead, Kate, who was after all still recovering from childbirth, made her way through the dunes to the beach, walking barefoot, and sat for a long time staring out to sea as little sandpipers scampered nearby, barely ahead of the waves.

A chapter in her life was closed. It was time to move on. She had known it was coming, but that did not make it easier to bear.

She still had no job, despite sending out scores of résumés. But at least it was true that someone still needed her; Pearl was totally dependent on Kate, and Kate felt empowered by the baby's need. Morgan and Pearl provided a bridge to the new life that would eventually come. Kate was as dependent on them as they were on her, which was fitting and right.

Change would come—eventually. Kate knew it was inevitable, and she was sure Morgan did, too. For now, they could help each other and perhaps they would always form part of each other's support network.

They had briefly discussed the advantages of living in Morgan's house in the city.

"If we stayed at the Tradd Street house, you would be near Joanna. She could help you with the baby," Morgan had said.

"I can take care of the baby myself," Kate replied, prepared to be stubborn.

"You said you weren't good with babies," he reminded her.

"I *like* taking care of Pearl," Kate said, a statement which Morgan believed because she had become skilled at it.

Finally Morgan had agreed to live on Teoway Island, which pleased Kate tremendously. She preferred the wide open spaces of Teoway Island because it was so much like her own beloved Yaupon Island, and also, she was reluctant to live in the same house that Courtney and Morgan had occupied together.

Morgan watched and waited for some sign that Kate loved him.

He had thought that Kate was beautiful before, but now—now! Her figure was sylphlike and graceful, her cheeks rosy and rounded, and he desired her more than ever. The six weeks of her recovery could not pass fast enough for him; he wanted to make love to her now more than he had ever wanted to make love to anyone in his life.

These days Morgan was privy to all the intimate details of living with Kate. He knew how she hummed to herself so that he always knew what part of the house she was in. He knew that she wore the most unattractive underwear he'd ever seen. Kate professed that it made no difference what underwear looked like, that underwear wasn't for looks, it was for practical purposes. Morgan had to admit that when he saw Kate in her underwear, he didn't think about the underwear—he thought about what she would look like out of it.

She was a terrific cook. This surprised him somewhat, but she gloried in the large well-appointed kitchen on Teoway Island, swooping here and there bearing big copper pans and presenting him with meals that rivaled the finest gourmet meals he'd ever eaten.

Morgan dreaded the day when Kate would leave.

She was his wife. After several weeks of coming home from the office to find a humming Kate in his kitchen and baby Pearl in the nursery bicycling her legs and spitting bubbles out of the corners of her mouth, he could not imagine either of them not being there.

He knew that Kate received a lot of letters, replies to the letters of job application that she had sent, and she never discussed the contents with him. He supposed it was her business. But was it really? Didn't he have some say-so in the matter of when, or even if, she would leave? Didn't she owe something to him and to Pearl?

JOANNA BABY-SAT for Kate while Kate went to the doctor for her six-week checkup, and afterward Kate had a pleasant visit with Joanna and her children.

"Your baby is *so* little," Melissa said, peering into the old cradle where Joanna rocked her.

"She's *much* better than our baby," Christopher said.

"Wouldn't you like to leave Pearl with us for the night? You could come to pick her up in the morning," Joanna said.

"I'm nursing her," Kate said,

"She took the bottle very well for me today," Joanna assured her.

"Please let her stay!" Christopher said.

"Please?" asked Melissa.

"Do," urged Joanna, and Kate, who was feeling the strain of too many night feedings, thought how well-loved Pearl would be among her cousins and how good it would feel to be able to sleep all night and late the next morning.

"Okay," Kate said, still reluctant. She couldn't imagine being apart from Pearl even for so short a time, but maybe this would be a good rehearsal for the time when she'd have to go away forever. Tears poured down her face all the way back to Teoway Island, and she missed Pearl terribly. Even so, she fell into bed as soon as she let herself into the house and slept like a rock.

When she woke up she saw a light on in the dressing room and knew that Morgan had come in from work. She sat up as he was tiptoeing past the bed.

"I tried not to wake you," Morgan said.

"I was already awake," she said.

He sat down on the edge of the bed, and in the dimness of the light from the next room, she saw the smile on his face.

"Joanna told me she was baby-sitting Pearl overnight," he said, stroking her arm.

"I miss her," Kate said.

"I know. When I came home tonight, the house seemed so quiet without you and Pearl waiting for me when I came in the door."

"I went to the doctor today," Kate said. "It was my six-week checkup."

"And?"

"And he gave the go-ahead for us to resume sexual relations."

"Resume sexual relations," he said, drifting his fingers down the curve of her throat. "It sounds so clinical."

"To make love," she whispered, her eyelids fluttering closed as she imperceptibly leaned toward him.

"Oh, Kate," he said. "To think that I wouldn't have known you if Courtney hadn't recruited you as the mother of our child. To think that I would still be walking around with that great emptiness in my life and not even knowing it."

He cupped a hand around her face and looked deep into her eyes for a clue to what she was feeling in the depths of her soul. If he read her right, she loved him. Why didn't she say it? Why couldn't she admit her emotions?

Her arms went around him, and he drew her close, pleasure filling him up and spilling over into desire, as she pulled him down upon the pillows.

Outside the sea rushed to the shore, and inside the tides of passion flowed in their veins. It had been so long since they had made love, but the moves were familiar, as though they had known these things about each other all of their lives. Her breasts were full and firm, her body was slender and practiced in the ways of love, and Morgan thought there could never be anyone else in the world for him, ever. And she was smiling, so he kissed her smiling lips.

"Dearest Kate," he whispered because that was how he thought of her now all the time. "Dearest Kate, I love you so much," and he heard her breath catch, the words perhaps sticking in her throat when she tried to say them, and she didn't speak after all. But she trembled violently in his arms, and he knew this was her climax, and in a moment he collapsed against her, drained and gasping for breath.

They lay together for a long time, neither of them talking, only touching, and each thinking private thoughts.

KATE WAS SO GLAD to see Pearl the next morning when she went to pick her up at Joanna's that she nearly danced across the sidewalk as she carried her to Morgan's car. For her part, Pearl's eyes lit up and she smiled.

Since they were both in such a good mood, Kate decided to drive to Preacher's Inlet, both to see Gump and to pick up her mail.

She carried Pearl in her arms and met Gump at the ferry dock as he returned from a run to the island. A few tourists filed off the boat, and Gump stumped down the ramp after they had left to hug Kate warmly and chuck Pearl under the chin.

"That's a good-looking baby," he told Kate with a twinkle.

"Do you think she looks like Morgan? She has his blue eyes." Kate said.

"Nope. She looks like her own self," Gump said. "Say, why don't you ride over to the island? See how Willadeen's museum is coming along?"

Kate's expression darkened, and she shook her head. "I don't want to see it. I'd rather remember it the way it was. The reason I'm here is that I came for my mail," she said.

"I've been saving it for you. Wait a minute and I'll get it," Gump said before boarding the ferry and disappearing momentarily into the wheelhouse.

Kate stood on the dock, inhaling the familiar scents of tar from the pilings and salt air from the ocean. Yaupon Island was a blur on the horizon, and Kate wondered if she would ever go back. Probably not. Some things were best remembered as they were.

Gump returned with a stack of envelopes. "Here you are. Could I interest you in lunch? The Merry Lulu serves snacks these days. We could have a sandwich together."

"Thanks, but it'll have to be some other time, Gump. I'm glad to hear about the sandwiches, though. You keep your nose out of beer mugs."

"Haven't tied on a good one since you left," Gump complained.

"See that you don't," Kate warned him.

"Hey, after I retire I'm going to move to North Carolina to live with my sister. No booze allowed in her house. You don't need to worry about me," he said.

Kate shifted Pearl to her other shoulder and stuffed the envelopes in her purse. "I'll be back for lunch before long," she called as she left.

When Kate got home, she had to feed Pearl, and then she ate her own lunch and took a short nap. Afterward there was Pearl's bath, and then she tossed a load of laundry in the washing machine. It wasn't until almost dinnertime that she remembered the mail.

The letter from Northeast Marine Institute nearly jumped out at her. With its distinctive logo, she spotted it right away. She thought perhaps Pegeen was writing her a personal congratulatory note about the findings of the FHF, but the letter wasn't from Pegeen. It was from the new director of the institute.

> Dear Dr. Sinclair,
> Recently you received a letter from the Federal Health Foundation stating the results of that agency's investigation into matters concerning falsified data.
> I have recently been appointed director of Northeast Marine Institute in order to fill a vacancy created when the former director of the lab, Dr. Deakin Cleveland, resigned. I'm pleased to inform you that I am now in a position to discuss the resumption of your valuable research under the auspices of Northeast Marine Institute.
> Please call this office as soon as possible to arrange an interview.
>
> Austin J. Follett, Ph.D.
Director, Northeast Marine Institute

Kate sank down on a chair in the living room, tears stinging her eyes. Finally! It was clear from the letter that she could have her old job back for the asking.

She stared out at the ocean, wishing she felt happier. She had won the fight; she had prevailed in the end. Now she knew for sure that she would soon be leaving Morgan and Pearl.

She walked softly into the room where Pearl slept, her tiny fists curled into balls. Pearl wore a nightgown printed with pink teddy bears, and her favorite mobile swung over her crib. In a while she would wake and grin a big toothless grin, waving her arms and legs as Kate changed her diaper. Then she would suckle at Kate's breast, her breath warm upon Kate's skin, her sweet talcum-scented body curved to Kate's as it had been all those months that Kate had sheltered her in her body.

So engrossed was she in thoughts of Pearl that Kate didn't hear Morgan come in, didn't hear the door close behind him. Suddenly he was behind her, his arms sliding around her as they both gazed down at the sleeping baby.

Morgan nuzzled Kate's neck, and swiftly she pulled away. She shook her head at him and laid a finger across her lips, leading him outside and gently closing the nursery door. He slipped his arms around her waist and tried to turn her toward him for a kiss, but she evaded him once more and led the way into the living room.

"You're early," she said faintly.

"I know," he said, smiling. He picked a gaily wrapped package up from a nearby table. "I thought about you all day and couldn't wait to get back to you. Last night was—well, more about that later. I went shopping and bought you some things. Open it." He handed her the box.

He sat down across from her—dear Morgan, always kind, always thoughtful. How was she going to break the news to him?

As he watched expectantly, a wide grin on his face, she slid the wrapping paper free of the box and lifted the lid. Lacy underthings, all kinds—bras, panties, slips, garter belts, camisoles. She raised her eyes to his, unsure how to respond.

"Things you need. Things I'm going to enjoy seeing you wear. Plain vanilla underwear is okay, I suppose, but why not have fun? I like to see my wife wearing pretty things," he said.

"Your wife," she said heavily, touching one of the camisoles. It was a confection of peach silk, ivory lace and blue satin ribbon. She looked at him. "Morgan, there's something I must tell you," she said.

His face grew serious, and overlaying the seriousness was a look of dread. She didn't take time to figure it out. Instead she plunged ahead.

"Morgan, I received a letter today," she said, pushing the box with all the lacy underthings aside and retrieving the letter from the floor where it had fallen. "It's from the new director of Northeast Marine Institute. He wants me to call for an interview. I'm going to get my old job back."

It seemed as if all the air left him. He sagged against the plump cushion of the chair where he sat and stared at her.

"I see," he said.

"You knew I would be leaving eventually," Kate said. "It was our agreement."

"I know."

"And the opportunity to resume my work is important to me."

"How about Pearl? Isn't she important to you?"

What could she tell him about the sweet pleasure that filled her when Pearl nursed at her breast? How could she justify leaving the child who so occupied her days and nights that sometimes Kate didn't know where Pearl began and Kate ended? There was no way, and so Kate merely stared at the floor.

"I suppose I'd better get a list of prospective nannies from Joanna," Morgan said at last.

"Yes," Kate said.

He stood up abruptly. "I'm not hungry. No need to cook dinner," he said. He strode out of the room and disappeared into the TV room, slamming the door after him.

Kate sat in the darkening living room. She wouldn't be able to eat anything, either.

Well, perhaps the best thing to do was to write a letter to the institute. Or perhaps she should phone tomorrow. Yes, that seemed like the wiser course to follow, but she wanted to organize her thoughts beforehand. What she needed was one of those large yellow legal pads that Morgan carried in his briefcase.

Morgan's briefcase was on the chair in the foyer where he had left it when he came in from the garage. She flipped on the overhead light and opened the briefcase, removing one pad of paper. A document fluttered from between the pages, and she stooped to pick it up.

As she slowly stood, her eyes fell on the letterhead. "Saldone Detective Agency," she read softly to herself. Her name, Katharine Sinclair, was on the first page. She pushed the briefcase aside and sat down on the chair, her eyes skimming the report.

Pegeen's name was there, and Kate flipped the pages over, one after another, stunned to be reading what appeared to be a complete account of her activities at Northeast Marine Institute, as well as a rundown of her personal life, including the address where she had once owned a house, the full name of her former fiancé and finally, and this astonished her, the information that the lab was certain to offer her her old job back.

She leafed through the pages and noted the date. Why, Tony Saldone's surveillance of her had ended before Pearl was born, before she and Morgan were married! And Morgan had known—he had known then that she was going to be offered her old job!

The report fell to her lap as her mind raced. Morgan had let her think that the detective's investigation into her background had ended with the report that she hadn't been seeing other men when she became pregnant. In fact, Tony Saldone had been investigating her the whole time that she and Morgan had been together on the island, while they were cohabiting at the lodge, while they had been falling—no. They hadn't fallen in love. Morgan *said* he loved her—but how could he love her? You didn't investigate people you loved.

Slowly she stood up and walked to the door of the TV room. She listened for the chatter of the television set but heard nothing. A narrow band of light showed beneath the door, so she pushed it open and walked in.

Morgan looked up sharply. He was sitting at the small desk in there, his face illuminated by the reading light. His eyes were red, and his expression was strained. When he saw her standing there, he looked hopeful.

"Kate, come in," he said, and she stalked over to the desk and tossed the report down in front of him. His expression changed.

"Suppose you explain this," she said coldly.

He was silent, staring at the report. She saw him swallow. "You've read it?" he asked, his eyes scanning her face.

"Yes. All of it. You told me you'd called Saldone off."

Morgan sighed deeply. "I did, but he convinced me that he might be able to turn up information concerning what was happening with the Federal Health Foundation's Office of Scientific Ethics investigation into irregularities in research at Northeast Marine Lab. He said that he might be able to find out something that would help you."

"And he did, didn't he? He told you that I was going to get my old job back, right?"

"Right," he said, measuring her fury.

"You didn't tell me," she said.

"I thought—" He didn't finish the sentence when he saw the angry glint in her eyes.

"You thought what?"

"That you wouldn't marry me if you knew you could leave as soon as the baby was born," he finished lamely.

"I would have! I wanted to prevent you from having another court battle with Courtney."

"I didn't only want that, Kate. I wanted us to have a chance. If you'd known there was a job waiting for you, you would have gone, and I wouldn't have had a chance to show you how much I love you. For that I needed to be with you every day for a while. I wanted you to see how well the three of us, you, me and Pearl, would function as a family," he said.

"That's pretty underhanded, don't you think?"

"You've never understood how much I love you, Kate. And it's been good, hasn't it? We've been happy living here on Teoway Island. You love taking care of Pearl, you said so yourself. Last night you told me how you hate being away from her. Can't you see that we have a good life together, that most people would give anything to know the happiness that we've created for ourselves—"

"*You've* created," she said. "Morgan Rhett gets what he wants. And now I know why. He'll stop at nothing." She turned to go, but in that instant Morgan was out of his chair and spinning her around.

"Don't touch me," she said.

For an answer he pulled her roughly into his arms and kissed her, kissed her until her knees turned to water, kissed her until her head spun.

"When you think about what's true, think of that," he said. "You and me. That's the only thing that's real, Kate."

Shaken, she backed away. "I'm leaving," she said. "Tonight."

"We need you, Kate," he shot back.

"I'm tired of—of people *needing* me. I'm sick of dealing with human beings. It gets so messy. I want to spend my days and my nights with something clear-cut and unequivocal—my work. Goodbye, Morgan." She spared him one last look and went out of the room, closing the door firmly behind her.

She tossed clothes into her suitcase, pausing only to call a cab. When she had packed, she carried her suitcase down the hall and deposited it next to the front door. She hadn't intended to say goodbye to Pearl; she didn't think she could bear it. But as she waited for the cab, Pearl began to cry, and Kate hid her face in her hands in despair. Whenever she heard Pearl cry, her milk began to flow. Oh, God, what was she going to do?

She ran into the bathroom for a tissue to stuff in her bra, and when she came out she met Morgan, stiff faced and pale, carrying Pearl out of the nursery.

"Kate, I'll take you into the city. If you'll feed Pearl first, I'll—"

"No," she said over the baby's cries, trying not to look at him, trying not to look at Pearl's puckered little face.

"How can you do this?" Morgan said in desperation.

"I don't know. I don't know!" Kate cried, her own ears flowing down her cheeks.

Pearl hiccuped, her chin quivering, and in that moment Kate almost wavered. But then a pair of headlights skimmed the edges of the driveway and they heard the bleat of the taxi horn, and Kate looked despairingly from Morgan to Pearl and back to the taxi.

Without a word she lifted her suitcase, spared Morgan one last frantic look and stepped out into the night. The last sound she heard was Pearl's crying.

Chapter Fifteen

Would she ever forget those last moments with Pearl and Morgan? Would the baby's cries ever be erased from her memory? Kate, as she resumed her work at Northeast Marine Institute, as she was welcomed back by her former co-workers, thought that she would not. She resigned herself to sleepless nights. She replayed that terrible scene over and over in her mind.

With Pegeen's help, she managed to find a lovely house to rent on the coast, where she could walk the lonely, rocky beach to her heart's content. And walk it she did, but it only reminded her of another beach in another place, and the crash of breakers on the rocks could not soothe her like the soft lapping of tides on a South Carolina beach.

It was hard, resuming her work. But she threw herself into it full force, knowing that only work could dull the pain.

She thought about Morgan all too much, about his treachery and deception, but mostly about the good times they'd had. Now, removed from the experience by time and distance, she had to admit that her weeks with Morgan and Pearl had been some of the happiest days of her life.

Certainly they had run the gamut of experience, from the throes of childbirth to the ecstasy of lovemaking, from the beaches of Yaupon Island to the luxury of a Charleston mansion. It was, she thought ruefully, a life that would be the envy of any soap-opera character.

She never heard from Morgan, even though she had written him a brief note with only her address on it. She supposed that he was going ahead with the adoption of Pearl, which would soon be final, but what about the divorce?

Not that Kate cared about the divorce. She didn't want to go out with other men. She still wore the beautiful wedding ring that Morgan had placed on her finger because her finger had felt too naked when she'd taken it off. Her life consisted of her work at the lab, a good book at night, walks on the beach when the weather was warm.

One month went by, then two, and Kate found herself daydreaming about Pearl. She wondered what Pearl looked like, who was her nanny, how much Pearl weighed. She wondered if Pearl had missed her when she left.

Morgan would probably remarry after their divorce, Kate thought. He was too nice a man to remain single. Someone would snap him up soon, no doubt, someone who had social ties similar to his, someone who fit in with the kind of people Morgan knew.

Kate lost weight, which she attributed to being too busy on the job to eat. Her cheeks molded more sleekly to the bones of her face, hollows appeared under her eyes, and she began having gnawing pains in her stomach, which her doctor said were due to stress. In an attempt to alleviate it, she painted the kitchen of the house where she lived a bright cheerful yellow, and she joined a health club. To raise her spirits, she even bought a red winter coat in preparation for the snow that began to fall in November.

Her Thanksgiving was spent with a group of single friends, and afterward they all went outside and had a snowball fight. Kate had snow rubbed in her face, and Pegeen's cousin, a handsome man five years younger than Kate, asked Kate to go to dinner with him sometime. She liked him, but she put him off, and when he pressed her for a reason, she fled.

Walking home that night with the snow falling upon her face and melting into tears, Kate tried to be thankful for everything she had—her work, her friends and her house. But all she could really think about was a sunny beach in the south where Morgan Rhett had appeared in his pin-striped suit and told her he was going to adopt the baby, and when she got home that night, she impulsively called an airline and made reservations to fly to South Carolina the week before Christmas.

Why am I doing this? Kate asked herself after she hung up the phone. *What will it prove?* More importantly, what would she do there?

She missed the balmy southern climate. She wanted to see Gump, certainly, while she was in South Carolina, although she wouldn't go to Yaupon Island. She might visit Joanna and ask for a progress report on Morgan and Pearl—that is, if she dared.

As for Morgan, she could communicate with him, if necessary, through his attorney.

KATE STEPPED OFF the plane in Charleston into a warm day so different from the snapping cold weather in Maine that it took her breath away. An airport shuttle deposited her at her downtown hotel, and she spent the afternoon wandering around the historic part of the city through streets decorated for Christmas, marveling that people were actually walking around wearing no more than a sweater in the middle of December.

She rented a car with the idea of seeing Gump, which she did the next day when they met for lunch. He was happily retired and packing up to go live with his sister.

"She's planning to drag me to AA meetings, you can bet," he said gloomily.

"Good," Kate told him.

"Humph," was all Gump would say as she kissed him goodbye, although she thought he seemed pleased that his sister was laying down the law to him. No one had tried that with Gump for quite a while.

As she drove out of Preacher's Inlet, Kate actually intended to turn back toward the city when she got to the highway. But somehow she maneuvered into the wrong turning lane and found herself trapped in front of a tractor-trailer rig and unable to change lanes. In the space of seconds, she was headed toward Teoway Island and thought, *Why not? I'll just have a look around, maybe take a few pictures of the place to show Pegeen.*

The entrance to the island was planted with bright red flowers, and the trees hung low over the road as they always had, and the marsh glittered on one side, the sea on the other. Kate remembered Teoway as beautiful, but surely it hadn't always been *this* beautiful.

She cruised slowly, feasting her eyes on Spanish moss and palmettos, thinking that she had her emotions completely under control until she saw the house where she'd lived with Morgan and Pearl. A blue spruce, a Christmas tree, was propped against the side of the garage, its trunk in a bucket. Morgan's car sat in the driveway, and hanging from one of the trees was a baby swing.

Pearl is old enough to swing? she thought to herself, slowing the car to watch the small blue swing sway in the breeze. She tried to imagine Pearl in it, which was impossible. Pearl's legs would be too short, and surely such a swing wouldn't be comfortable, would it?

Pearl was almost five months old. What did five-month-old babies do? Did they eat a lot of solids? Did they crawl?

Kate had slowed the car almost to a stop and was staring at the house, wondering what the occupants were doing. Not that she wanted to see them—she had no intention of that. She was curious, that was all. Curious, and—

And lonely. She missed them. Or did she merely miss the happiness of their life together?

"Kate?"

In her surprise, Kate almost hit the accelerator instead of the brake. Her head whipped around to see Morgan approaching the car from behind. He was pushing a stroller and in it sat Pearl, wearing a sunny yellow suit with a peaked cap. But why was Morgan here? He should have been at work at this time of the afternoon.

An eternity passed in those few seconds. Morgan looked unsure of himself, and Kate felt like sinking through the floorboard of the car.

"Kate, please come in. Please." Morgan's voice held a quiet urgency. Pearl gazed up at her with big blue eyes, eyes as blue as Morgan's, her mouth hanging open and drooling. When Kate looked at her, Pearl chortled and kicked her feet into the air.

"Please?" Morgan said as he opened the car door.

Kate stood up, uncertain of what she should say. "I—" she started, but there were no words to describe how she felt. Looking at Morgan, seeing him for the first time in three months, she was overwhelmed by a sense of déjà vu, caught up in a time warp where she and Morgan and Pearl were once again a family—or playing at being a family, which was hardly the same thing.

She lifted her shoulders and let them fall. "Pearl is— so big," she said helplessly.

Morgan reached down and lifted the baby out of the stroller. Pearl's pacifier fell on the ground, and Kate reached down to pick it up at the same time as Morgan. When they stood up, she and Morgan bumped heads.

"Sorry," they both said at the same time, and then they laughed self-consciously.

Morgan jounced Pearl expertly. "We've been for our walk," he said, "and now we're going in. It's time for Pearl's nap."

"She still sleeps a lot?" Kate asked, following Morgan up the path to the door, thinking that this was an inane thing to ask but unable to think of anything else.

"She even sleeps through the night," he said proudly, holding the door for Kate. "And guess what? I'm teaching her to play pat-a-cake."

"That's nice," Kate said. She walked around several boxes labeled Xmas Ornaments. The sight of them made her feel pensive because she knew she would be utterly alone for the holidays.

"I'll put her in bed while you get yourself something to drink," Morgan said over his shoulder.

Kate wanted to watch him put Pearl in her crib. Fleetingly she wished Morgan had invited her. Under the circumstances, however, she could understand why he hadn't.

Kate stared for a moment at the dirty pacifier in her hands before carefully setting it on the coffee table. She went to the bar and poured a glass of ginger ale for herself before mixing Morgan his favorite Scotch and water. When he came back, he said, "Pearl will fuss a little until she settles down, but then she'll go right to sleep."

"You sound like an experienced hand at this," Kate said after Morgan sat down across from her.

"I didn't hire a nanny," he said. "I've been staying home and taking care of Pearl myself."

Kate stared. "What about your business?"

"I set up one of the extra bedrooms as an office with a computer, a fax machine, the whole works. Phyllis comes over a couple times a week and I keep in close touch by phone. It's not easy, but Pearl needs me," he said.

"I never expected you to jump into this fatherhood bit with both feet," Kate said slowly.

Morgan smiled a wry smile. "Neither did I, believe me. Only I wouldn't have it any other way. I was supposed to go to England in the fall—remember? When it was time to go, I found I couldn't leave Pearl. I would have missed her too much. Do you know she does something new every day?"

"Amazing," Kate said.

"How about you, Kate? Are you happy?"

"Reasonably so," she said, avoiding his eyes.

"Your job is as you expected?"

"Yes. And I've rented a nice house, I have a group of friends, and—" She paused. She couldn't go on lying. "And I hate all of it," she finished, meeting his eyes bleakly.

"What went wrong?" he asked in a low tone.

She set her glass on the coffee table and walked to the wide window. "I don't know," she said in a troubled voice. She twisted Morgan's wedding ring around and around on her finger.

He approached her, his footsteps silent on the thick carpet.

"I think I do," he said quietly.

She didn't speak, and she didn't look at him. Their history was so deep and so complicated; their love—if that's what it had been—had strangled on its own problems. She didn't want to talk about regrets. It was better to let it go, to slough off her past life like an old skin.

"You miss us," Morgan said. He turned her to face him, his eyes searching her face. "Don't you?"

Her heart beat rapidly in her chest, and she forced herself to remain calm. She didn't trust herself to answer because she was haunted by the specter of what might have been if only the circumstances had been different. Of course, if the circumstances had been different, they might never have met at all.

"Kate," Morgan said as if reading her thoughts, "what we had together was wonderful, and I don't regret any of it. I never will."

She felt the unraveling of her defenses as he gazed deep into her eyes. Then, without knowing quite how it happened, she was in his arms, her face crushed against his neck, his heart beating in her ears.

"Kate, oh, Kate, you should have known you couldn't leave us behind. You're part of us, of Pearl and me, part of our lives."

Kate felt dampness on her cheeks and realized that she was crying. She tried to wipe the tears away, but Morgan beat her to it, kissing the tears one by one.

"I thought it would be all right once I got to Maine," she said, sobbing, "but it wasn't. Oh, Morgan, I thought I was incapable of loving anyone or of being loved. Before, when I was engaged to Mitch, I felt betrayed when he faked the research results. I was outraged and angry."

"That has nothing to do with us," Morgan said.

"It does, because after I began to love you, I didn't trust you, and all my worst nightmares came true when I found out that you'd hidden Saldone's investigation of me. In my mind you'd done almost the same thing Mitch did," she said.

"Keeping Tony's information to myself was stupid and ill-advised. I thought I could use my money and influence to help you, Kate, but I realized after I'd done it that all I'd accomplished was to dig my own hole deeper. I would have done everything in my power to make you stay. I love you, Kate. You've known that for a long time," he said.

"And I love you. I've known *that* for a long time, too, only I couldn't admit it. Oh, Morgan, can you ever forgive me?"

He cradled her close. "We both have things to forgive, I think. Won't you come back?"

She wound her arms around his neck, glorying in the length of his body pressed against hers. "I *am* back, Morgan," she said. "I love you and Pearl so much, and she's my responsibility. I brought her into the world, gave her life, and I can't just *leave* her the way my mother left me or the way Courtney ran out on her. Didn't you tell me that Rhetts always live up to their responsibilities?"

"Always," he said, kissing the tip of her nose.

"I love you, Morgan," she said, getting a feel for the words.

His lips brushed against her hair. "This day is a new beginning for both of us," he said.

"For all three of us," Kate said, smiling through her tears.

Epilogue

"Happy birthday, dear Pearl, happy birthday to you," they all sang, and Pearl, her paper party crown slipping down over one eye, plunged both fists into her birthday cake. Kate, foreseeing this development, had snatched the one candle away barely in time.

"Who will blow out the candle?" she asked.

"You, and make a wish on Pearl's behalf," Morgan told her, curving an arm around her shoulders.

Kate thought about the things she could wish for her child. A happy life? No, Pearl had never known anything else. A family who loved her? No, this gathering of the Rhetts and Dumonts proved that Pearl had that in abundance. In fact, Christopher and Melissa were even now encouraging Pearl's tentative steps in the direction of her presents piled high at the end of the living room.

"Blow the candle out, Kate, or it will burn your fingers!" Joanna warned.

Kate wished and blew, and the flame went out. Morgan, Charlie and Joanna clapped, and Kate went to help Pearl open her gifts.

That night, when they were alone in their darkened bedroom, watching the reactivated beam of Yaupon Light in the distance, Morgan said, "What did you wish for Pearl today? I saw the expression on your face, and you looked so happy.''

Kate stood behind him and slid her arms around his waist, resting her head on one of his broad shoulders. She wore only a lace nightgown, sheer and held up by two straps of narrow satin ribbon.

''Guess,'' she said.

''Well, was the wish for Pearl or for yourself?''

She lifted her head and frowned at him. ''It wouldn't be fair to wish for something for myself on Pearl's birthday, although in a way it was for me, I suppose. Anyway, I have everything I ever wanted. The Marc Theroux Fellowship and the chance to direct meaningful research, a handsome husband who adores me and a darling little daughter. No, I'd say this wish was for something Pearl needs.''

''I give up. That child has everything any kid could want.''

He turned around to take her in his arms, and she smiled up at him.

''She doesn't,'' Kate said as she began to unbutton Morgan's shirt, ''have a brother or sister.''

''That's true. Does she need one?''

''Most definitely. I don't want her to grow up a lonely only child as I was.''

''I didn't think you were too eager to repeat the child-birth experience,'' he said, kissing her temple.

''Actually, I'd rather have babies the way oysters do. It's a whole lot easier,'' she said.

''But it's much more fun to fertilize eggs the way people do, and I missed that the first time around.''

''Then,'' Kate said, ''perhaps we should try it as soon as possible.''

Morgan laughed. "Are you sure you haven't been eating oysters? They're well-known for their aphrodisiac qualities, you know," he said.

"I haven't noticed that I've needed an aphrodisiac," Kate said as he slowly untied the ribbons at her shoulders. "And neither," she said pointedly as the nightgown rippled to the floor, "have you."

Morgan laughed again, and then, by the light of the lighthouse, he swept her off her feet and took her to bed.

#453 RAFE'S REVENGE by Anne Stuart

In Hollywood, where only winners survived, Rafe McGinnis was known as a fighter who never gave up. And neither did film critic Silver Carlysle. Theirs was a battle of wills—but each new skirmish only fueled their mutual desire. Despite the danger, Silver couldn't surrender. For Rafe had laid out his terms: Nothing less than a night in her arms would satisfy him.

#454 ONCE UPON A TIME by Rebecca Flanders

With buccaneer blood in his veins and a savage thirst for adventure, Chris Vandermere loomed like a modern-day pirate to his sassy stowaway, Lanie Robinson. She thought such men lived only in her dreams, but then she met Chris's lips and fantasy threatened to become reality.

#455 SAND MAN by Tracy Hughes

Like the Sand Man of her childhood dreams, Jake Abel brought a special magic into Maggie Conrad's life. Jake was anything but a myth. When he sprinkled his magic dust, Maggie almost believed that wishes could come true—despite their differences. But Jake was unstoppable and he'd made up his mind. He wanted Maggie in his life . . . and in his bed.

#456 THE COWBOY'S MISTRESS by Cathy Gillen Thacker

In the battle for the Bar W Ranch, Travis Wescott employed his devilish, double-edged tongue—using one side for witty repartee and the other for kissing his flame-haired adversary, Rachel. She meant to show him no one could rein in her ambition. And now Travis dreamed of claiming his ranch and branding Rachel his forever.

HARLEQUIN
American Romance®

American Romance's year-long celebration continues.... Join your favorite authors as they celebrate love set against the special times each month throughout 1992.

Next month... If Maggie knew college men looked this good, she'd've gone back to school years ago. Now forty and about to become a grandma, can she handle these sexy young men? Find out in:

SEPTEMBER

S	M	T	W		F	S
						5
						12
						19
2						6
27						

SAND MAN
by Tracy Hughes

Read all the Calendar of Romance titles, coming to you one per month, all year, only in American Romance.

HARLEQUIN SUPERROMANCE®

A PLACE IN HER HEART...

Somewhere deep in the heart of every grown woman is the little girl she used to be....

In September, October and November 1992, the world of childhood and the world of love collide in six very special romance titles. Follow these six special heroines as they discover the sometimes heart-wrenching, always heartwarming joy of being a Big Sister.

Written by six of your favorite Superromance authors, these compelling and emotionally satisfying romantic stories will earn a place in your heart!

SEPTEMBER 1992

#514   NOTHING BUT TROUBLE—Sandra James
#515   ONE TO ONE—Marisa Carroll

OCTOBER 1992

#518   OUT ON A LIMB—Sally Bradford
#519   STAR SONG—Sandra Canfield

NOVEMBER 1992

#522   JUST BETWEEN US—Debbi Bedford
#523   MAKE-BELIEVE—Emma Merritt

AVAILABLE WHEREVER
HARLEQUIN SUPERROMANCE
BOOKS ARE SOLD

BSIS92